PRAISE FOR THE NOVELS OF
GERARD STEMBRIDGE:

What She Saw

"Gerard   ly new
way to   aborate
conspir   rceful,
unreasc   *hat She*
Saw is   sometimes n   *Foxtrot*

"Extraor   anville

"One of   s produced i   idable
talent."   *endent*

"What   har-
riage   my
books   *Mail*

"A whit   *Metro*

"Skillfu   first
century   *imes*

WHAT

SHE

SAW

WHAT
SHE
SAW

GERARD STEMBRIDGE

HARPER

NEW YORK • LONDON • TORONTO • SYDNEY

HarperCollins books may be purchased for educational, business, or sales promotional use. For information, please e-mail the Special Markets Department at SPsales@harpercollins.com.

P.S.™ is a trademark of HarperCollins Publishers.

FIRST EDITION

Designed by Leydiana Rodriguez
Film strip illustration on page 128 © Sharapanovochka / Shutterstock

Library of Congress Cataloging-in-Publication Data

Names: Stembridge, Gerard, 1958- author.
Title: What she saw / Gerard Stembridge.
Description: First Edition. | New York, NY : HarperPerennial, [2017]
Identifiers: LCCN 2016035894| ISBN 9780062568984 (paperback) | ISBN
  9780062569004 (ebook)
Subjects: | BISAC: FICTION / Suspense. | GSAFD: Suspense fiction.
Classification: LCC PR6069.T419 W47 2017 | DDC 823/.914--dc23 LC record
available at https://lccn.loc.gov/2016035894

ISBN 978-0-06-256898-4 (pbk.)

17 18 19 20 21   LSC   10 9 8 7 6 5 4 3 2 1

To Gráinne
For the road we travelled.

WHAT

SHE

SAW

FRIDAY

OCTOBER 26, 2012

Ferdie hated the way Vallette moved. Right now he was padding around the Suite Imperial, nose up, accusatory eyes flicking left and right, a Doberman bred to notice something everyone else had missed. The place had already been swept twice by his own meatheads, for fuckssake. Bending slightly, he probed underneath a random cushion, fingered a lampstand like he was about to reveal an undetected mic or camera, then padded out onto the terrace to lean over the barrier and discover . . . what? An army of intrepid Front National wall climbers? Then back inside, holding himself so still, apart from that god-awful clicking of fingernail on fingernail—Ferdie really, truly hated that—chin up, left ear cocked, detecting sounds inaccessible to the mere humans in the room, especially any sounds that might suggest danger for his master. Always alert, potentially lethal. What a prick.

Then Vallette did the thing Ferdie hated most of all. He walked toward him without looking directly at him. He pointed—accusingly?—at the leather folder on the coffee table.

"All cleared except for numbers seven and fifteen. Denied."

Ferdie didn't open the dossier to check the head shots of numbers 7 and 15, nor ask for a reason why they were not acceptable. He knew it was just Vallette's little power trip,

controlling everything while at the same time making it cold-
ly—no, neurotically—clear that he wanted nothing to do with
this party: that he despised the very idea of it, that it turned his
stomach, that it was only because it was his master, Monsieur
Fournier's desire . . .

It was Vallette's mode to treat all underlings as underlings,
but Ferdie recognized the special contempt reserved for him, as
if he was not just workaday inferior but *morally* inferior, not so
much chauffeur as pimp, to be tolerated only because Monsieur
Fournier wanted him around. So when Vallette demanded a
dossier of all the party girls Ferdie had arranged for tonight it
had given him special pleasure to withhold one photo: Caramel
Girl, as Ferdie liked to think of her, remained a JPEG on his
laptop. Vallette had not been given the opportunity to veto this
one. Ferdie, knowing this was a potentially dangerous thing
to do, had nonetheless decided to take the risk. Caramel Girl
would not arrive with the other girls. He would meet her alone,
later, in the hotel bar, and would bring her up to the party
when Vallette was no longer around and the dossier had been
forgotten in favor of Monsieur Fournier's urgent requirements.
If Ferdie knew his master then Caramel Girl would flick his
inner switch. He had seen enough of him on these occasions
to recognize the special moment with the special girl when
suddenly the master's body became slightly hunched and hard,
the focus in the eyes narrowed, the hands taking on a life of
their own. Ferdie was banking on his luscious crème brûlée
having this effect and more. All going well, he'd earn kudos
from Monsieur Fournier and maybe even a little gratitude from
Caramel Girl. Vallette would find out about it, but too late.

Of course Ferdie would then have to be very, very wary.

What was it about these number-two guys like Vallette?

Something in the head with all of them. He'd seen it before in other employments. They were like crazy wives: a top layer of unctuous, cloying loyalty to the master, but a little digging discovered something else entirely. Ownership? Jealousy? Homoerotic impulse? Or was the real truth that they all thought they were the puppeteers and the Master owed them everything? *Ev-er-y-thing.* Whatever the reason, from Ferdie's perspective, their attitude made them a real ass-pain to deal with and sometimes, as was more and more the case with Vallette, genuinely intimidating. It was one thing to be casually despised by him, quite another to make him your enemy.

After Vallette and the meatheads had left via the Suite Imperial's private elevator—without even the most perfunctory goodbye—Ferdie took particular pleasure in immediately stretching out on the silk-covered chaise longue *in his shoes.* He turned on his laptop and opened the JPEG of Caramel Girl to full screen. He gazed at her impossibly delicious skin and couldn't resist leaning in to tip his tongue to her lips. Tonight in the hotel bar he would brush close to her once more, speak to her, one on one. Then cross the foyer together, into the elevator, and up to the Imperial suite. A minute alone with her was better than nothing.

Ferdie forced himself to focus on work. He opened the leather dossier to remind himself who numbers 7 and 15 were: Cecile and Denise, pretty, dirty bitches naturally, but neither of special interest to Monsieur Fournier, so no great loss. He removed their profiles and dialed Cecile's number first. It would be basic courtesy to call directly and let them know the bad news.

• • •

IN THIS MOOD, RUNNING YELLOWS IS FUN. OH THE BIG FAT YES OF THAT moment, no more than a wink, a come-on before the brake-slamming red. With any luck angry horns would cheer her on. She had run through three on her way to the airport. At least one and a half minutes of her life won back.

The security line steals that and more. Finally through the screening without a beep, but then the grim face. Open the bag, please. Mouthwash. Three hundred milliliters. Forbidden. How was she supposed to know that was in there? She had packed so fast. Oh take it, take it, but don't give me that look!

Lana knows enough not to say that out loud.

On the plane at last and it's hard not to glare at the fat suits and giddy families who have stolen the first three rows. Seat 4D is fine, she tells herself, for a last-minute reservation. And no one in 4E. Good. All good.

As soon as possible after takeoff Lana slips earbuds in and pumps up *Siamese Dream* as loud as she dares. Her eyes shut, the Pumpkins angsty stoner energy crowd-surfs her all the way back nearly twenty years to unstoppable sixteen. One more time around the whole album gets her all the way to the final descent. The tap on the shoulder from the stewardess. Yeah, turn off all electronic equipment, I know! I know! It's hard not to say that out loud.

Left now to its frenetic self, Lana's brain flashes with those images of the Suite Imperial on the Hotel Le Chevalier website. Seventh-floor penthouse, all silk and velvet, gold thread by the yard, the sumptuous canopy bed, and outside, an enormous terrace with the Eiffel Tower looming. No online booking, contact the hotel. She'd had no patience for that, obviously. For a few seconds, though, she'd craved its excesses and considered it an outrageous treat.

The landing bump high at Charles de Gaulle gradually deflates during the endless approach to the gate. They must have taxied to Belgium by now. Lana sings "Luna" under her breath as the lyrics urge her to take chances. She slyly unbuckles her seat belt so that the moment she hears the *bing!* she springs from 4D and retrieves her duffel while wriggling forward until her momentum is halted by a wedge of fat suits. In what airline world does a wheelie case, a laptop shoulder bag, a little briefcase, and a bulging duty-free bag count as one piece of hand luggage? Still, third in line to exit is hardly a worst-case scenario.

Once disembarked it's earbuds back in. Lana overtakes the fat boys and, with "Today" pounding at full volume this time, opens an impressive gap hurtling along the great looping, moving walkway that sags way down as if depressed by the weight of so many millions of passengers, then surges up resolutely at the end. Recurring images of a model in severe profile wearing a little Eiffel Tower strapped to her head are eye-catching, but Lana doesn't slow down to check out what the radical millinery is advertising. She silences the Pumpkins at Passport Control, which is default surly, but at least hassle-free, unlike back in her old single days when the Lana Turner passport always produced a crooked grin and a fun comment and required the fakiest fake feminine giggle from her in response. You guys! Never heard that one before! Lana remembers how at every hotel, car rental office, *bureau de change*, and airport, she would, again and again, try not to curse poor, drug-crazed, now-deceased Josh and Rosie Turner, who in the uninterrupted high of the summer of 1977 had thought it would be such a supercool outta-sight idea to name the newborn accidental child of their love Lana. The same child who by 1980 they would only discuss through their respective lawyers.

But now at Charles de Gaulle Passport Control, just like everywhere else since she became Mrs. Lana Gibson, her passport scarcely merits a glance before it's slid back to her. Briefly registering the bland, contented married-lady mug shot before she slaps it shut and sails on, Lana is struck by the chasm between that image and the real woman clutching it and is buzzed to feel more Lana Turner than she has for quite some time. The *Bad and the Beautiful* Lana, the *Postman Always Rings Twice* Lana.

Of course she knows that this feeling is not a good thing. Lana Gibson knows that too well. But it's such a good feeling.

With no luggage to collect, she's through Sortie 34 in less time than it takes to listen to "*Geek U.S.A.,*" which means more of her life snatched back. A ray of late afternoon sun nudging into a corner under the joyless gray concrete overhang outside Terminal One entices her. She could hop a cab immediately and keep the momentum going, but Lana Turner needs a cigarette.

The recent urge to buy her first pack of cigarettes in over a year had been her own first warning of the mood change. The actual purchase of that pack had been confirmation. And yet, and yet, it had been several days later before the defiant lighting up and luxuriant draw that signaled a great big "hi!" to the buzz. That lovely buzz. Welcome back, take me out, honey.

Lana opens a new pack and plucks one out and lights up and she's thinking of Brian now, though she doesn't want to. Even when he'd noticed the signs of elation, even when she'd told him to butt out and try not to be *so* lame—she'd be fine and this needed to happen every so often, it was part of who she was, right?—even when she'd laughed at his tentative suggestion to go see her doctor and get the necessary meds, Lana had still hidden the cigarettes from him, knowing that particular fall from grace would have made her husband so sad. It might have even made him feel that the ship had finally sailed. She couldn't be one hundred percent sure about that part, but still she could not, would not, do that to him, even though in this mood, Brian's feelings meant about as little to her as anyone else's feelings. Which was to say, pretty much not at all. So here, now in the sterile no-man's-land of CDG airport's smoking zone, alone, framed in that encouraging little rectangle of sunshine, she enjoys lighting up and sucking, sucking, sucking.

As she blows smoke and holds her hand aloft in a studied pose, she notices her wedding band next to the cigarette and has a sudden memory of just such a gesture, just such a moment. *Nathan.* Her last time in Paris. Forget that. Lana Turner is in charge now and she revels in the villainy of flicking the half cigarette away before plucking the band from her finger with élan and aiming for the taxi line.

The Suite Imperial is not available," the receptionist at Le Chevalier tells Lana in perfect, almost accentless English. Though the young woman's skin is crème fraîche and her eyes are pods of luxury bath oil, her smile is enamel-sealed, and she makes Lana feel rather foolish for having even considered that such an awesome prize could be had just for the asking. To anyone.

"But the junior suites are superb, superb, Madame. You will be very happy." Lana had known all along that the Suite Imperial would not be available. The whole *point* of such a facility is that access to it is almost impossible. But what if? Would she really have gone for it? At any price? How expensive could it be for only one night? How would Brian have reacted to that indulgence?

The bellhop's smile seems more genuine than the receptionist's, its warmth rising all the way to amber eyes she'd like to crawl into and be preserved in. Lana's wheelie duffel feels so light—holding only a cotton dress and bow pumps, extra underwear, and anything else it had occurred to her to toss in before she got bored with packing—that having it carried seems a little embarrassing, but you get what you pay for and it would be plain wrong not to enjoy the pleasure of that gorgeous face smiling her to the fifth floor. As he explains how the room keycard also operates the elevator, she wonders why a certain kind of French accent in English manages to sound naïve and erotic at the same time. She wants to close her eyes and let it shiver through her, but instead tries to affect an interest in *what* he is explaining to her.

"And the card only works for your level. You cannot, for example, use this to go to level three or six or . . ."

Lana now notices that the elevator only goes as far as six.

"Am I wrong? Did I read on the website that this famous Suite Imperial is on the seventh floor?"

"Yes. This is correct."

His quizzical look is adorable. Lana smiles.

"But the elevator only goes to six?"

"There is a private elevator to the Suite Imperial."

"Of course there is." Lana steps out and looks round. "Where is it?"

Now the poor guy looks mystified. Adorably so. "You want to see the private elevator?"

"Only if we mere mortals are allowed to gaze?"

"Pardon?"

"I'd love to."

As they squeeze through the central lobby, already crammed for cocktail hour, Lana's eyes are drawn upward, way up high, above the wave and curl of the art nouveau furniture and fittings, to where gold angels flutter at each corner of a dizzying ceiling fresco of gardens as seen from above. Tuileries Gardens, she guesses, by an artist of the early Google Earth school, perhaps? Anyone with vertigo or even just one cocktail too many should be warned *do not look up*. The bellhop stops and points through a tall picture window to a quiet corner. The private elevator looks disappointingly like the regular one, apart from the fact that it's placed so discreetly—more or less invisibly—around a corner in a space that leads nowhere else.

"How disappointing, not burnished gold or anything. Just discreet enough to keep the riffraff at bay."

"Pardon?"

"Riffraff."

"Rrriffrrraffe?"

"It's a special word. You should use it. American tourists will understand much better if you explain the whole keycard idea by telling them it keeps the riffraff away."

Now those eyes tell her he knows he's being toyed with as well as flirted with. A quiver of lip makes a half smile. He turns to lead her away but Lana stalls, needing more. Like seeing the doors of the private elevator open to reveal its mystery VIP resident.

"So, who's staying there now?"

A very French shrug, hovering at the corner of who knows and I'm not saying. Is such information simply above the bell hop's pay grade or is discretion a condition of his job? Now he walks away and Lana has to follow, but some movement right at the edge of vision makes her glance back through the tall window. A man is stepping into the now-open private elevator. Where had he emerged from? No one had walked by her. Had he been hovering out of sight, aware of her presence, waiting for her to turn away? Why? Infuriatingly, he doesn't turn as the doors close, so Lana doesn't get to see his face. Maybe he's so instantly recognizable, his celebrity so overwhelming that he fears anyone seeing him in case they could not control their hysteria. Or maybe just the reclusive type.

BACK IN THE RIFFRAFF ELEVATOR, SUCH QUESTIONS ARE FORGOTTEN thanks to the frisson caused by her proximity to the charming bellhop. Lana finds herself eyeing him openly, smiling all the way to the fifth floor, and can see that he is in no way embarrassed by this attention, and simply accepts it as nothing more than his due. And quite right too. Lana figures he's planning how to maximize his tip, the way a bellhop back home would, or just enjoying his own perfection, the loose elegance of his movement, a limber performance repeated over and over to ones and twos and small groups. What does he see when he looks at her? Are blondes his thing? Does he like thin? She had put on hardly any weight in the last five years, apart from in her breasts, which feel so much more attractive now. In fact she wishes for just a little plumpness in the cheeks as, for a year or more, she has felt skin tighten against bone, her smiles now brittle, almost forced, with a sourness about her mouth and— she was sure at this very moment—a little craziness in her eyes. The bellhop would hardly find her irresistible, but maybe he enjoys the attentions of—that egregious category—the Attractive Older Woman, and takes it for granted that someone like her might make certain advances. The situation has a whiff of Tennessee Williams about it, but let's not run away with ourselves, Lana thinks, it could also be a porn movie setup. Or what she imagines might be a porn movie setup, never having actually seen one. Out of completely nowhere she remembers Vince Litzow, Jesus, *Vince Litzow!* The poor dope trying to show her that adult video belonging to his parents, *Curse of the Catwoman.* When was that—was she fifteen? She'd laughed and lashed him with that seriously scary teenage tongue of hers and poor Vince had flushed so bad and drummed her out of his house really quickly as if he'd been afraid she'd see him cry. She could be such a bitch back then. Back then? What about now, flying the coop to Paris without bothering to inform her husband? She would call him, of course, in her own good time: it's only an overnight and genuinely a one-time-only opportunity. And the point is to see the definitive Hopper exhibition, which makes the whole escapade seem almost reasonable. Okay, the hotel is an extravagance, but Brian never worries about things like that and, in the context of her present state of elation, is a short bout of reckless spending so very bad? And what's wrong with playfully considering if a toothsome willowy bellhop was sizing up how old she might be?

Lana guesses the age difference at maybe thirteen years. Not so wide when viewed from thirty-five, but she wasn't so locked out of reality as not to realize that what she saw and what he saw were very different things. What a chasm thirteen years must seem from the point of view of immortal twenty-two or whatever, even though in her teens and early twenties she hadn't given any guy under thirty a second glance. But it was different for girls, wasn't it? Some of those names and faces suddenly come bouncing back, *Jesus no!* and she tries to refocus on now, this moment, on the bellhop's ass exiting the elevator—Lana wants to give him a name . . . Laurent? . . . Vincent? . . . Laurent—managing to look desirable even while rolling a bellman cart on which only a tan duffel sits, deflated and lonely. But Laurent makes it seem somehow important, as if the little bag could not have been transported any other way.

He unlocks 511, leads her in, sets down the bag, and, in what to Lana becomes a kind of dance accompanied by a purring monologue in that kissable voice, describes the art nouveau influence on the interior design. Lana pays little attention to the detail, enjoying instead the music and choreography of the

performance. Why it is that even young French men have oozing, cello-like voices, never that hectoring insistent American
horn blast: Brian on the phone braying to his pals about the
latest Seahawks game. "He's a super-intense guy and *hey!* I'm
all over that . . . he's gotta learn to channel that *competitive-
ness!* . . . The whole four-quarter-*total*-commitment thing . . ."

Laurent has so transported her that he is already saying
"Bonne soirée, Madame," and opening the room door on his
way out when she realizes she hasn't offered a tip. It's amusing
how her sudden apologetic cry and scramble for her purse, the
possibly gross generosity of the offering—Lana doesn't notice
what number is on the euro note she grabs and presses into his
soft hand—are acknowledged with nothing more than polite
equanimity. Merely his due, is that what he is thinking?

Lana misses him when he is gone and suddenly needs a
cigarette, so, as a distraction, she directs her attention very deliberately back to Brian.

It would be only kind to let her husband know where she
is, rather than leave him mystified, but he's still at work now
and never appreciates being interrupted. When he arrives back
to the very comfortable Edwardian house the company had
sourced for them on Dublin's north coast, her absence won't
be an immediate red flag, but if he calls and gets her voicemail
several times, he might become concerned enough to make a
"casual" call to their two Dublin friends, hoping she'd be with
them, trying not to reveal the stress that Lana knows will have
already begun to throb along his shoulders and up his neck.

To be fair, Brian was not the kind who would immediately
jump to the worst-case scenario, although he had been picking
up on and getting more anxious about her mood in the last day
or two. Lana had felt the drag of his uneasy attention. He'd

asked if she was worried at all at how long this "current phase" was lasting, and she was definitely taking her meds every day, wasn't she?

Does he have any idea how condescending his concerned smile looks? What about his own obsession with his work? Doesn't he ever think that's "excessive," that it needs "taking in hand"? Maybe he needs some meds to help sort out that fever. After all, it's the thing that occupies most of his waking hours and it was certainly what had uprooted them from Seattle to Ireland, whether she'd wanted to make the move or not. Actually she had very much liked the idea, the suddenness and freshness of it, but that was not the point. If Lana had refused to fall in with his plan—the complex sideways-upward career trajectory that involved fixing whatever was wrong at Dublin HQ, before triumphantly returning to Seattle and a certain promotion in six months or so—how would Brian have handled that? Lana knows exactly how: he would have nodded sadly, but resignedly, as if accepting her decision, then the pinpricking campaign would have begun, him scratching and hinting and nudging and nagging until he'd have gotten his way, somehow. That's as much a mania as hers is, isn't it? So Lana Turner thinks, let him suck it up for a few hours, let him stress about her, it'll do him good. Meantime, she'll get on with it, shower, change, go to the exhibition, and call him afterward, or—yes, better—just text him.

Fifteen minutes later, with her mind mostly on Hopper, Lana Turner still can't resist drifting across the lobby before exiting the hotel, drawn like a pig to a truffle toward the private elevator, hoping, though not believing, that this time there'll be some action. And *yesss*, there is. A slight-framed guy is standing waiting for the doors to open. His back is to her and it is definitely not the back she had seen earlier. This suit is a different cut and color, and it's much, much cheaper. Lana finds herself speeding up, trying to time it so that she will pass close by as the guy enters and turns. Just to get a nice close look at his face. The elevator doors ping open. He steps in. Lana accelerates, enjoying the ridiculously pointless rush of it all; the doors start to close and the guy turns and—something trips her. She stumbles forward. After several hotel guests converge to help her up and she assures them "It's okay, thank you, I'm fine, really, just a bit embarrassed that's all. How stupid of me!" the possibility occurs to her that it had been some*one*, not some*thing*, that had tripped her. She even asks herself if it is one of these concerned ones, then in a gap between the solicitous faces Lana notices an arm a shoulder and a big ear, a very big ear, protruding from a nearby high-backed armchair. This guy had not leapt to her aid, nor even stood to see what the fuss was about. She had passed close by that armchair on her impulsive dash toward the private elevator. Could this guy have stuck out a foot and caught her? Yes, but why would he have?

As Lana moves away, she can't resist choosing a moment to glance back casually, but the face is hidden behind today's edition of *Le Monde*.

Ferdie was gleeful. It was fun fitting Vallette's face to the body of the guy on all fours being fucked, then to the guy over him, thrusting, then back to the first option. The guy being fucked was definitely the better choice and technically the match looked pretty seamless. But the expression on Vallette's face in the photo he was using wasn't as hilarious as it should be. It needed to have more of that squinting disapproval that, Christ knows, Ferdie had seen often enough. It was just a matter of trawling through his gallery of Vallette head shots for one with just such a demeaning expression. But there was no time because he saw Monsieur Fournier approach the car and had to quickly power down his laptop and slip it under his own seat. The Photoshop efforts were very much for his own vulgar amusement, and he knew his employer wouldn't smile on them.

He hopped out to open the rear door and, listening to Monsieur Fournier's side of the phone conversation, understood that he was talking to Vallette. It pleased him that his boss's mouth traced a familiar smirk and his tone was sarcastic.

"So is the plan to assault any hotel guest who passes near the elevator? . . . Yes, yes, Arnaud, I understand completely how careful we must be, but let's also be careful not to create drama where there is none."

An hour ago, Ferdie had just stepped out of the elevator at the Suite Imperial for a final check when Vallette had phoned, barking at him to stay where he was until he came to him. Then he was subjected to an interrogation. Was he aware that he was being followed? No, in fact, Ferdie was fully aware that he was not being followed. Really? What about an American woman, blond, thirties? Ferdie was certain there was no such woman following him.

He turned onto boulevard Sebastopol and inched along in the rush-hour madness, which he never minded because it gave him more time to enjoy the regular sidelong glances from other drivers at his 1970 DS21; looks of fascination and envy for the classic favorite. Four years ago, when he interviewed for the job and was shown the car, he would have accepted any salary to be allowed to drive the black beauty with its sun-bouncing silver roof. Fortunately, Monsieur Fournier's rates were also generous. And the perfect threesome he had enjoyed with car and boss continued until the campaign made Vallette a much more oppressive daily presence. So it was a pleasure now to hear the master bring the overprotective guard dog under control; a double pleasure, because at the same moment he saw two heads in a brand new Citroën in the next lane turn and gaze with affectionate nostalgia.

"If you think it's worthwhile, Arnaud, then of course. And where is she now? . . . Really? How amusing, hm? . . . Well, an American comes to Paris and what does she want to see? An exhibition by an American artist . . . Frankly, unless your men would appreciate seeing Monsieur Hopper I don't see any need . . . It does seem obvious that she's just a tourist, yes?"

Back at the hotel, Vallette had claimed this woman "had been observed" pursuing him as he entered the elevator. He had made it sound like a catastrophe had been averted and didn't seem to feel any explanation was necessary as to why some American woman should have Ferdie under surveillance.

"If Oscar had not taken action she would probably have reached the elevator before the doors closed. What then?"

What "action" had Oscar taken? Ferdie did not know. More important, why had he been hanging around there at all? The answer to that one was clear. Vallette's instructions.

Then Vallette had done that infuriating thing he always did: repeat the question in precisely the same tone, like it was a recording on a loop, while never, not once, looking directly at Ferdie.

"Well . . . what then?"

"If some strange woman hopped into the elevator? I'd have stopped her, of course. Pressed the emergency stop if I'd had to, explained to her that she'd made a mistake and allowed her to exit. This woman was probably a tourist who thought it was just another normal elevator she could use."

Ferdie couldn't have cared less about what sounded like a farcical incident, but it had alerted him to a much more important matter. He had to stop Vallette from monitoring the elevator to the Suite Imperial. He didn't want any complications when he brought Caramel Girl to the party later.

"Anyway, we'll soon find out more. Oscar and Marcel are tailing her."

Ferdie had wanted to sneer openly at the lunacy of Vallette's favorite meatheads wasting time following some American tourist, but he held back. Confrontation now would not be useful. He wanted Vallette reined in, at least for tonight, and there was only one person who could quietly make that happen. Monsieur Fournier would have to persuade him or instruct him to back off. To encourage this, Ferdie reported the incident to his boss as an amusing anecdote while planting the idea that Vallette's approach was mildly embarrassing, just a touch heavy-handed in the circumstances. Was *indiscreet* too strong a word? These he knew were grievous errors in Monsieur Fournier's playbook.

"But Arnaud, Arnaud, listen to me, tonight, Arnaud, let's keep all security away from the hotel interior . . . Yes, yes, I understand, but nevertheless."

Ferdie stalled at a red, tense now. Vallette was arguing back as usual. Would he have his way after all?

"No, no, no . . . Yes, call it that if you wish. *Adamant* is a good word, Arnaud . . . Do I need to . . . ? Very well, my view is that such an arrangement seems a little *indiscreet* . . ."

Ferdie tingled when he heard his boss echo his exact word, with emphasis.

"Please, Arnaud. Let's not talk in terms of orders and instructions. Say it is my wish."

How many times had Ferdie heard Vallette push and push like this? And how many times had Monsieur Fournier rolled over? But it seemed not this time. "Outside the hotel is sufficient . . ."

For once, Ferdie wasn't impatient for the lights to change. He was happy to sit and eavesdrop.

"Naturally if there is some development with the American lady, that would change everything, but I don't seriously foresee a difficulty there, do you? I think we are in agreement on that at least."

Monsieur Fournier clicked off. He sighed. It seemed like everything was all right, but Ferdie looked in the rearview eager for confirmation. Say something!

"Ah, Ferdinand."

"Monsieur?"

"The light is green."

• • •

LANA CANNOT BELIEVE HOW MANY PEOPLE ARE WAITING IN LINE, CREAT-
ing a wide human spiral. The evening is mellow orange, but
she has no intention of hanging around outside for what might
be an hour or more. This could never happen back in Seattle,
where fifty thousand of Brian's too easily earned tax-deductible
dollars had bought the Gibsons their coveted Gold Circle status
at Seattle Opera, with free tickets to dress rehearsals and an invitation for two to the "intimate" director's salon, where they
could "mingle with the artists while enjoying cocktails." All
this and heaven too: season-long access to the Norcliffe Room,
complimentary valet parking, and so on and so on and so on.

But she is not in Seattle now and she knows the long lines
will be here tomorrow too, probably even longer on a Saturday,
so she puts the brake on her impatience and steps through the
first barrier. The young attendant looks at her Internet ticket
printout, smiles, points, and explains something. Lana understands enough to work out that the girl seems to be sending
her to a different line. But of course. The French would never
be satisfied with one line when they could create several. The
good news is that this second one, reserved for online bookers,
is much shorter. The great spiral is for the losers paying cash
at the entrance. A phrase floats into Lana's mind: "In the famous French triad of values, Egalité is the most abused." Then,
remembering who had said that to her, her smile disappears.
Nathan. This is precisely the memory of Paris she wants—
needs—to avoid on this trip. At all costs. She finds distraction

in the discovery that there is a line even more privileged than hers. The third, reserved for holders of something called Sesame Pass, is scarcely a line at all. Mostly these lucky patrons just drift in without having to wait. Almost all are women of a certain age, their lines and wrinkles complementing their air of grace. It helps that they all seem to be an enviable size six. Several arrive at the same time and fall into seemingly spontaneous conclave, which soon takes on the rhythm and intensity of an enthusiastic seminar. Lana figures they can't all be university lecturers or art critics, although they sure as hell come off like they are. But their anticipation of the pleasure ahead seems genuine.

Her own line shrinks quickly: fifty, twenty-five, fifteen. Lana is cold now, darkness is falling fast, and she has no energy left to be interested in either the privileged enthusiasts on one side, or the slow-shuffling herd on the other. Her only desire at this point is to get to those Hoppers. When the attendant finally waves her group on, she springs forward, a culture hound in full cry.

Lana realizes very quickly that the exhibition is more extensive and complex than she'd anticipated. The first display is an old black-and-white newsreel of 1921 Manhattan's heaving streets projected on a wall of a darkened room. Lana scans it very quickly; the world of Hopper, urban America, yeah yeah yeah. She pushes on, bundling through the gawking crowd, past painfully worthy early efforts from Hopper's Paris years. Moving right along. She flashes through a roomful of etchings, though their long-shadowed gloom carries a certain temptation, but Lana is clear about what she wants to see and has no intention of falling in with the exhibition's carefully structured narrative of Hopper's slowly maturing style. Not for her. Not today, thank you. So she cuts a swathe through the milling, whispering crowds, floats past a giant slide show of Hopper's work as a commercial artist for magazines, and skims a long line of East Coast watercolors, all the while wanting to scream, "Where are the Hoppers? The real Hoppers! Come on, curator! You know what everyone is here to see."

When they finally arrive, they do so with Christmas Day overabundance. Lana steps through an unassuming gap in a wall and is suddenly surrounded by the mother lode: images as familiar as home and secret as memory.

Now, finally, Lana stops racing around. She even breathes more slowly, although her eyes can't stop flicking around the treasure-filled room. Okay, here we are, settle now, she thinks, take your time. A thick semicircle of heads draws her eye first and, peeking through, she's not surprised to discover that they are gathered in front of *Nighthawks*. She negotiates a better view, but doesn't stay long. Nor does she linger at another favorite, *Gas*. Sure, there's the joyous tickle of recognition, the intake of breath at the solidity of its close presence, the texture of the paint itself so tangible. But then after no more than a few moments Lana just moves on, without quite understanding why, until she comes to *Compartment C Car 293* and loses herself. It can only be the woman's story that holds her: *who is she*, where is she going dressed in black on that late evening train? What's she reading? And thinking, her eyes hidden behind the brim of her black hat. Above all, Lana would love to know why she's alone.

Reluctantly, she tugs herself away, because she spots another favorite, *Office by Night*. A young woman is removing papers from a filing cabinet while glancing toward a man at his desk. There is such an undercurrent of longing in the young woman, as if she's wishing and hoping the man would give her the same attention he seems to be giving the document. Now, so close to the original, Lana notices detail that had never struck her before: how moistly scarlet the little smudge of lipstick glows amid the gloomy browns and subdued greens and creams of the cheap little office. The young woman's voluptuous bottom seems even more so, and the downturned eyes scream even louder of loyalty tormented by lonely desire. Working late, always there for him, waiting, waiting, waiting. For what?

One by one, Lana introduces herself to Hopper's solitary women, drawn from each one only by remembrance of another. The flowering sensual redhead in *Summertime*, who stands outside some forbidding old civic building, its gray stone and columns burnt almost white in the heat, seems even more aching with desire and yet more virginal. Alone among his women, Hopper had not painted her with downcast eyes. This girl lifts her face to the sun and allows a warm breeze to flutter her diaphanous dress between her legs. But, like all the others, she is alone. Even the ones Hopper pairs with men still seem somehow separate, in a lonely place. A woman on the edge of a tiny bed stares dejectedly at the floor, oblivious of the joyous morning sun pouring in the window and the man behind her sprawling naked on his stomach, his face buried in a pillow.

It occurs to Lana that she has no idea how long she's been drifting about the room and that her elation seems to have relaxed into a melancholic communion with these women. Now a work she has never seen before jolts her: the raw loneliness of *Hotel Room*. Once again a woman alone, sitting half-dressed on a bed, staring at a piece of paper. Lana admires how the bareness and cheapness of her room is created with rigid vertical and horizontal lines. What a contrast to the curvaceous ostentation, the billowy opulence of her Le Chevalier junior suite. But she and the sad lady share something: the woman has as little luggage as Lana does and what she has is strewn just as carelessly—shoes kicked away, a hat askew on a cheap bureau. What is this woman escaping, for surely she's hiding from something or someone? What has she lost or left behind?

The cell phone that appears right in Lana's eye line is a shock and her concentration is shattered by its camera's *click, click, click.* It's no surprise that the snapper is a student type, aglow with peachy-skinned youthful deliciousness, carrying all the requisite accessories including the cutest little scarlet heart-shaped purse. She could not be less like the woman in *Hotel Room.* This is a child raised on positive reinforcement, comfortable with her beauty, no doubt creative, and generally all-around amazing. Lana feels an impulse to slap that cell phone from her hand, kick in and gush forth like James Dean's oil strike in *Giant.* Instead, somehow, she manages to speak calmly.

"You know you shouldn't do that."

"Oh really, yeah?"

It's oddly relieving to hear an English tone rather than American. The contemptuous "yeah?" at the end is little princess-speak for "who are you?" Even as she hears herself snapping back, Lana regrets that she hasn't kept a dignified silence and hates how her own accent now grates with upward-inflected aggression.

"The signs? No photography? Just for other people, huh?"

The little princess wheels away, with a forced sigh, a twist of the nose, a dismissive swing of her purse and Lana tells herself, let it go, the moment is over. Except it isn't.

"Excuse me."

Lana turns and *click.* The little princess flips the screen to show her the photograph, just to be that much more of a mean girl. She has framed Lana's face side by side with that of the desperate woman in *Hotel Room*. In the background, incongruously, is a man turning his face away, obviously smirking. It can only be at Lana's humiliation. She spins round to lash out at him, but he is no longer there.

"Just like sisters, aren't you? Two pathetic women, yeah?"

There it was again: "yeah?" How could one harmless little word make this teenager sound so insufferably superior? She pops the phone into her little scarlet heart and skips away. What fun she'll have with that shot on her Facebook wall. Too late Lana thinks of an answer, not a zinger exactly, but what she should have said, wanted to say. "When I was your age I didn't *need* to snap or tweet or Facebook my life. I was in it, living it. In ways kids like you can't ever understand. Yeah?"

And that was true, wasn't it? Her memories are too powerful and detailed and clear for it not to be. But what if at thirty-five all that's left is a memory of living?

Lana deliberately does not check her own cell after she leaves the Grand Palais. Floating rather than pushing through the crowds, for once not bothering to turn and gaze with pleasure at the shimmering bending lines of car lights up the Champs-Élysées, red one way, yellow the other, she works hard to still her brain and focus on what she saw in each of those women before the student princess intruded. Why is she utterly convinced about one thing: that none of them are mothers. What had put such an idea in her head? It had probably never been in Hopper's, but that was of little significance. She considers if any of them had ever experienced pregnancy and decides that the woman in *Hotel Room* was the most likely. Yet she might not be a mother. She might, like Lana, have had a miscarriage.

Definitely time for my meds, she jokes with herself, but still, the conviction has lodged. And isn't she entitled to it? Isn't that what art is all about?

Exhausted from standing in line and hustling through crowds and visual overload, Lana doesn't feel remotely guilty at the thought of succumbing to the delicious indulgence of high-thread-count cotton and embroidered silk. Arriving back at the hotel, she feels like a nap is priority number one, but before reaching her elevator, abruptly changes her mind. Even if she does succeed in calming her jabbering brain sufficiently, the end result of going to sleep now would be to find herself awake at three in the morning, on full battery, buzzing for action. Far better for her to check out the hotel bar, have a Badoit, and see what's what, before escaping the hotel, maybe crossing Pont Neuf to Buci for dinner and—no, no, not the Left Bank. That would be asking for trouble. No point in walking herself into exactly the scenario she'd sworn to avoid on this trip. The nightlife at Les Halles and Montorgueil has its own special atmosphere and anyway, it isn't as if her brain, fevered though it may be, is demanding excitement or even adventure. All she wants to do is stroll about, enjoy the pleasure of listening and looking at how easily Parisians make it seem worthwhile to be alive, and expend enough energy to give her at least a fighting chance of a few hours' sleep later.

Waiting for the bartender to notice her, Lana tries to work out what the jazz trio is playing. Judging by the satisfied nodding to the beat and the knowing little smiles on their faces, none of the bar clientele is having any such difficulty. They are surprisingly young, their clothes striking a pitch-perfect balance between Le Chevalier chic and jazz casual. Even though the dark-wood walls and high stools and rows of spirit bottles jostling in front of a long beveled mirror behind the bar speak of an earlier age when more drink-hardened "Yanks" spewed out dollars and brawled in bars like this one, the pampered young French who fill the place tonight are clearly getting off on reliving that era and its music at a more luxurious remove. Only one young woman, sitting on one of the high stools at the bar, offers a whiff of what seems recognizably authentic cool. The unctuous maple of her skin gives her bare arms and long neck an almost viscous sheen. But it's the eyes that really fix the attention, even though Lana can only see them reflected in the beveled mirror: two amber pearls on plinths of sculpted cheekbones. Standing at the bar waiting for service, Lana feels like a tense small-town librarian finding herself backstage accidentally during Paris Fashion Week, standing awkwardly next to a supermodel. Lana can't be bothered with pointless and frankly dishonest self-deprecation. She knows that men have always found her attractive and are still genuinely surprised to discover that her thirtieth birthday was a very distant memory, but in her present mood, she can't help feeling that, next to this stunning creature, she simply withers on the vine.

Wanting to get a better look at this remarkable young woman, Lana decides to speak to her. But in English or French? Lana's warm and fuzzy liberal arts education had left her with the belief that an effort should always be made to say something in the language of the host, as a sign of respect, and this was quadruply true in the case of the French. The problem is, that tends to create the impression she can manage an adult conversation of reasonable complexity, which she cannot. A newer school of thought argues that rather than forcing the proud French to endure hearing their beautiful language mangled, the better option is to wave the white flag from the start, with: "You know what, I'm just not very good at this. Do you by any chance speak English?" Those who argue for this approach claim that present-day Parisian youth have abandoned the linguistic fascism of their elders and are all only too delighted to show off their English, or, more accurately, given that mostly they learn it from the movies, their American. This flawless young woman is certainly no more than twenty-five, and Lana guesses that she must be part Moroccan. She seems like the kind of girl who'd make hearts pump faster in any happening bar from Manhattan to Buenos Aires to Moscow. All things considered, the second approach seems the correct one, yet Lana still hears herself blurting out some embarrassing-sounding French.

"Quelle scène de foules. Très intéressant."

It takes the young woman a few seconds before she realizes that the crude noises have been addressed to her. She looks at Lana, puzzled, and then says something that Lana figures is broadly in the area of, "Did you speak to me?" Clearly, it's time to abandon the effort at conversational French.

"I'm sorry. Excuse my terrible accent. I was just saying what an interesting-looking crowd it is here. In the bar."

The young woman answers so rapidly that Lana doesn't catch much or any of it, but from the soft-voiced, yet icy dismissiveness of tone and the way, drink in hand, she swings her body away when she finishes speaking, Lana guesses that either the girl doesn't speak English, or has zero interest in speaking with her. All Lana's friendly curiosity, all her honest, disinterested admiration of the young woman's beauty, evaporates into a simple enraged under-the-breath mutter. "Well bite me!"

The poor bartender chooses that unfortunate moment to smile in her direction and gets burned by the back draft. "Badoit!" she blazes at him, but deciding mineral water won't satisfy her mood, barks an equally inflamed "Non. Champagne!" without even the most perfunctory "s'il vous plait." Lana figures that one champagne will be fine. One glass does no one any harm. A hearty meal will soak that up—she really is hungry now—and the meds can wait another few hours. No harm at all.

She has almost finished her glass and has finally recognized one of the jazz trio's numbers—a tricksy fun take on "You're

Nobody 'Til Somebody Loves You"—when, at the furthest corner of her vision, she senses a man approaching the unfriendly young woman. Lana allows herself no more than the merest turn of the head and a sideways look toward the mirror. The guy isn't so tall: barely eye to eye with the girl, who's still sitting. He's late twenties, in a suit way too cheap for Le Chevalier. Most unattractive of all, as far as Lana is concerned, is his receding chin, which in profile gives him the look of a nervy but potentially vicious bird. Bottom line, the guy isn't within several leagues of the young woman. Yet after only a few whispered words she's standing—now several inches taller than him—and together they head for the exit. Lana is stunned. Tasered. Is that her date? Is he very, very rich? Not in that suit.

Looking at how they move together, something doesn't feel right. Lana can't detect any intimacy or chemistry. Apart from his lips close to her ear when he spoke quietly at the bar, there had been no hint of physical connection. Lana keeps watching them as they cross the lobby and, when they shift direction, she can't help sliding from the barstool and trotting forward to keep them in sight. Now, from behind, she recognizes the guy. Earlier today she had seen that frame, that cheap suit, stepping into the elevator to the Suite Imperial, and that's where they seem to be heading. Well now. Lana follows as casually as she can and, through the giant picture window, sees Weak Chin produce the keycard, open the elevator doors, and usher the beautiful girl in. Still no touch, not even a hand on an elbow. It all begins to make sense to Lana. Weak Chin is not her date and certainly not the real occupant of the suite. He's a little helper, some kind of staffer for the seventh-floor celebrity. So, what's the deal with the young woman? Business or pleasure? Perhaps a family member? Lana doesn't even pretend to give that idea traction. Of course it may possibly be work-related: an actress meeting some movie producer? Unlikely, at this hour. His yoga instructor? Speech therapist? Singing teacher? Same. The only serious question is whether she's an actual girlfriend or a working girl and maybe Lana's inclination toward the less flattering option is because of the way she'd been iced by her at the bar. Also, a scenario of high-grade call girl and fabulously wealthy client getting it on with the Eiffel Tower in the background would make for a much more entertaining tale to tell. Arriving back to her barstool she notices that the beautiful young question mark had left a pack of Gauloises behind. She picks it up. Three left. Smoking one wouldn't be any kind of revenge for the way Lana felt she'd been insulted, but it could serve as a neat coda to the story, when she retells it.

Except that, out on the cold terrace, it doesn't feel like any kind of coda at all, more of an unsatisfactory trail of dots, a dying fall. Lana can't stop thinking about what might be happening on the seventh floor and it suddenly occurs to her that the encounter might involve genuine escorting, as in maybe the couple is planning to go out. In which case they'll pass through the lobby, in which case Lana would miss them if she stayed outside. So, after just a few savage drags at the Gauloise, she stubs it out in a plant pot and leaves the pack behind. Lana recognizes that a needle indicating her elation levels right now would be right up there in the red zone, but of course being elated means she couldn't care less about it. What's there to worry about? *Nothing is going to happen.* Which is actually a matter of slight regret to Lana Turner as she sidles past the picture window, eyeing the elevator and thinking, is there really no other way up to the seventh floor? Surely there has to be a fire exit. Imagine if she could locate it and . . . Lana *Gibson* knows this is just the crazy stuff ding-donging in her head and doesn't take any of it too seriously. A more relaxed and sensible way to find out more is to get herself a comfortable chair in full view of the elevator and wait for the doors to open and the answers to spill out. On the other hand, a better idea might be to forget all about it and take off into the magical Parisian night. Lana makes a deal with Lana. She'll give her fevered curiosity five minutes, no more.

She is about to sit down when the elevator doors open.

Disappointingly, they reveal nothing other than that she had been right about the little helper. Weak Chin steps out alone having delivered his presumably valuable package. He passes so close to her, their shoulders brush, but it doesn't seem deliberate or even conscious. His mind is elsewhere. She watches him cross the lobby. He doesn't look back. Lana cannot help edging closer to the elevator, though she has no plan or purpose other than to peek inside and confirm absolutely that it's not possible to use it without the privileged keycard. A quick scan like this seems perfectly safe: Weak Chin has now vanished into the crowd, and if anyone else suddenly appears she can just act foreign and confused. Where are the restrooms, please?

She steps inside the private elevator and immediately the doors close. It doesn't seem to be such a problem until she realizes there is no obvious DOOR OPEN button and it occurs to her that none of the buttons will work without the correct keycard. Feeling something a little more like panic, she presses one anyway. Nothing. Then another. Nothing again.

The elevator lurches and begins to ascend.

As if to say, "I'll teach you, missy, to mess with private stuff that doesn't belong to you," the elevator suddenly picks up speed. Lana tries to stay cool, telling herself there's nothing to do but wait helplessly for the journey to the seventh floor to end. While sincerely regretting the brash folly of her mania, she forces herself to surrender to it. What the hell, might as well enjoy it now. What's the worst that can happen? Some angry rich guy will rant at her, although, given that she'll be dealing with someone obscenely rich, it's more likely that the words will drip with politesse in a tone so icy that the elevator back down will feel like a freezer truck. On the plus side, she might get some confirmation on her call-girl theory and maybe even a quick peek at the glories of the Suite Imperial. Who had summoned the elevator? If it was another visitor, now departing, Lana might bluff her way past whoever it was, smiling and saying, "Sorry to intrude, but the gorgeous young woman who's just come up here with the ugly little guy left her cigarettes at the bar and I wanted to give them back to her."

Her cell phone rings, sudden and loud. Lana is shocked and for a moment irrationally assumes the call is coming from the Suite Imperial. She wrestles the cell from her pocket with giddy hands. The caller ID flashes: Brian. Of course, he's home by now, without the slightest idea where she is. The elevator stops with the politest of jolts. Nothing to do but send him to voice-mail. The doors slide and what is revealed had not, nor could ever have, flitted through even her most manic imagination.

Lana hears music before anything else registers. Hip-hop. Now that's a surprise. The elevator doors open to a little window-less lobby. On the facing wall, impressive white wood entrance doors are also open, revealing the suite itself beyond. Despite the dim lighting, she registers that the people she can see, at least a dozen or so, are all naked and in erotic attitudes, flickering silhouettes, bending, thrusting, writhing. But in seconds that shocking sight dissolves as she registers what is happening a couple of feet in front of her. The beautiful young woman from the hotel bar is struggling with a man. He grips her lower arms and speaks urgently, his eyes locked on her with hypnotic determination. The man is entirely naked, fully exposed.

The nightmarish energy of the scene before her reminds Lana of one of those grotesque medieval cartoons: the goat-man lunging, the predator having his way. His hair, silver-gray and too long, is a bag of rats' tails shaken free in the frenzy of his assault as the girl flails, desperate to escape.

There is the impulse to reel away in revulsion and there is the impulse to leap forward and wrestle the beast from his victim. Lana does neither. She cannot move, not even to look away. The young woman sees her now and opens her mouth, but no sound comes. Her expression no longer has any trace of the cool indifference of her demeanor in the bar. She frees one arm and stretches a hand toward Lana. It is clutching her purse. The goat-man's hand flays at it, too, and Lana sees he is determined to wrest it from her. Suddenly she becomes aware of something clutched in her own hand, gripping so hard it hurts: the cell phone. It is a struggle even to lift it up and beyond imagining to turn on the camera. Now the goat-man notices her. The last thing she registers as the elevator doors close again are his eyes, a chill of blue, and the pucker of lips as they form an expletive that would have been comprehensible in any language. Somehow, though unable to keep her hands steady, Lana manages to lift the cell phone and click-click-click-click as the doors close.

IT COULDN'T HAVE BEEN MORE THAN TEN SECONDS. THE ELEVATOR SHAKES and plunges in uncomfortable imitation of that stomach-churning moment when the roller coaster begins the dizzying descent from its highest point. Lana can't stop the elevator, but even if she could what would she do? Return and rescue the young woman? Whatever was happening up there couldn't end well. But right now Lana just wants to retch, although there's every chance that if she does she'll only heave up her hopping heart.

When the elevator door opens back at ground level, Weak Chin is there to meet it. Lana abandons any thought of going back up. The way his expression changes from that of an un-attractively bored teenager to "Jesus! There's zombies coming at me!" would, in other circumstances, have been cartoon-funny. His reflexes are impressively quick all the same. He manages to slap a hand against the side of the elevator and step forward to prevent Lana exiting. But he can't guard against her hysteria-fueled foot stamp. Her heel grinds into his instep with all the force of survival panic. His mouth opens with a yelp, his eyes pop, and the hand barring her way drops.

Lana decides her room is the safest place to be and power-walks through the lobby, staring straight ahead, praying that her elevator will be waiting on the ground floor and her hands won't shake too much when she tries to use the keycard.

The elevator is there. She lunges in and glances back. No sign of Weak Chin in pursuit. Probably not walking too well. Her pleasurable thrill as she recalls the foot stamp disappears when the keycard doesn't register. Lana swats it hopelessly and, glancing up, sees Weak Chin standing in the crowded lobby, eyeing her directly, but not moving closer. He looks away at something else, then turns back to her again. Why isn't he coming for her? The absence of immediate threat steadies her hand holding the keycard. At last the green light flashes. As the doors close, Weak Chin still stands in the throng, staring at her, then away, then at her, then away again.

•   •   •

BLOND, THIRTY MAYBE. WHEN THE ELEVATOR DOORS HAD OPENED FERDIE had been totally thrown. Even the shock and agony of her vicious attack had been less excruciating than the realization that this could be the same woman Vallette had been ranting about. If so it meant . . . what the fuck did it mean? Whatever was going on, Ferdie sensed he had tumbled headfirst into the kneading trough. What was this woman doing in the elevator? What had happened upstairs?

Something had told him the seventh floor was not where he wanted to be just now, so he'd pursued the blonde instead, although with what felt like some part of his instep smashed there was little chance of catching her now. He limped as fast as the pain allowed, but she was out of sight. Vallette and Oscar and Marcel were watching outside. If she left the hotel surely Oscar would recognize her. And if they caught her would that make things any better for Ferdie? Somehow he didn't think so. Maybe he should go up to the Suite Imperial and face the music.

As he turned he had the feeling that the blonde had flashed by somewhere in his field of vision, but before he could check again, something else caught his eye: the bellhop, his young pimp, was crossing the foyer toward some guy wearing a porkpie hat, who then gripped the bellhop's arm and whispered urgently to him.

Anyone in a porkpie had to be a prick, was Ferdie's opinion. His attention split between this pair and the blonde. He glanced over his shoulder and now he spotted her in the other elevator, desperately swiping her keycard. So she was a hotel guest. Ferdie looked again to Bellhop and Porkpie. They clearly knew one another, heads close together, a hand on a shoulder, as they headed for the smoking terrace. Ferdie swiveled back to the blonde. She'd stopped swiping the keycard because she was staring at him. Now she knew he knew. What to do? What to do? Too much going on at the same time.

And there was more. Vallette marched in through the main entrance, Oscar and Marcel scuttling behind. They were coming straight toward him. The only thing Ferdie was certain about was that *none* of this could be good for him. A last stare at the blonde. The elevator doors were closing. Ferdie didn't have to concern himself with her for now. She had just trapped herself. Vallette approached and passed without a glance, but clicked his fingers and pointed for him to follow. Oscar's and Marcel's smirks as they passed were not reassuring.

Ferdie was obviously in deep shit, but had no idea why. What was going on? What had happened up in the suite? It had something to do with that blonde, for sure. His knowledge that she was a guest—information no one else had—might help him wriggle off whatever hook he was on. Getting her room number would be easy enough—not for him, of course, a mere chauffeur, but for Monsieur Fournier or, more likely, Vallette.

Ferdie had followed too slowly. The doors of the private elevator were closing as he arrived, and the others didn't bother to hold it for him. While he waited for it to return, he thought about Bellhop and his pal. Whatever they were whispering about, it seemed urgent. Could it have something to do with his problem?

When the elevator arrived back in the foyer, it was not empty. Three middle-aged men in two-thousand-euro suits scampered out. He wanted to advise them that if they were trying to look like they were leaving some business meeting, they should lose the scared-rabbit faces and not move like there was an angry bear in pursuit, but though the party regulars knew Ferdie well, none of them acknowledged him.

It was even more clear now. Trouble awaited upstairs.

More party gentlemen were hovering when he arrived to the seventh floor and entered the foyer of the suite. No one made eye contact with him, and the place stank of nervous embarrassment. Oscar, who seemed to be managing the evacuation, gestured and three nervous ex-bacchants raced to the elevator. He offered Ferdie a quick pitying look, but said nothing. The interior of the suite itself felt like the aftermath of some flood or natural disaster with the female survivors taking refuge in a safe house. The girls had dressed and were sprawled on the couches, whispering and sniggering.

Caramel Girl was not among them. Where was she?

He was peppered with moany questions.

"Ferdie, at last. What's happening?"

"Ferdie, you gonna sort this out? When can we go?"

"Ferdie, we're still getting paid, right?"

The attitude was friendly, which was a relief. He didn't need a coven of party girls baring their teeth right now. He made appropriate reassuring noises and managed a big smile, but his attention was elsewhere. No sign of Monsieur Fournier, no sign of Vallette, and no sign of Caramel Girl. This was not good.

The master bedroom was the only part of the suite he had not checked. Ferdie stared at the closed door, not sure he wanted to find out what was on the other side. But he had to. He tapped. In just one word, "Yes?," Vallette's growl was recognizable. "Ferdinand, sir." Silence, then the relief of Monsieur Fournier's mellow "Come in, Ferdinand."

Monsieur Fournier was sitting on the bed fully clothed, bending forward to stare down at his dangling feet; they didn't quite reach the floor. His hair looked like he'd been scratching his scalp in a frenzy. Vallette stood at the end of the bed, looking at Caramel Girl, who was tied to a chair, gagged with tape. Ferdie wasn't sure what to feel. It didn't look like she'd been harmed, at least not in the way he had begun to fear. Nor was there anything like fear in her eyes. They flamed, an emotional cocktail composed of equal parts rage, bile, and contempt.

"You know this girl." It was not a question. "Monsieur Fournier tells me you brought her here and introduced her. But she did not feature in the dossier. I never saw this face."

Ferdie knew that if he opened his mouth now he would just tell some stupid lie. So he stayed silent, staring at Vallette, aware that if Vallette bothered to return his gaze, how obvious the terror in his eyes would be.

"I will want to know everything about this girl. You may need a little time to think about this. Take Monsieur Fournier home. Then return immediately."

Return? To what? Nothing good, for sure. He might have a better chance of survival if he made some sort of plea to both of them. Monsieur Fournier had always been an ally. If he could shift the conversation away from Caramel Girl. The information about the blond American: now was the time to lay that mouse proudly at his master's feet.

"Yes. Of course. But the other woman. The blond American. You were right about her—"

"I said, take Monsieur Fournier home now—"

"I was at the elevator when she came down. She stamped on me."

Even as he pointed Ferdie knew it was ludicrous to think that in the circumstances either of these men would have the slightest interest in his foot injury.

"Go. Now!"

Vallette clearly wanted to be left alone with Caramel Girl. Ferdie didn't have time right now to be too concerned about her. His words came tumbling fast.

"But wait, listen. I followed her. When you passed me in the foyer, I had just seen her use the other elevator. She had a keycard, so she's a guest. We can find out her room number."

Ferdie wished he hadn't said *we*, that was a mistake, but still, Monsieur Fournier now turned to him, suddenly interested. Even Vallette seemed to be considering. He and Monsieur

Fournier eyed each other briefly. Then Monsieur Fournier stood and offered his quiet, sad smile.

"Thank you Ferdinand. Very good."

Ferdie thought, *prayed*, that his information had saved him for now.

"So, take me home and return, as Arnaud suggests."

It hadn't.

• • •

HEART DRUMMING, LANA DOUBLE-LOCKS HER ROOM DOOR AND LEANS against it. She slides to the floor, terrified and laughing. Or at least it's a spluttering sound that might be laughter. What had just happened was terrifying and . . . *thrilling*. She breathes deeply, slowly through her nose, trying to get a grip. Could she be in trouble, in danger even? Whatever she'd witnessed in those few seconds on the seventh floor, it was something ugly and secret, for sure. Jesus, what had she just *done*? The photos— how had she had the presence of mind to grab those shots? Presence of mind? No way. Mad, blind instinct. The elation driving her on. Scary, but intoxicating. She fumbles for the cell phone. Its camera is one of those that takes shots in quick succession and Lana has managed to fire off four. The first shows a section of wall and what might be a bob of silver hair in the bottom of the frame. Annoyed, she clicks to the next: the elevator doors closing and, in the gap between, an outstretched hand. Damn! The third and fourth are just shots of elevator doors almost, then fully, closed.

Useless. The young woman's panic and distress; the naked man's aggression; the photos captured nothing of what she saw. Lana recognizes that if she reports the incident she will have to do so without any evidence to back it up. Her brain is a jumble, total gridlock, a tangle of wires. What to do? What time is it? Really hungry now, but isn't she somehow . . . doesn't she have to report this thing? Who should she report to? Hotel management? There's no chance they'll do anything. Whoever is paying for that suite has to be one of their most valuable clients. What about the police, then? Will they just think she's a nut job? What about the language difficulty? What would she even say? Once again Lana remembers the whole weird playlet she'd witnessed. Would it be out of order to use the word *rape*? Was that what it was? Assault for sure. A further doubt now enters her head. If she describes it moment by moment, would she be describing a crime at all? Her instinct says yes, absolutely, in the United States, but is French law the same? The incident was beyond question horrible, ugly, distasteful, and violent, or certainly potentially violent. Is "potentially" enough to bring the police here? It's probably already too late. The naked man saw her, and his little minion knows how feral her survival instinct is. He'd have limped back to report to his boss, so surely they haven't just carried on doing . . . whatever? If Lana calls the police, assuming she can even get through to the appropriate person and make herself understood, by the time they could get to the hotel and go up to the suite, there would be nothing to find. Whatever had been going on between the young woman and the naked old guy is surely over by now.

Lana is aware of just how frantically her head is spinning and tries again to control it. She forces herself to stand still for as long as she can—about three seconds—and breathes slowly and deeply. At the heart of this mess, she asks herself, what is the one thing, the only really important thing? She had witnessed, however briefly, what seemed, on the face of it, to have been an act of violence against a young woman. It might also be true that she fervently wishes she hadn't stepped into that elevator and seen anything, but now she has some kind of duty, responsibility to the young woman, even though Lana had been iced by her earlier at the bar, even though she can't be certain that the girl is a completely innocent party. Had she known she was going to an orgy, or had she been invited up there on false pretenses, gotten a shock, and tried to leave? Is there some other angle? What was in that purse the naked man seemed so anxious to get a hold of? Had she stolen something? What precisely did those few seconds Lana had witnessed actually mean?

At least by calling the police she'll have done *something*. If the young woman makes a complaint, then Lana's testimony could be important corroboration. What about an anonymous call? Say something dramatic, so the police will have to respond immediately: "A young woman's life is in danger in the Suite Imperial at the Hotel Le Chevalier. Come quickly." Could she manage that much in French? Could they trace the call to her room? Is her cell the better option? Lana picks it up several times and throws it down again on the bed. Just make the call, she tells herself, anything is better than pacing around trapped and hungry and stressed out. She forces herself to sit and, as calmly as possible, checks the hotel information book for the emergency number for the police. When the moment comes, the hotel phone seems safer to use for some reason. She gets an outside line and dials. As soon as the French voice comes at her, too fast, too peremptory, she feels panic.

"Ah, gendarmes s'il vous plait."

Another burst of quick-fire French. Lana doesn't know exactly what's being said, but guesses that she is already talking to the police.

"Ah . . . d'accord. Il y a un urgence . . ."

What, what is it she wants to say? The voice at the other end sounds impatient. A woman in danger at Le Chevalier. Suite Imperial. Jesus, just get it out.

"Pardon, je suis dans L'Hotel Chevalier, je suis une étrangère—"

No, already too much information. She's interrupted again. Would the guy not let her even try to explain? She catches one word, *ville*. Is he asking her what town?

"Hotel Le Chevalier à Paris. Le premier arrondissement. Une situation terrible . . . violente. Allez vite, vite."

She sounds like a babbling idiot. This is utterly hopeless. Once again the questions come at high speed and that's when Lana hears a loud ring and everything stops in her head. She slams down the phone. Another ring. It's her cell, of course. The relief when she sees it is only Brian makes her sink to her knees. But of course it's Brian: who did she think it would be? She's surprised to realize that she wouldn't mind hearing his voice right now, but knows it would be crazy to talk to him. Not now. Not until she has achieved some kind of calm.

The call goes to voicemail. She waits a beat, then checks the screen. Three texts: the first, two hours ago, is casual: *Me home where U?*

The second had followed right after with proper spelling and punctuation, always a definite impatience indicator for Brian: *Will you be home soon? Should I go ahead and eat?*

Nearly an hour had passed before the third, the tone of which performs a little uneasy dance between annoyance and concern: *L hon are you picking up your msgs? what's happening?*

What's happening? There's no way she can tell Brian. He'd totally lose it. Which is why a conversation has too many dangers right now. Lana decides on a simple cheerful text. She types rapidly: *Hi. Srry, phn off. Ovnite Paris for Hopper Exhibit. See you tmrw.*

Lana had barely hauled herself from the floor when the reply comes: *WTF!*

If that's his reaction to the fun part, imagine telling him what else has been going on. Another text pops up: *You serious?*

She answers quickly: *Dont worry. All cool. Exhib was transcendent!*

Lana knows this won't be the end of it. Moments later the phone rings, and once again she lets it go to voicemail. It rings again. Then another text arrives.

Where you staying? Did you bring meds? Call me.

The comfort of a familiar voice is so tempting. But she knows any conversation would become a sinkhole because no way would Brian leave it at, "Enjoy yourself, honey, see you tomorrow!" He'd keep pushing and pushing and they'd argue and inevitably she'd let something slip and make things worse. But another voice keeps prodding: isn't it only fair to reassure him, at least tell him she's brought her meds? Okay, so she hasn't taken her dose yet, but she has them, by her side, waiting. So Brian can relax. She taps out another message: *Have meds. Hopper sooo great. It's all good, honeybabe. Relax.*

Lana sends it before, too late, she regrets *relax* at the end. It's exactly the kind of thing Brian hates being told.

His response is more even-tempered than she feared but still persistent: *Call me. Let's talk. PLS!*

Can she risk it? She is feeling a little calmer. By reassuring him she might reassure herself. Also, a little chat is probably the only way to end the texting tennis. What the hell. She dials. Brian answers halfway through the first ring. The tension in his voice is certainly not calming. "Lana, baby, what's going on?"

Apart from seeing a young woman assaulted at a sex orgy? Apart from being locked away in her hotel room in a panic?

"Nothing, Brian, really."

"Nothing? Okay, look, let's not, you know, let's not dance around this. You're elated. You've been this way for a couple of weeks now. You can deny it all you like—"

"I'm not denying it, Brian."

"Right. Okay. Well . . . So . . . When I get home and you're not here, isn't it . . . you know, it's not surprising if I'm a little— call it concerned."

Lana can tell Brian is on a roll, attackattackattack, so she steps into the bathroom, clicks him onto speaker, and places the cell on the toilet seat. She runs the tap and douses her face with cold water, telling herself to keep it steady, it'll soon be over.

"So, I text you. No answer. I text again. And I hear nothing for nearly two hours, then I get this, this breezy 'hey I flew out to Paris today' TEXT! So now what? You've seen this exhibit and you're alone at night in Paris and in no condition—I mean Jesus, Lana. I'm worried about you, can't you understand that?"

After a few seconds of dead air, Lana, mopping her face with a hand towel, realizes that Brian has finally run out of words. She leans in closer to the phone.

"Okay, I know you're worried, but you know that I'm— you know—in this certain mood right now, okay? Elated. All right. So you know what goes with that and I'm sorry, Brian, but the reality is it doesn't matter that much to me what you're feeling, because I know that what you're feeling is misguided and you've got nothing to worry about. But I called you, didn't I? And now you know I'm fine, everything is fine, and I'll be home tomorrow. So there is no problem."

"But you're on your own over there. You are on your own, aren't you?"

"Jesus, Brian. I'm staying in Le Chevalier, not slumming it in some pension out in the banlieue."

"Le Chevalier? Oh. Okay."

At last, she hears a meaningful shift in Brian's tone. To him, an expensive hotel in a foreign city is a vaccine against unknown threats. Just like how first-class flights or Michelin-starred restaurants ward off all evil.

"Surely you figured that there's no way I'm going to be high in Paris in a cheap hotel?"

"Oh. So you're going to eat there? Is that the plan? Just relax in the hotel and . . ."

Relax? If only. If only her brain would slow a fraction. She slumps on the floor next to the toilet.

"That's exactly right. I just want a little time on my own . . . to . . . to ponder, to think about what I saw today." Yes, steer it back to Hopper. Safer ground. "Like I said, the exhibition was so amazing, a real once-in-a-lifetime kind of deal, you know—"

"Of course, and I know you're a big Hopper fan. I understand. Really. I mean I guess I'm just a little, I don't know, disappointed . . . You know if you'd told me about it, I could have organized something really amazing for both of us. Maybe I'd have liked to see it—"

"Let it go, Brian. Let it go now."

"Okay. Sure, okay, honey. So . . . you'll eat in the hotel, right? Relax. And you have your meds."

"If I'm a good girl tonight, can I do some shopping in the morning?"

"Sorry?"

"If I stay locked up safe tonight, can I step outside the hotel before I have to go to the airport?"

"Oh come on, honey. Don't be like that. I love you, I'm worried about you. You know you're not . . . well. You have to work on getting better, that's all I'm saying. Please don't make me the bad guy."

Dumb, dumb, dumb, dumb! So near to bringing this to a nice neat end, why had she shot off her stupid mouth?

"I know. I'm sorry."

Lana doesn't mean this, but she needs to end this call NOW, to hop off this nerve-jangling carousel. But she's also aware that it has to happen peacefully, so as not to alarm her husband. She stands up, grabs the phone, and clicks it off speaker, returning to the bedroom as she speaks.

"It was wrong of me to take off the way I did, but you know by now how this thing works and hey, at least I'm aware of it. I have to get myself back in balance. But believe me, baby, this little trip, the exhibition, it's helped already. I promise. I'm feeling more . . . grounded already."

She almost makes herself believe it. She shakes the contents of her bag onto the bed until the little prescription bottles tumble out.

"I'll take my meds and then go eat, okay . . . okay? Listen."

She rattles a bottle close to the phone: a thirty-day supply of Risperdal.

"I'm taking them as soon as I get off the line, yeah? And I'll see you tomorrow."

"Well . . . okay. You want me to pick you up at the airport?"

"Why not, yes. That would be lovely. It's the last flight."

"What time?"

Lana's lips tighten. What time, what time? She plucks the boarding pass from the mound on the bed.

"Oh, let me see, just finding the . . . Oh here we are. Arriving at ten forty tomorrow night. Terminal Two. And I'll call you from Charles de Gaulle before we take off. Say . . . eight o'clock your time?"

There are a few more wearying okays and love-yous before Brian finally hangs up. Yet Lana feels better for having spoken to him. It has put some distance between her and the situation she's found herself in. Maybe she should just get out on the streets and try to forget the whole mess. Is that possible? Is it the right thing to do?

The knock on the door answers the first question. Someone has caught up with her. A clear voice, deep notes, speaks her name.

"Madame Gibson."

Can she hold her nerve and her silence until whoever it is goes away?

"Madame Gibson. This is the police."

• • •

DRIVING WAS PURE AGONY AND NOT JUST BECAUSE EVERY TIME FERDIE had to touch the brake pedal it felt like someone was jabbing a knife into his instep. Generally Monsieur Fournier loved to chat, loved the sound of his own voice, though he would also occasionally fall silent, lost in thought. But this time, he maintained silence for the entire journey. Ferdie wasn't foolish enough to break it with attempts at badinage. This did not feel like a lost-in-thought silence. It was more of a freeze-out-Ferdie silence.

He parked and limped around, wincing, hoping to garner a little sympathy, but when he opened the rear door Fournier stepped past him without a word. As he keyed in the code to his building he spoke without glancing back. "She was an adorable piece of ass, Ferdinand. Such a pity." He stepped inside. "Now go talk to Vallette." The door swung shut.

Alone, sore, frustrated, and scared, Ferdie wished he knew what had happened with Caramel Girl. Clearly, the blond American's little trip in the elevator was part of whatever the problem was. Now Ferdie recalled that when he met Caramel Girl in the bar earlier he had half-noticed a woman sitting alone on a nearby barstool, but had paid little attention and could remember nothing about her, not even the color of her hair. But it could have been the blond American. Now it was clear. Vallette had made a connection between them and Ferdie . . . Oh Christ!

· · ·

THROUGH THE FISH-EYE PEEPHOLE LANA CAN SEE TWO MEN. THE ONE IN the foreground, the older of the two, is presumably the one who had spoken. He's staring straight at her as if he knows she's watching.

"We need your help, Madame Gibson. Please open the door."

This is spoken with utter confidence that she's inside, listening and looking. The distortion of the lens doesn't, for some reason, make this man's face look fatter. Instead the lines of his forehead, the haunting prominence of his cheekbones, and the weary sympathy in his eyes are magnified into something rather powerful-looking. Lana opens the door a crack. Face-to-face, the man looks mid-forties, with serious wrinkles, although the gray in his hair is only beginning to take hold. A man who compels attention.

"Pardon the intrusion, Madame. I am Detective Inspector Fichet. You would prefer if we speak like this?"

His ironic half smile and little gesture make Lana feel foolish, but even still she doesn't open the door any farther.

"What do you want, Inspector?"

"We need your help. Pardon my English if I do not explain well. Would you prefer if we spoke in French?"

"No. My French is pretty terrible and your English sounds just fine. Just tell me how I can help you, Inspector?"

Fichet leans in closer and speaks very quietly, as if discretion is his highest priority. His cologne, Lana is surprised to notice, is just as discreet. Expensively scented cops? Only in Paris, she can't help thinking.

"There has been an incident in the hotel. A certain gentleman has been taken into custody. We understand that you may have witnessed something . . . ah, pertinent. I am sorry. This is difficult. It is such a delicate matter."

The detective seems genuinely embarrassed and uncomfortable standing out in the corridor. Now that she knows it's about what she'd guessed it might be about, Lana figures it's really not an option to conduct the conversation like this. She opens the door the rest of the way.

"Thank you, Madame."

He turns to his large colleague and speaks rapidly. Then he smiles reassuringly at Lana.

"He will wait outside."

He hadn't actually been invited in, but could hardly be refused now. Inspector Fichet closes the door and strolls past her into the room. Lana can't help feeling some loss of control already.

"Until tonight I have never been in Le Chevalier. Now in

a little space of time I have seen the Suite Imperial and ah . . . well, a more, shall we say, normal room. But even the normal room is special. Art nouveau is not to my taste, but the air of opulence is necessary for a hotel such as this, yes? You arrive today? From the U.S.?"

"No."

Fichet waits, but Lana says nothing more. Fichet laughs.

"Ah, I understand. You are not under interrogation, Madame. No, excuse me. It is my habit to ask questions. Forgive me. All right, but there are some things I must ask."

Lana's not sure she likes the way Fichet's eyes flick about the room. Is it just her paranoia or have they come to rest at the bottles of pills on the bedside locker? Can he read the labels from that distance?

"Did you travel in the private elevator reserved for the Suite Imperial approximately . . . half an hour ago?"

"I did."

"Ah, wonderful. I see you are a very direct woman. I ask a simple question, you give a simple answer. So my work will also be simple. If only more people understood this. *Donc*, the elevator went to the seventh floor?"

"Yes."

"Will you tell me what occurred?"

So, it's happening. Suddenly she's a witness.

"Of course."

"Thank you. May I?"

Fichet gestures toward an armchair. Lana nods and it's only when he sits down that she realizes how much closer it brings him to the bottle of pills beside the bed. But he doesn't seem to notice them.

"Are you going to take notes?"

"Not now. I want you to be comfortable telling your story. I'm sure you will be willing to make an official statement later if necessary."

"I see. Well . . ."

The difficulty for Lana is where to begin. In the private elevator, or at the bar with the young woman? Or even the earlier conversation with the bellhop? She decides to keep it simple. More than anything, she needs to avoid babbling. She had stepped into the elevator, it had suddenly taken off, the doors had opened at what she'd assumed was the Suite Imperial, and . . . well, she'd seen what she'd seen. The incident, if that was the right word, had lasted maybe ten seconds. Then the doors had closed and the elevator had descended to the lobby floor. Lana doesn't see any point in mentioning her encounter with Weak Chin. Fichet nods helpfully throughout and doesn't interrupt, although he has a curious and distracting habit of excavating his fingernails with the thumbnail of the other hand, without ever taking his eyes off her, almost as if he's unaware of the action. The thumbnail burrows under each fingernail, slides across, and emerges with a click, one that sounds oddly sinister.

When she finishes, he says, "If you do not mind, Madame, please describe again exactly what you saw when the doors of the elevator opened on the seventh floor."

Exactly what she saw? This time Lana becomes very conscious of precise detail and weighs her words more. She highlights the violence of the old man's grip, the girl's hand outstretched, the struggle for the purse. Even though Fichet's gaze is still friendly, she feels as if it is warning, "Don't lie to me because I will find you out." The steady click of thumbnail on fingernail doesn't help her feel any more at ease. When she finishes, he nods, but says nothing for what seems a very long time. Finally he stops the nail picking and stretches back in his chair looking around as if imagining himself as a guest, luxuriating in all Le Chev' has to offer. He'd enjoy the courtesy manicure set, she smirks. Though it seems quite accidental that his little visual survey brings him to the bottle of pills, his gaze at it for what seems a very long time is deliberate.

He smiles again and says casually, "Very good. Very clear. Nothing more you want to add?"

"No."

"Tell me. Do you think you would recognize the young lady or the man, or both if you saw them again?"

"Oh yes. Well . . ."

"Yes?"

"The man was naked so I guess that complicates things a little, but his eyes and his hair . . . yeah, I think I'd know him again."

"Excellent. Oh, I did not ask—I should not presume, but you did not say if . . . Do you know either of them?"

"No."

"So, you had never seen either of them before?"

For some reason Lana really notices just now how strong his face is, weary experience etched in the lines and creases, warning in the steady gaze. She suspects the question is a test or trap and Fichet already knows that she had encountered the young woman beforehand. It's entirely possible that he had found this out, but just as possible she's extracting meaning where there is none. It's amazing how quickly under even the friendliest interrogation guilt starts to play a role. The question seems important to Fichet, for whatever reason. What's clear is that, just as she'd thought the thing had been concluded in a relatively straightforward way, her story now seems more complicated.

"Well, no . . . yes. I hadn't mentioned this because it didn't really seem to be . . . well, I didn't think it was important. But earlier on, I was sitting at the bar and I, ah . . . I did notice the young woman. Actually she was sitting quite close to me."

Fichet offers no reaction to this information. He waits for more. Lana hangs on to silence.

"Oh. That is all? You saw her."

"Yes . . . well, I said something to her actually, you know I guess I tried to make conversation, just something stupid you know but she, ah . . . well, she wasn't interested or maybe she didn't speak English, I don't know. But anyway, she just . . . well, frankly, ignored me. Which was no big deal actually. And then this guy came and she left with him."

"A guy? The same man you saw with her later?"

"No, another guy. Little thin guy, weak chin."

It's nothing more than a flutter across his eyes, but Lana guesses she's just told him something of interest. Again he waits for more.

"She went with him to the private elevator."

"Ah. Sorry, am I understanding you? You saw her in the bar?"

"Yeah, she was sitting at the bar, so was I."

"But you said you saw them go in the elevator?"

Too late, Lana knows she has complicated things again, even though Fichet's tone is no more than one of polite confusion.

"I am trying to imagine, but I don't think it is possible to see this elevator from the bar."

"No . . . no, you're right. I was curious so I . . ." She really didn't want to say "followed." "So I suppose I stepped out after them, just to see where they were going."

Fichet stands. He seems pleased about something.

"Ah, yes. Forgive me, but I think I understand now. I wished to ask you something, but I was not sure how to ask. I did not wish to be . . . intrusive. But it is okay."

"What is it? I don't understand."

Something is nagging at her about Fichet now, something hard to frame as a sensible thought, but it's as if his voice and his smile tell her one thing, while those steady eyes are pursuing another wholly unspoken agenda. What that might be, Lana has no idea.

"Hm? Oh. It was just my strange curiosity. Always I think *why*. So, when you tell me your story the first time, you do not say why you go into the elevator. *Alors*. Maybe the reason is not important, but I cannot help asking myself. And now I see. This young woman, she was interesting to you, and then a man comes and you follow them and you see her going in this special elevator and now she becomes more interesting, yes? I see now. You were curious, that is all."

He says it with a kind of triumph in his tone, as if he had just solved some great puzzle in his head. Is he insinuating, or rather taking for granted, that Lana's interest in the young woman had been sexual? Jesus! But Lana knows not to get into that with him. She'd just sound stupidly defensive. Who cares as long as he thinks he has it all figured out? Hopefully, this means the conversation is wrapping up. One thing is clear: whatever had happened up on the seventh floor the police are all over it, which is good. If what she had seen was of any value to their investigation they'd ask for a statement, tomorrow presumably. Fine. She should warn Fichet that she'll be leaving Paris in less than twenty-four hours. But right now, it seems that she can relax and safely leave her room and the hotel. Just enjoy what's left of the evening and eat, finally. Lana is ravenous.

"Madame, you have been so helpful. Thank you. I'm sure as a woman you appreciate that in a case like this the police should act with urgency. Perhaps we could have got to the scene more quickly. It is of no importance now . . . of course I can comprehend your dilemma . . ."

What's this now? What's he implying?

"However, I'm sure that you want to do everything you can for justice. I cannot compel you to agree to my request, so I will simply request you and you will give me your answer . . ."

Lana doesn't like the sound of this at all. There's something in Fichet's tone that's not quite threatening but . . . weirdly moralizing.

"Obviously, as I already said, we would like you to make a statement. There is no particular urgency except perhaps how long you will be in Paris."

To her shock he picks up her boarding pass from the bed. So casually.

"I notice this already. You are leaving tomorrow night. To Dublin."

Unsettled though she is at this intrusiveness, Lana is distracted from any protest by what he now asks.

"Then perhaps my request is more urgent. The gentleman you saw, he is in our, ah, custody. It would help if you come with us now to identify him, from a . . . you say a lineup, no?"

So it ain't over yet. Lana shakes her head firmly.

"No, no. I'm sorry. Really, but it's impossible. An hour ago I was intending to go for a walk and find myself a nice bistro—and then—I mean, it must be nearly eleven now and I haven't eaten yet. You can't seriously think I want to see this man again—"

"But you will not be face-to-face. He will—"

"I know that, I've seen the movies, I know how it works. Look, maybe tomorrow. But right now I just want to forget about this. Go eat. Try to relax."

Fichet shrugs, but the eyes are boring into her now.

"I comprehend. It is okay. It was only that tonight, now, it is easy. We are only five minutes away. In fifteen minutes it will be over for you. After we will bring you to any restaurant you want. But of course, I comprehend."

"Tomorrow. Call me tomorrow morning."

"No, do not worry. It will not be . . . A man like this, you see, he has the special lawyers. If it is only what the young woman claims, then the lawyers, they will say, ah, this is not evidence, he must go free tonight. Then tomorrow they make another delay, de-dah de-dah. You see? You will go back in Dublin. Maybe you will want to forget this. It is normal."

Lana knows exactly what Fichet is doing. The sorrowful but resigned tone, the cynical shrug are transparent tactics, but potent all the same, the eyes probing for weakness. It's working. How can she enjoy a meal now, while dwelling on her refusal, her guilt at turning away when another woman needed her support. Should she just get it over with? Even if he's lying about the fifteen minutes, which of course he is, how long could it take? Won't she eat better afterward, if she's helped bring the whole affair to a more satisfying conclusion?

"You're not really five minutes away, are you?"

"There is a car outside. At this time of night, of course, five minutes, I promise. If you say yes, I will arrange everything now, so they are ready for you when you come. No delay."

How curious: There's the voice, friendly, wheedling. Then there's something beneath the voice, like a tremor, a warning. And behind the eyes, something colder, more frightening. But

Lana knows well that after all that had happened and with her meds way overdue, her own instincts are utterly untrustworthy. What the hell.

"Oh, all right. Can you give me a moment to get ready?"

"Of course, Madame. And thank you."

He takes out his phone and speed-dials as he marches from the room. After the door closes Lana can hear his murmur outside. She tosses one Risperdal and one Trileptal into her mouth and swigs Evian from the courtesy bottle. She should have done this hours ago. But she hadn't, so there you go. Lesson learned, Lana. Or not, as the case might be. She throws her phone, keycard, and some money into her purse, puts on her coat, and opens the door. Fichet is with the other one near the elevator. What is it about the way his voice is a whisper? It registers with Lana as a boys' club conspiracy. It makes her nervous, but only for a second. Fichet's turn and smile dissolves the tableau and everything seems perfectly ordinary again.

"We are very grateful to you, Madame Gibson."

•　•　•

BACK AT THE HOTEL, FEELING NO LESS NERVOUS, FERDIE PARKED BEHIND Vallette's car. It was unoccupied. He had no desire to return to the Suite Imperial, but what choice did he have?

On the seventh floor, the elevator doors opened to silence. The place seemed unoccupied. The door of the master bedroom hung open. Ferdie approached it carefully. What now? The first thing he saw was the chair that had held Caramel Girl. It was overturned and her gag and ties were scattered on the floor. Then he saw the foot visible at the end of the bed. A highly polished oxford shoe. Ferdie's instinct was to exit quietly, but he couldn't help wanting to confirm that it was Vallette. Dead, with any luck. He took as few steps as needed to see . . . Marcel. Knocked out but still breathing.

Ferdie backed quickly out of the room. Then ran to the elevator. The way his luck was going, he'd be caught here and nailed for this mess too.

Reaching the cocoon of the DS21, he had to control his breathing, wait for his heartbeat to slow, tell himself over and over that, whatever had happened up there, he had an alibi, he had just returned from driving Monsieur Fournier home, he knew nothing about anything. Suddenly he remembered the JPEG of Caramel Girl on his laptop. He needed to trash that immediately. As he bent to retrieve it from under his seat, a knock on the window nearly stopped his heart. Oscar. He rolled it down.

Oscar flicked his eyes toward the hotel entrance and whispered, "You recognize her?"

Her, what her? A quick check in the side mirror showed it was not Caramel Girl. Thankfully. Even in the shadowy light there was no mistaking the American blonde. With Vallette. Jesus. He nodded.

"Good. We'll take her in your car. I'll drive. You sit in the back with her."

Apart from objecting to anyone else driving his beautiful car—even Monsieur Fournier, who fortunately never seemed interested—this instruction made no sense to Ferdie. Why not take her in Vallette's car?

Oscar whispered, "Stay down until she gets in. In case she recognizes you."

Ferdie continued watching in the side mirror. He guessed from Oscar's languid demeanor that neither he nor Vallette knew anything about Caramel Girl's escape. As Vallette and the blonde approached, a shadowy figure appeared from the hotel entrance calling, "Madame! S'il vous plait!" There was no mistaking the shape of the uniform: a bellhop.

His bellhop.

. . .

CROSSING THE LOBBY, LANA IS ALREADY FEELING MORE LIGHTHEARTED. Perhaps it has something to do with the jazz trio's latest number, which is fast and playful. She knows it, she's sure she knows it, although it's impossible to get past the trio's flourishes and hum the basic melody, so the title eludes her. Perhaps she's feeling not just safe now, but a little bit Hollywood, flanked by two Parisian detectives escorting her to the exit. Perhaps she really needs to get out of the hotel and onto the streets, so being requested to attend a police station to identify a possible sex offender seems a reasonable trade-off.

Outside, the mild Parisian night air intensifies Lana's desire to go walk around the city. Soon, she tells herself, soon she will be that happy wanderer, that flâneur breathing in the graceful old beauty of every street, enchanted by the hum from the corner cafés, those serious faces and voices for whom every conversation has the urgency of a life-changing encounter. Of course, she's not quite free yet. Things had veered alarmingly off course in the last hour or so and in a kind of shocking way, but now were back on track. And she had learned something: keep the crazier whims in check. And chill. Chill, chill, chill. A gorgeous meal and definitely no alcohol; relaxing with a decaf grand crème; observing the beautiful inhabitants of a beautiful city meander by would be excitement enough. In truth, now that it's a reality, Lana is also kind of looking forward to the lineup, even if it feels like something from one of those

dumb lists that magazines and blogs love to feature: Top Ten
Weird Experiences Everyone Should Have at Least Once. As
long as, she hopes, the thing doesn't drag on and is reasonably
hassle-free.

Inspector Fichet guides her to the left, still under the arches
outside the hotel. His colleague moves ahead toward a beautiful
old Citroën that looks like it's from a 1970s French movie. She's
surprised that the police are still using them. He bends forward
and taps the driver's window. There's something about him in
profile. Lana had glanced his way in the elevator a minute earlier and had the same feeling, but had decided it was just the
surprising subtlety of his fragrance, Serge Lutens or something
like it. Like Fichet. Do all Parisian detectives wear expensive
cologne?

"Madame. S'il vous plait, Madame Gibson!"

Lana looks back. The figure standing in the hotel entrance
is no more than a silhouette against the warm gold of Le Chev's
interior light, but she instantly recognizes the slim frame and
cello-like voice of the bellhop. Laurent, as she liked to think of
him, is holding up something.

"Your cigarettes, Madame. I think you have lost them."

What's this about? She couldn't have dropped a pack of cigarettes she didn't have. Why would Laurent think they were
hers? Yet something in his tone is saying this is not any kind of
mistake. She hears Fichet telling his guy to get the cigarettes
and at the same time Laurent speaks again and now she detects
real urgency. "Your Gauloises, Madame."

Is this the pack the young woman had left at the bar and
Lana had left on the smoking terrace?

"It's all right, Inspector. I think I can get my own cigarettes."

Close-up, Laurent's eyes look wary, but his voice remains loudly cheerful as he places a pack of Gauloises in her hand.

"I am happy I found it in time, Madame."

And his sweet smiling lips scarcely move as he whispers.

"They are going to kill you."

Lana searches for the wink in the eye, although it's pretty clear that she's not being punked. The idea that a bellhop at an exclusive Parisian hotel would mess with a guest's head is just as outlandish as the idea that two French detectives intend to murder an innocent American tourist, yet it was as if Laurent, or whatever his name is, had turned some unformed, unacknowledged fear into actual words. She stares at him with intensity, while speaking as casually as he.

"Thank you for that."

When she turns back, Fichet and the other no longer seem like the musky clean-cut forces of *Law and Order*, but something more predatory hovering in the shadows. And that old Citroën now looks all wrong. Her instinct, already unsettled, shifts in favor of the bellhop's warning. Her eye is drawn to Fichet's colleague, still at the car window, muttering to a driver she can't see. That profile, just like in the elevator only minutes ago, what is it about him?—and a surprising image flashes in her head: the high-backed chair where she'd been tripped earlier, the arm sticking out and . . . What *big ears* you have. And now she has another flash: the photo that young brat had waved so contemptuously in her face at the Hopper, with the man in the background, smirking as he turned away, his face in profile:

It can't be the same guy? In the hotel, at the Hopper, now here? But you think it is, don't you, Lana?

What is going on? Who are these people?

The questions and doubts are like the kind of leak that doesn't gush, but seeps through cracks and dribbles down walls: obvious stuff she should have considered before. Fichet had arrived so quickly after her police call. Sure, the young woman might have told him, but could he have tracked her to her room so fast? She hadn't asked for identification. How dumb!

Though she'd promised herself to avoid anything connected with her last Paris misadventure, and especially not to even think about Nathan, she can't prevent a sudden memory: the arrest they'd both witnessed on rue Serpente one afternoon, a bust involving two wailing Eastern Europeans and four undercover detectives, all unshaven, in jeans and sneakers. No crisp suits or expensive cologne. Of course these guys are not detectives. It's obvious now that they are somehow linked to the naked man on the seventh floor and that for some reason they have been watching her since early this afternoon.

The urgent whisper behind her has the effect of a starting gun.

"Believe me, Madame Gibson. Run!"

And she flies. At least it's a head start. Behind her she hears the grunts and bumps of some kind of scuffle, but doesn't dare look back to check if poor little Laurent is getting himself hurt trying to delay those guys. It's hard enough in the shadows under the arches to stay upright at speed, especially in pumps not made for fleeing a posse of phony cops. Running had never been one of Lana's talents. Back in high school, athletic activity of any kind had been the least cool thing in her set, and though elation makes her more hyper, it's never going to turn her into

Flo-Jo. She takes the first turn up a narrower street, praying to spot a taxi, or a real police car, or maybe a bar or café big and crowded enough to allow her some chance to . . . to what? It's hopeless. Her only surprise is that none of them has caught up with her yet.

She's wheezing now and maybe hallucinating because she sees a little yellow car that looks like a loaf of bread on wheels cruise slowly by, with a young woman in the driver's seat hanging her head out the window, jabbering at Lana in French and gesticulating behind. She dares to check over her shoulder and sees Big Ears pretty much in grabbing distance. When she turns her head again the yellow loaf car is still keeping pace with her and the female driver now reaches back and pushes open the back door. There's no doubt that her jabbering is an invitation to get inside and, with Big Ears bearing down, there's no time to question it. Lana switches direction, lurches between two parked cars, and lunges toward the hanging door, but her efforts to clamber in are frustrated by the young driver's inability to keep an even pace. The loaf of bread shudders, the open back door swings with every jerk and jolt. Now Lana feels a meaty paw almost grip her jacket. She has to take a chance. She dives and gets her head and arms in. Her hand stretches and finds the corner of the driver's seat. The young woman squeals delighted encouragement and the car picks up speed just as determined fingers claw at Lana's ankle. Clinging to the driver's seat with one hand, she whacks him frantically with her purse in the other. The yellow loaf is now going alarmingly fast, given her precarious situation, but at least it's making things a lot harder for Big Ears. He loses hold, but his flailing hand snatches her purse away.

Lana wrenches herself inside and stares miserably out the

back window at the men and her lost purse. Her phone, her money gone. Stupefied by the turn of events, she is only barely aware of the young woman shrieking something over and over, but finally recognizes some actual words and pulls the door shut as requested.

· · ·

IT FELT PECULIAR TO BE SITTING COMFORTABLY WATCHING THIS SUDDEN commotion in a side mirror. Ferdie didn't know exactly what the young pimp had said to make the blond American run away, but it confirmed they were in collusion. Oscar and Vallette would catch her without too much exertion, despite the laughable efforts of the bellhop to slow them down. A collision with Oscar's 110 kilos was never going to end well for the boy. He went down hard. Vallette and Oscar careered round the corner. Ferdie had no desire to join in the chase.

The bellhop was still on the ground. He could hear his groans and was reminded that it was the boy who introduced him to Caramel Girl. Oh Christ, had he helped her escape too? As one of the staff he could access the Suite Imperial. That whispered conversation with the guy in the porkpie might be part of this after all. As quickly as jabbing pain would allow, Ferdie got out of the car and limped to the bellhop. He knelt and grabbed him by the hair, then remembered that he was outside an exclusive hotel with CCTV cameras capturing everything; also, that he was hopelessly unconvincing at threats. Vallette would return shortly having nabbed the blond American. It was not the time or place to try to extract useful information from this little prick. So Ferdie smiled and turned the hair grab into a tousle.

"Hey, my friend. Come on, can you stand?"

He put an arm around the bellhop and helped him up.

"Did you hit your head off the ground?"

"No, but my wrist. I think it might be sprained. And my jaw hurts."

Contact with Oscar's head at full tilt would do that, Ferdie thought. They staggered together into the hotel. Modestly he accepted the thanks of several horrified staff and limped back out. Before he had a chance to light a cigarette, Vallette and Oscar appeared around the corner, still in a big hurry but without the blonde, though Oscar was clutching her purse. Ferdie bit his lip; now was not the time for a witty comment. Oscar ran past, but Vallette stopped and pointed a finger at him.

"Report to me at seven in the morning."

He didn't move for another few moments, almost looking at him, his eyes fixed somewhere close to Ferdie's left shoulder. It seemed like he had more to say. Or do. It was easy to imagine him turning violent right now. The sound of Oscar pulling away broke the spell. Then, to Ferdie's shock, Vallette marched to the DS21 and got into the driver's seat. It was only when the engine started that it dawned on him he was being left behind.

How dare Vallette take his—touch his—beautiful DS21 without permission? This was not right. Why was he the one suffering, left in the cold, without his car? And who knew what would happen to him in the morning if he didn't have answers? But to what? He didn't know what the fuck was going on. He had never seen the blond American until she stepped out of the elevator and assaulted him. Okay, Caramel Girl was his responsibility, but he had no idea what she'd done and where she was now. He would have to dig up something worth telling Vallette before facing him again.

The bellhop was his best chance. He was visibly injured,

so surely he'd be released from work? Ferdie would wait for him. He limped under the arches beyond the camera gaze and chose a pillar to lurk behind and keep watch. He was lighting up when it occurred to him that the boy would, of course, leave by an employee exit. Fuck! Had he missed him already? Frantic, he hopped and hobbled and lurched to the corner and turned right and right again. Then he had his only piece of luck all night. Two figures emerged from a service door only a few meters ahead, but they were walking so fast and talking with such fierce intensity that they didn't notice him. In the darkness they looked weirdly similar. Something about the heads? Neither wore a uniform, but one had what seemed to be a bandage on the left wrist and the other had a feminine swing in her step.

Ferdie chased them as quickly as he could and when he managed to get the fast-gliding figures in his sights once more in the brighter light of rue St.-Honoré, he grew more certain that it was indeed the wounded bellhop and Caramel Girl he was, with considerable discomfort, pursuing.

· · ·

IT'S DOING NOTHING FOR LANA'S ALREADY DIZZYING STRESS LEVELS TO see the curls bouncing gleefully as her doll driver goes faster and faster, taking turn after turn. Her perky little frame and shrill, gleeful, and utterly incomprehensible chatter contrast with Lana's grim silence and crumpled posture. What outrageous nightmare had she stumbled into? She needs to wake up now, perspiring but relieved, to discover that she'd actually dozed off on her luxurious bed in gorgeous room 511 and the last hour had not happened.

But the doll driver's gush and the eager laughing face remain all too real. And the curls swish as she turns far too fre-

quently in Lana's direction. Shouldn't she be looking at the
road? What's she asking now? The wide eyes and questioning
brow are clearly expecting an answer, but the only thing Lana
wants to say is, "Would you please look where you're going!"

Instead, as calmly as possible, she explains.

"Ah, pas de Français?"

"Pas d'Français?"

The doll driver repeats it like it's the most unbelievable thing
she's ever heard. Lana is about to offer her usual self-effacing
"un peut" but decides not to complicate matters just now.

"Yes. No French. I am American."

Now the curls shake as if this explains everything.

"Ah! I speak American. No way! Yes way!"

"Please, please! The road."

The street is narrow and Lana can see a car approach. Doll
driver looks around casually, then shrieks, then swerves. The
cars skim each other, Saran Wrap close. As they flash by, Lana
catches the naked terror on the other driver's face. The curls
bounce and the voice giggles.

"Fun, yes? Now I ah . . . I ah." She points two fingers at
her eyes and then directs them ahead of her. "I look. I see for
Guillaume. My eyes. You also, please."

She can't sustain the linguistic effort any longer and continues in breathless French. Lana wishes there was a cord at her
back to pull and turn her off, but still, grateful to have been
saved from danger, she concedes that the somewhat melodramatic circumstances of their meeting might be a factor.

Now the headlights reveal a young man in the middle of
the otherwise empty street, hat in hand, waving it wildly. Lana
braces herself, knowing that the doll driver will either swerve
dramatically or brake dramatically. It's the second option and

despite her precaution she still finds herself flung forward, almost into the front passenger seat. The young man jumps in, jabs a finger at Lana, and announces, "Wonnerful." His face disappears into the curls as the pair kiss for an unnecessarily long time. Then in intimate breathless tones they exchange excruciating little chirps of love. Amid the overlapping gush Lana recognizes certain words enunciated with boastful clarity: *sensationelle, audacieux*, and *ange courageuse*. Just when she is certain they have entirely forgotten her presence the guy pops his stupid little hat on at a cheeky angle and turns to her. Close-up, his young face is clownish, with a wispy beard, a crooked mouth, and moist, laughing eyes.

"She is fantastic, my Pauline, yes? I am Guillaume. And you?"

"Oh . . . Lana."

In the breathless babble that follows between the couple, she hears "Lana Turner" quite distinctly but figures it's most unlikely that Pauline is suddenly revealing surprising knowledge of her birth name. Still, given the shocks of the night so far, it's worth checking out.

"Did she say, Lana Turner?"

"Ha, yes! Pauline says she never hear of someone with this name, Lana, except for the movie star, Lana Turner. She loves her. Me? Veronica Lake, always."

"Yes. Well, actually there are lots of people in America called Lana. . . . Look, I'm not feeling very good right now—"

"*Non?* But you are a very lucky lady."

"Am I? Really?"

"Yes, Pauline comes just in time."

"But I've lost my purse, my cards, phone, cash."

"The phone—you lose your phone?"

Guillaume suddenly looks like the little boy who's been told the candies are not for him.

"Yes. It was in my purse."

Now his speech sounds very unchildlike, shrugging and mugging. Lana isn't at all sure what to make of this.

"Too bad. A pity. Anyway, you are here. Claude was clever, *non*? And brave. He tells me you are a nice lady."

"Sorry, who says this?"

"Claude."

"Who is Claude?"

"Claude. At the hotel. The brother of Odette."

"Odette?"

"Oh, of course, you do not know her name."

"Who are you talking about?"

Guillaume's hesitation is surprising. Then he makes the grin even bigger.

"Claude's sister. The beautiful girl at the hotel bar. You spoke to her, remember?"

It hits Lana that the beautiful girl and the bellhop—who is Claude, it seems, not Laurent—do resemble each other. Except the smile—Lana had not seen the sister smile. Odette. Odette and Claude. Odette is fine, but Claude doesn't feel right at all. Laurent suits him much better. It's a pity.

How much does this couple know about what had happened in the Suite Imperial? Now that she thinks of it, how does Guillaume know that she had sat next to Odette at the hotel bar?

The headlights of a car coming toward them freeze suddenly about twenty yards away on the narrow street. A second set of headlights is visible behind. Guillaume and Pauline look toward the cars, then at each other. Smiling again, Guillaume turns back to Lana.

"The camera, the camera."

He gestures toward Lana's feet, where she notices an open leather bag. There's a video camera inside. She picks it up. He grabs it, checks something on the side, then turns back again, his manner suddenly very professional, snapping his fingers.

"The memory card."

"Sorry?"

"A card, a little card. Quickly!"

Lana rummages and finds two identical slim black rectangles. She holds them up. Guillaume says, "Wonnerful!" and snatches one. Despite the glare of the headlights ahead, Lana can see doors opening and shadowy figures moving. Guillaume mutters to Pauline as he slides the card into a panel at the side of the camera, turns it on, rolls down the window, and holds it out, pointing toward the other car. Pauline starts the engine and revs up.

Two large black shapes now appear in front of the headlights, moving toward them, unhurried. With their cars planted in the middle of the street, nothing, not even the yellow loaf, can get past. Pauline looks over her shoulder, but this time there is nothing doll-like in her expression. She stares past Lana at the road behind, laser focused. The car jerks and reverses at frightening speed. The black shapes start running, then stop and turn back toward their own cars. Terrified as she is, Lana cannot but be impressed at how cleanly and directly Pauline guides the little yellow loaf backward. The doll can drive, that much is clear. But the headlights of the other cars are blinding as they get closer and closer. Guillaume, still hanging out the window as he films the pursuit, whoops loudly.

At a quiet intersection Pauline spins around and changes gears like a pro. The loaf leaps forward and flashes across the front of the first pursuing car as it emerges from the street. Guillaume sits back inside, howling his enthusiasm.

"*Incroyable!* I think perhaps the light was too bad for my camera. I don't know if I can use any of these shots. We can only try, yes?"

"Why were you filming that?"

Guillaume gives her the mystified look of a clown. "Because I am a filmmaker."

"Sorry?"

Lana is genuinely beginning to suspect she's either going insane or has found herself in some French version of *Candid Camera.* The two black sedans are gaining on them, panthers closing on a chicken. They can overtake the little yellow loaf with ease and force it off the road.

"Yes. And you will be in our movie also, I hope."

"What movie? Hold on. I was told that those men want to kill me—"

"Yes, I know, I told Claude to tell you this."

"You told—wait. Claude is the bellhop at the hotel?"

"Of course."

"And you told him to tell me that I was about to be killed."

"Yes, me."

"So, is that actually true, or is this just happening in some little movie in your head?"

Guillaume pauses and Lana's heart sinks. These are just crazy people. It's all some terrible misunderstanding.

"Well, of course I cannot show perfect evidence if they will kill you—"

"Oh Jesus."

"But what do you think? They were taking you out to dinner?"

"But they are the police, right?"

"Ha. Flics? They tell you that? You see? No. No. They are not flics. They are with Fournier. Believe me, I know Vallette. They want to take you from the hotel—"

Fournier? Vallette? Too many names. But it's hard to interrupt Guillaume's flow.

"—they want you out of the way. I think maybe you saw something they do not want to—"

Everyone lurches to one side as Pauline spins left onto yet another narrow street. When Lana sits upright again she sees headlights zooming toward them. They are going the wrong way on a one-way street and the black sedans have followed. Instead of braking and hoping the oncoming car can stop in time, Pauline now accelerates. Horns blare as the distance between the two cars shrinks fast. Just as Lana is convinced that a collision is inevitable, Pauline veers suddenly left, into a tiny gap between two parked cars. The other car shoots by, horn still blaring, its driver just a terrified gaping mouth screaming French obscenities. Never has Lana been more impressed by the legendary parking skills of Parisians. Had Pauline really spotted the little gap ahead and speeded up so as to get to it in time? Is she that coolheaded behind the wheel? She's even more impressed when the clamor of two sets of brakes tells her that the pursuing black sedans have been blocked by the other car. Pauline pulls out of her parking space and starts chattering as happily and inanely as ever to Guillaume as she hurtles down the one-way, still in the wrong direction, before correcting that at the next intersection. They're in the clear, it seems, pursuers finally shaken off.

Lana no longer has even the remotest sense of where they are. The only thing she's certain of is that they hadn't crossed the river, so they must still be on the right bank, right? But they'd zigzagged about so much she has no idea if they are traveling north, south, east, or west, if they're still in the 1st, or in the 8th, or the 18th. It hardly matters at this point. She must have relaxed at least a little because suddenly she feels ridiculously hungry again.

"Where are we going?"

"Our little nest."

"Where is that?"

"Not so far. Rue d'Aboukir. We hope that Odette will be there."

"You hope?"

"Yes, we do not know what happened. Perhaps you do. Maybe you will tell us for the camera?"

"What?"

Lana does not like the sound of this at all. Guillaume now gives her an amused quizzical look followed by an incline of the head and a coy angled smile: the naughty little boy who has been found out, but is still confident he will charm his way out of trouble as always.

"Oh, I am desolate. Of course. Please. I do not explain myself well."

He reaches into the top pocket of his denim jacket and takes out a little card, which he offers to Lana. It says Productions Liberté, and underneath in quotation marks "le camera ne ment jamais." There are two names, Guillaume Pelletier and Pauline Garrel, and an email address.

"I am in the hotel tonight because of Fournier. Three months ago Claude tells Odette about a sex party. She tells me. We say,

'Claude, if Fournier is coming to the hotel again you must tell us.' It is perfect, if only we can get some pictures. So—"

Lana is beginning to follow. Fournier must be the naked old guy. Guillaume is unstoppable now, his every word nailed to some gesture of hand or face.

"—so Claude meets the guy who fixes special girls for Fournier. He tells him Odette is a girl like this. She is so beautiful, yes? We know Fournier will want her. This is our plan: she will go with a special little camera, hidden. So, tonight Odette waits at the bar. I am in the foyer. I see you speak to her. The chauffeur, the little pimp, he comes. He brings her to the Suite Imperial. I see you take Odette's cigarettes. It is nothing, but then later you are also at the private elevator. You are watching and walking, up and down, up and down. So, now I think, who is she? Is she also interested in Fournier? Ah no, she is following beautiful Odette—"

"Well, no, not that it matters, but that wasn't why—"

"It's okay, Odette is very extraordinary."

It's not worth explaining. Guillaume now has the expression of someone who has just seen a dog with two tails. He holds up a finger dramatically.

"But then, what is this? Oh! You go in the elevator. It goes up, then it comes down and you are there again. I see you *eungh!* on the chauffeur's foot. That makes me laugh. How will the *putain* drive now? But I know from your face something is wrong. There is something bad. I wait for Odette to return. Fournier and the chauffeur leave the hotel. Then I see Vallette go to the reception. I am watching all the time, oh yes. They talk. They look at the computer and ha! I understand. I am clever, me. They are looking for you. But where is Odette? What has Vallette done with her? What will he do with you?

Now I am thinking fast. My brain is buzz buzz buzz all the time—"

"Wait. You keep saying 'Vallette.' Are you talking about the man who told me he was a police inspector?"

"He told you this?"

"Yes. He called himself Inspector Fichet."

"Fichet?"

"Yes."

"It was a lie . . . Fichet?"

He turns and jabbers at Pauline. Lana hears "Fichet" at least four times, then Pauline shrieks laughing. Lana begins to feel her blood boil. What is it with this girl? Does she have to behave like she's battery operated?

"Excuse me, do you mind telling me—"

"I am desolate. But it is a good joke. Vallette, he is mad, but clever, too, you know. Let me explain, Lana. You say this name, Inspector Fichet, I think I remember this name. So I say to Pauline. Fichet, Inspector Fichet, what is this name? Pauline says, Fichet, but you know. I say I cannot remember. And she says, *Les Diaboliques*, Inspector Fichet. Of course! Of course. I am an idiot. *Les Diaboliques*. Do you know this movie? It's a good joke from Vallette, yes?"

Lana cannot speak. She's definitely all out of laughs having just survived an attempted kidnapping. Maybe an attempted murder, too, though she doesn't really buy that, but it sure ain't funny either way. Who is this Fournier? If her weary spinning brain had been following the story correctly, that was the name of the old naked guy. Fournier.

Lana is flung sideways this time as Pauline brakes hard, changes gear, and backs into another tiny gap between cars. They have arrived at their destination, wherever that might be.

Guillaume and Pauline say more pretty things to each other, kiss, and step out. Lana guesses she should too. The street is silent and, by Lana's notion of Paris, featureless. Guillaume points toward the top floor of a building across the road.

"We are there. Let us hope Odette is returned."

Lana hopes so, too, although nothing she has heard has made her confident about that. It seems stupid to just follow this pair into a strange building, but as she has no wallet or phone and no idea where in Paris she is, Guillaume and Pauline are her lifeline right now. Their smiles might be neighborly or marionette crazy, but they are all she's got. And she is awesomely, horribly hungry.

"Do you have food at your place? Because I have to tell you, I haven't eaten for, like, ten hours. I can't go on without—I have to eat."

"Eat? Of course, no problem."

Naturally, this new idea requires another powwow with Pauline, which takes a lot longer than can possibly be necessary.

"Pauline says when she is feeling hungry like this, her favorite plate is boeuf bourguignon. She asks if you like boeuf bourguignon also?"

"Yes, I love it. Frankly, Guillaume, shake a little salt on your arm right now. I'd happily take a bite out of that. I just need to eat."

"Perfect. Then we will go to Le Tambour."

"There is something else . . . remember I lost my purse, so I have no—"

"Do not worry about that. We will pay, of course. You are our important guest."

He speaks quickly and quietly to Pauline, who nods and skips across the road.

"She is going to the apartment to find Odette. I hope she is there."

"Why haven't you phoned her?"

"We agree before, she will phone me. If I phone her, it might be the wrong time. It might make trouble. Please tell me, Lana. I am a little worried. When you went up to the suite, did you see her? What was happening?"

Lana doesn't know if she can trust him enough to tell him what she saw.

* * *

EVERY SECOND STEP WAS A DAGGER, A RED-HOT NEEDLE. FERDIE TRIED pressing his weight on the heel of the injured foot, which was a little less painful, but made it harder to keep up with Bellhop and Caramel Girl, whose long, infuriatingly languid strides were taking them farther and farther away. The pursuit was becoming hopeless until they veered toward an entrance to the Palais Royal metro station and pranced down the steps. Might be bad, might be good: it would be harder for Ferdie to avoid being noticed in an enclosed lit space, but there was at least the possibility of enjoying some rest on a metro journey while tracking the pair to their destination. Of course he had no ticket and the bureau was closed and the machine would take too long, but—a little luck at last—an emerging passenger gave Ferdie a chance to hop through before the exit door swung shut.

No sign of them in the empty tunnel. Palais Royal had two lines, so four platforms. He went to the nearest: Line 7, direction Mairie d'Ivry, and immediately spotted Bellhop on the opposite platform, direction Villejuif, jigging a little impatiently. Why was Caramel Girl no longer with him? Ferdie dragged himself up the steps, trying to decide if he should keep looking for her and risk losing both. Reluctantly he decided to stick with Bellhop. There was only so much he could do with this fucking foot and already he was near the limit. He hobbled across and down, then lurked at the platform entrance out of Bellhop's sight. When the train came the last car would stop just a few agonizing steps away. Boarding unnoticed wouldn't be a problem, but monitoring where Bellhop got off and tracking him without being caught mightn't be so easy.

Ferdie had a clear run to the almost-empty last carriage so, as soon as Bellhop got on, he hopped on the good foot, pulled himself in, and fell onto the nearest seat. He stretched the injured foot, taking the weight off. Heavenly relief. Closing his eyes he imagined Caramel Girl massaging the foot gently, whispering, "Tell me where it hurts, my angel." All too soon the train stopped. Ferdie dragged himself up on his good foot, stretched out a hand, and released the doors. He peeked out with extreme caution. No sign of Bellhop departing. Ferdie sat back again. He repeated the procedure at every stop until, at Crimée, Bellhop appeared on the platform, walking toward him. Ferdie quickly sat and leaned forward, elbow on knee, hand on forehead, shielding his face. The warning horn for doors closing had already started as Bellhop passed. Ferdie had to tumble out so fast his injured foot landed agonizingly on the platform and he fell to his knees. Bellhop was already disappearing into the tunnel. Ferdie scrambled up. If he could keep him in sight until he reached the street he might not have to follow much farther. It would be enough to see him enter a building somewhere and get the address. Then Ferdie could grab a taxi to the nearest emergency room. What he really wanted was to wake up in his bed and discover that all this had been a nightmare.

Instead, he had to continue pounding along several tunnels and up an out-of-order escalator. Bellhop seemed to be moving even faster now. What the fuck was the kid's hurry? Ferdie thought, knowing he wasn't hurrying at all, just gliding with long, easy strides, while he winced, felt tears, and smothered squeals, only a stumble away from total collapse.

Which, at the top of the steps, right under the MÉTROPOLITAIN sign, he did. Face forward. He heard himself let loose one pathetic dog whine before blacking out.

Then, after how long he had no idea, Ferdie felt himself being turned over. He blinked. Caramel Girl's eyes had never looked more liquid, tender, sympathetic. She had returned. What miracle had brought her back? He blinked a few times, focusing more clearly. The eyes, still golden, so caring, still gazed down at him, but somehow her hair didn't seem . . . what was wrong? And the mouth . . . Christ! Why had he never noticed the resemblance before? Of course he had never seen Caramel Girl and Bellhop together and certainly he had never, ever looked into Bellhop's eyes the same way. He hadn't looked into his eyes at all. He was, as far as Ferdie was concerned, just a young Arab on the make, whereas Caramel Girl . . . Were they twins? Looking at the boy now there was no doubt he and she were family. Which meant Bellhop had pimped out his sister or his cousin.

"I will help you to my building. It's just around the corner."

Ferdie was not dreaming this, even though it sounded too friendly to be true. When he attempted to answer he was surprised at the croak that had replaced his normal voice.

"Thank you. Help me up."

"Let me call the ambulance first."

Bellhop spoke quickly and quietly on his mobile so Ferdie

couldn't catch what address he gave. No matter, he would soon be there. Bellhop offered him his good arm.

"It's nice I get to repay your kindness so quickly."

Ferdie detected no sarcasm in his tone. He grabbed Bellhop by the hand and elbow and, putting all his weight on the good foot, forced himself up. Bellhop held him as they lurched across the road, and left onto rue de Crimée. He stopped outside number 187 and punched a code to open a gray door riddled with graffiti. The lobby was tiny and cold. He didn't bother turning on the light. He sat Ferdie on tiled stairs.

"There's no elevator and I'm on the fifth floor. The ambulance will be here soon. Do you agree it would be crazy to go all the way up to my apartment just to come all the way down again?"

Ferdie nodded. He had the address and now knew what floor. This information would be a nice meaty bone to toss in Vallette's direction. There was no added advantage in seeing inside what Ferdie guessed would be a smelly little fifteen-square-meter attic studio.

"If you need some kind of painkiller I can run up and find something for you."

"No, it's okay."

Bellhop sat next to him on the steps. Ferdie found it impossible now to look at those eyes in close-up without seeing Caramel Girl. It was a bit too freaky.

"So why were you following me?"

He said it so casually, without any trace of anger or threat, that it completely threw Ferdie. In the darkness his eyes glowed bright with what seemed nothing more than curiosity, but of course that was entirely misleading. How long had Bellhop known he was being pursued and why had he dragged him all the way to his building? Ferdie could hear how fake and hollow the denial sounded.

"Following you? No. We must have just ended up on the same train and then . . . hey . . . got off at the same stop . . ."

Bellhop's smile told him he would have to do a lot better. And now the wildest thought crossed his mind. Had the boy really phoned for an ambulance or was it a fake call, or—Jesus!—a coded call to someone else now on their way here? Ferdie could hardly stand up without help, and even this skinny-ass would have no trouble preventing his escape. Did he have a weapon? It had never occurred to Ferdie that tracking Bellhop might put himself in danger.

"It must have been very important to you, you know with your foot so bad. Do you want me to look at it for you?"

The offer was so soft-voiced it sounded sinister.

"No! No! Okay, sure, I was following you." Ferdie often kept trouble away by mixing dollops of truth with vital *soupçons* of deceit and misdirection. Now he realized this was how he should have handled the situation from the beginning.

"Okay, let me explain. A lot of stuff has happened tonight and none of it good for me, I can tell you. Worse than this, believe me." He gestured toward his foot. "That American lady—she did this to me by the way and it seems like that isn't all—she's put me in big fucking trouble with my boss. I could lose my job . . ."

The whine in Ferdie's head was getting louder fast. It was real: a distant siren. Bellhop had called an ambulance after all. Of course he had. Look at the kid. Maybe he really was an innocent, even if his sister, cousin, whatever Caramel Girl was, was not. No, that made no sense. It was obvious both of them were involved. Marcel had ended up unconscious in the Suite

Imperial. That had to be Bellhop. For now all that mattered was to get away safely in that ambulance. "You took so much trouble to help her outside the hotel, it occurred to me that you or your . . . girl might know something about what she's up to."

"It was nothing. She was nice to me earlier. A big tip." Bellhop sounded casually sincere. "And I don't think she meant you any harm. But you know Americans, they like to stick their noses in." He glanced down at the foot. "How did she do this?"

"A pointy heel."

Bellhop grimaced. The siren was very near now. He stood and stepped quickly to open the door. Flashing red and blue lights tracked along the building across the street. Bellhop stepped out and waved. The ambulance came into sight and pulled up. It was going to be fine. He would escape and get this fucking foot seen to at last. With Bellhop's help, how about that?

Ferdie did feel a little guilty that he'd be handing him to Vallette in the morning.

The sauce is so wine-dark it looks black, the meat falls to pieces on her tongue, the shallots are sweetly unctuous and make her head swoon. Lana cannot recall ever enjoying beef bourguignon so much. Hunger retreats and the crimson ambience of Bistro Le Tambour soothes her battered brain. A discreet rumble of voices to her left and right envelops her in a dream of normality, almost resembling the kind of Parisian evening she had, just a couple of innocent hours ago, expected to enjoy. The medication seems to be kicking in, too, allowing her to slow a little after the rather insane sequence of events that had brought her here. Guillaume and Pauline sip coffee, grin, and encourage her every mouthful as if she were a five-year-old with behavioral problems. Disconcertingly, their conversational duets, which sound quietly intense and full of portent in French, turn out to be entirely banal when relayed to her in English.

"Pauline says bon ap'. She is happy that you are enjoying your plate. She says it is her special skill to know what is the perfect food for the perfect moment. Pauline says you are lucky because her ah . . . metabolism—same word, yes?—will not allow her to eat such food at this late hour."

And on and on in that vein, Guillaume praising everything about Pauline to the extent that Lana doubts his sincerity just a little. But soothed and sated, she's inclined to be generous. Perhaps they are covering up the depth of their concern for Odette, who hadn't returned to the apartment and still hasn't made contact. She files the young man's gush under immaturity and the woman's narcissism under charming naïveté. And to be fair she's a hell of a driver. Is it such a rare or even a bad thing: two young people under the illusion that their relationship is the axis on which the world turns? And they had just saved her life. Hadn't they? They had, hadn't they? What had happened exactly? Her decision to run away from Fichet—or Vallette, if Guillaume is correct—hadn't been a decision in any proper sense, more like a fight-or-flight thing propelled by a melo-dramatic warning from a young man she liked and trusted. The most important question on Lana's mind is, does someone very powerful have her in his crosshairs? The way Guillaume had kept referring to the naked guy by last name only, *Fournier*, like he presumed Lana already knew him, suggested he was famous or, more likely, notorious. Who was he? Now seems as good a time as any to hear the worst.

"So, tell me, who is Fournier?"

"I am sorry?"

"You keep saying this name, Fournier. Who do you mean?"

For the tiniest moment Lana thinks she sees something dis-turb Guillaume's happy clown face. A ripple across the surface that's not quite anger, more like a suspicion she might be toy-ing with him. The shadow of a fast-scudding cloud, it passes quickly and the face is all sunshine and quirky delight again.

"You are not going to say now that you did not see Fournier?"

"I told you I saw a naked guy on the seventh floor of Le Chevalier, right?"

"Yes."

"And he was, well . . . manhandling the young woman I saw in the bar. Your friend Odette, right? Okay. But you keep saying the name Fournier, and what I'm trying to explain to you is that I don't know that's who it was."

"But you saw his face?"

"Yes."

"So, you mean you cannot be certain it was him?"

"Oh Jesus, Guillaume! What is so hard about this? I don't know anyone called Fournier. It's like, I don't know . . . okay, do you know who Kelsey Grammer is?"

"Sure. He's the guy, Frasier."

"Right, bad example. I was trying to think of . . . You see, I'm from a place called Seattle."

"Yes, I know this place."

"Okay, so I was trying to think of someone famous from Seattle that you've never heard of—"

"And Kelsey Grammer is from Seattle?"

"No, ah, sorry, no, actually, the character Frasier was, but—oh look, forget that. Just wipe that. Let's say, ah . . . does Stone Gossard mean anything to you?"

He gives it a lot of thought, like there's a cash prize on the line. Jesus! Lana really wishes she hadn't taken the conversation in this direction and when Guillaume starts discussing Stone Gossard with Pauline, she interrupts quickly.

"Anyway, listen, the point is that you haven't heard of him, whereas, to me, a Seattle girl, he's totally part of my growing up, right?"

They both nod, but it's not certain they've got the point at all.

"Likewise this guy Fournier seems to be famous to you, but I don't know who he is, or what he is, or what he looks like. The name Fournier means nothing to me."

Guillaume looks genuinely blindsided. He rabbits at Pauline and of course she does some more eye-popping and mouth-O'ing.

"So, I am sorry if we are idiots, Lana. What you are saying? You have never heard of Jean-Luc Fournier?"

"Exactly. Never. Should I have?"

"Ah, of course. A good question." Now for some reason Guillaume looks more delighted than ever, a child getting a surprise gift. "Now I see. It is the French attitude, of course. Ha, ha! We think if someone is famous throughout France then of course the whole world will know also. Please forgive me."

"No, really, absolutely not. I'm sure I should know who he is."

"No, please, Lana—"

"Think of me as just another one of those American tourist types who never know stuff—"

"No, no, not at all, but you see, just now he makes such controversy, so significant. Everywhere people talk, talk, talk about Jean-Luc Fournier. Everyone has an opinion about him—"

"Guillaume . . . Guillaume . . ."

"Yes?"

"Please tell me who he is?"

"Of course, yes. Well, you know in two months is the election for president of France?"

"I . . . yes, I did hear something about it, but to be honest, I haven't really been paying much attention."

"Jean-Luc Fournier is a candidate. Right now, he is the favorite to win."

• • •

IN THE AMBULANCE THE PARAMEDICS HAD CAREFULLY REMOVED HIS SHOE and sock. "Got some swelling there, pal." They gave him a couple of painkillers and began to dab at the foot with damp antiseptic-smelling cloths. Apart from inevitable stings this felt pleasantly cool. Then one of them cheerily pronounced, "Looking a bit ugly, but don't worry, you'll live." Ferdie looked down. The swelling had already given the instep the look of a pig's trotter, and the purple stain appeared to be a splat of spilt ink.

But by the time they rolled him into the emergency room, he was in the best mood he'd been in since those tingling moments earlier tonight, walking with Caramel Girl from the bar to the elevator and up to the Suite Imperial. While waiting his turn, Ferdie became slowly aware of an unusual process at work in his brain. Was it because the situation itself was so strange? He had not been in the hospital since he was a child. Even lying still, but awake like this, was unusual. Ferdie led a busy life, so when he went to bed it was either alone at a late hour, exhausted, and so he tended to fall asleep within a minute, or—by no means as often as he'd like—with a woman, in which case lying still was not what was required. Ferdie had never been subject to late-night terrors, and generally did not toss and turn, his mind dancing between this and that. Through the day he followed a clear, simple path, made any decisions he had to make quickly and easily, from what to eat to who he liked or disliked. Mostly he did as he was asked by whoever was paying and he rarely dwelt on the meaning or consequences of his actions. So when the night came, so did sleep. Easily.

But right now, sleep was not an option. The doctor might appear in five minutes or it might be hours. He was not in unbearable pain, but a steady throb or pulse, as if someone had captured his foot and was squeezing it gently but pointedly, prevented any drift into unconsciousness.

Ferdie was not a person to fret over how long it would be before help arrived. Hanging around was a big part of his job; he was used to it. Whether he sat calmly in the car or stood outside having a smoke, he enjoyed letting thoughts just drift in and out of his mind: always the same easy stuff. None of that was happening now. Sure, his brain had had a lot to cope with, but even the kind of thoughts he frequently enjoyed that *were* relevant to the events of the evening—such as his hatred of Vallette along with pleasing fantasies of the pain and degradation Ferdie might inflict on him—were not present. No, instead his mind returned again and again, unbidden but irresistibly, to Caramel Girl and Bellhop. Not individually, but as a pair. A very beautiful pair. Part of a family. How had he not seen it? They looked much more like each other than he and his brother or either of his two sisters did. And yet . . . Every so often he asked himself why he was thinking about them, but his attempts to shift attention to other subjects failed and the brother and sister loomed again and again. He decided that apart from the faces they were not alike at all, actually, unless they had deliberately presented a misleading impression of themselves. Obviously the girl had been playing a role, but even so, something about her playing of that role felt authentic; her brusque, incommunicative manner rang true, even if the details of her story turned out to be bullshit. And the boy's easy charm, his smile, his apparent desire to please equally felt like the real essence of him. He had to have known that Ferdie was following him and surely understood very well that this was not a friendly act. He could have left Ferdie lying on the street. Instead he shouldered him to his home, more or less, had called for an ambulance, and even offered to accompany him to the hospital. If Caramel Girl had her brother's personality, Ferdie could imagine really falling for her.

So these thoughts ran on and rewound and ran on. He was unable to load another film in his head and escape the brother-and-sister story. It disturbed and annoyed, but also charmed and amused and excited him. Ferdie began to recognize that this uncustomary mental turmoil was coaxing him into unfamiliar territory: he was experiencing a dilemma. This was not comfortable. Dilemmas were things he had occasionally advised others about, certainly not something he ever had to contend with. He also detected, hovering at the edges of this particular dilemma, a shred of feeling that he faintly recognized as a desire to protect. It was not the potent instinctive self-protection that was his daily companion, but a much-diluted, more apologetic thing, like Orangina was to a real orange: a strange urge to protect another person.

The doctor had come to him by then and Ferdie was pleased at her clarity, speed, and efficiency. No amiable interaction or sympathetic smiles, but he didn't expect either—the woman had far too many patients to see. When she asked, "Did something heavy fall on it?" Ferdie enjoyed answering, "A woman's heel." The doctor was turned toward his foot so he could not see her reaction, but there was a moment or two of silence before she continued, "Okay, now you will feel a little pressure," and her thumbs pressed right on the spot. "Aaaaeugh!" he screamed. Why could medical types never say it plainly: "You will feel excruciating pain"?

It was a surprise to discover that no bones had been broken or fractured, but there was serious bruising and the foot required complete rest. No weight on it whatsoever. The doctor fixed her narrow gray eyes on him and repeated "complete rest" as if she knew men and their determination to let nothing as trivial as pain interfere with their routine. He would be given crutches to be used for limited necessary movement, but otherwise—one more time—"complete rest." She instructed an equally expressionless nurse to bind the foot, wrote out a prescription for painkillers, and wished him well.

He admired this woman's professionalism, but knew he would forget her as easily as she no doubt would forget him, which was what he would have liked to do with Bellhop and Caramel Girl. The situation should be clear-cut: the possibility that he might be chauffeur to the next president of France had, in the last couple of hours, diminished alarmingly, and, at the extreme paranoid end of the scale, perhaps more than just his enviable job was in danger. He had urgently needed to acquire some significant piece of information that Vallette did not have, and had done so: the bellhop's address. Hopefully he would be told to take a few days' sick leave and when he returned everything would be normal again.

So why the dilemma? He cursed this unfamiliar sensation, but could not shake it off. Entirely against his own interests, Ferdie was seriously tempted not to give Vallette the bellhop's address.

• • •

LANA CAN'T THINK OF ANYTHING TO SAY. ONCE AGAIN HER MIND CONjures up those horrifying seconds. Elevator doors sliding open, R&B music, naked bodies, an eerie bacchanal, then the young woman's frightened face, and the old guy's flabby wrinkled skin and glittering eyes. Guillaume clearly is not joking, but he must be mistaken. He has to be.

"Then the man I saw must be someone else."

"I do not think so. But it is not a problem to find out, Lana. We can show you Fournier. Photos, video. With clothes, but still. Perhaps you can recognize him."

It's the second time she's been invited to identify the naked old goat she now fervently wishes she had never seen. It's like they've been handcuffed together and the key's been lost. Now the stakes have been raised exponentially. A presidential candidate. The front-runner. Lana recognizes immediately there can be no escape from this unwanted connection, not without a payoff of some kind. Right now it seems like her only choice is to stick with this pair, even if to do so is only the least of a growing assortment of evils.

On the way to their apartment, Pauline offers nonstop wisdom via an enthusiastic translation from Guillaume: It's good to confront things. She, Pauline, has that kind of personality and is happy to see that Lana is this way also, an independent proactive woman. Lana soothes her inflamed brain by imagining herself banging Pauline's head repeatedly against the peeling purple door that Guillaume is opening.

The apartment is a duplex. The lower level is one large living room, kitchen, and cluttered office and editing space. On a table are two computer screens, a keyboard, and what Lana guesses is a sound desk and other pieces of expensive-looking technology.

"Here, I am editing my film."

Lana finds it instructive that, despite his continual praise for his precious Pauline, it's still "my" not "our" film.

"So you want to see Monsieur Jean-Luc Fournier?"

Very quickly he finds a YouTube video with the title "Fournier humilie Dufour." It's a TV debate. Guillaume points to the man on the left of the screen who's doing most of the talking, while waving a dismissive hand at his opponent.

"Wait, there will be a close-up."

But already Lana can see that he is the right age, with the

right shape, the right hair. The hint of knowing amusement at the corner of the mouth makes him look more genial and the long silver mane is carefully back-combed with a leonine flourish. When the camera cuts to close-up his blue eyes seem direct, intelligent, and ferocious. It is the naked man. Lana can't follow the TV debate, but it looks like he's winning the argument. Or his manner suggests that he certainly thinks so.

"Tell me about him."

"You mean his *histoire*. It is a very normal one for this kind of politician in France. Fournier is *typique*: *Un gauche cavier*. He says, 'Yes, I am from a bourgeois family and that is why I am a socialist: because I believe everyone should have the same opportunities like me.' He went to the best schools, Lycée Louis-le-Grand and ULM and Sciences Po. If you are a clever boy in France, everything is more easy, and if you are bourgeois and clever there is a special road for you."

Not so different anywhere, Lana thinks. Certainly not in the United States. But she doesn't interrupt.

"And also, this is important, I think. He was a student in Paris in 1968. So—this is me, this is my theory—Fournier, he discovers politics and sex in one moment. On the street, crazy protest, on the campus, passionate free love. You understand? It was a cocktail, intoxicating, no? And so, I believe, always for him politics and sex are, ah . . . *entrecroisé* . . ."

"Intertwined?"

"Yes. My idea. Guillaume's proposal. I think so. What do you say?"

"Yeah, it's, ah, I can see how that might be. But please, tell me more about him."

"Then he is professor of economic history. At this time it is normal for a university teacher to join the Parti Socialiste. He marries also. You see. So, all is normal. This is the path for leaders in France. Mitterrand likes this clever young man. Now he is a junior minister. During this time there is no problem about his private life. But his first marriage, *phut!* And he marries again. Now it begins. Not public news, of course, but rumors and whispers, amusing stories for the dinner party. Soon he is a legendary . . . we say, *lapin chaud*. You have heard this?"

"I get it."

"When I am in university in 2000, no one speaks of Jean-Luc Fournier without a little joke about his sexual appetite. He is a kind of aspiration for many of my friends: Socialist— good. Big brain—good. Women cannot resist him—fantastic! It is impressive, no, for a fifty-year-old man? Then he becomes a European commissioner and now a big surprise. In Brussels, a woman complains. She says he forced her to have sex with him. What? Jean-Luc Fournier, force? No, Fournier does not need force, he is so irresistible. Ah, but there was no physical violence. This woman only says she could not refuse him, even though she wanted to. Why? Because she was a subordinate and afraid about her job. Ah, so. What do the friends of Fournier say? This woman is bitter about something perhaps? Revenge? Of course that is the solution. And so embarrassing for poor Fournier, that he must speak about such affairs in public. He says he was foolish. In France they say yes, foolish to trust such a dangerous woman who cannot keep her mouth shut. But after there comes another story and another. Again only whispers. No one speaks in public. A young journalist goes to interview Fournier in Brussels and she says he tries to seduce her in his office. She has to fight to keep him away. Could it be true? Cer-

tainly it is true that older women who work in politics, in media, in university, they now whisper to their young colleagues,
'Do not be alone with Fournier.'

"Then we hear the most crazy story. So crazy it cannot be
true. In this story a woman goes to hospital one night because
during sex the man bit off her ear . . . The man was Monsieur
Jean-Luc Fournier. Yes, Lana, I am serious. But okay, I cannot
discover if it is true for sure. But I know that it is true about
these sex parties. And now you know it also. In France you see
there are many who say it is wrong even to ask these questions.
These are private matters. Even if these things reveal a man
who is out of control, who will abuse his power? Have you
heard of satyriasis? That is what they say is the sickness that
Fournier has."

"I understand. And I have to admit what I saw tonight was
pretty sick."

"Would you want such a man as your president?"

"He's not going to be my president."

"Ah, but he is good enough for France?"

There is a harsh ringing. Sustained. Then it stops. Guillaume and Pauline look at each other. Then Guillaume holds
up a hand demanding silence and goes down the hallway to
the front door. Lana hears the door open, then an exclamation
from Guillaume. A few seconds later he reappears carrying a
woman in his arms. Her head is resting on his shoulders and
her face is visible. Her eyes are open and she is breathing. It is
Odette. Guillaume barks something in French to Pauline and
looks at Lana.

"The door, please."

She goes quickly to the apartment door and closes it. When
she returns Guillaume is carrying Odette up the spiral staircase

and Lana follows them into a large attic space with a steeply slanted roof. A corner section at the high end is painted a lurid green from floor to ceiling, with a chair on a little platform in front. There are studio lights on stands positioned all round. Guillaume gently places Odette on a bed in a dark corner of the room. She moans and Guillaume mutters soothing things. Pauline arrives with the bowl of water, a towel, and a bottle of some liquid. Guillaume dips the towel in the water and begins to wipe Odette's face. In the grim light Lana cannot see exactly what her injuries are. Guillaume pours liquid from the bottle onto the wet towel and dabs her forehead and her arms with it. Antiseptic? Odette moans again and both Guillaume and Pauline whisper sweetly. Lana feels out of place, almost like a voyeur. Then she is surprised to hear her name. Guillaume seems to be asking if Odette recognizes her.

Odette's eyes peer over his shoulder. Realizing how pathetic and trivial it would seem, Lana manages to stop herself from saying, "Don't you remember? We spoke in the bar. I tried to be friendly, but you weren't interested?" Odette is whispering to him now. Pauline cries out in horror at what she hears. Guillaume looks back at Lana.

"After you, they stopped the orgy. Even Fournier runs away. Vallette and his friends tie her to a chair and interrogate her. They did this. Then they leave her, except for one. He does not question her, but he insults her and touches her."

With her face turned away, Odette speaks in faltering English.

"He was not important."

"I am saying to Odette I should never have asked her to do this. It was too dangerous. We were hoping she could be at the party, safe for a little while, find some good shots, then make an excuse to leave, say she was nervous. The camera was in her *sac* . . . no, her . . ."

"Purse."

"Yes. A tiny hole. She holds it like this, this way, then this. She practiced."

"It was good. Perfect shots I am sure. . . . but then . . ."

Odette's English seems to fail. She continues in French, sounding strained. Guillaume translates rapidly.

"She almost escaped . . . she filmed Fournier . . . on his knees like a little dog . . . but he saw her go to the elevator . . . he was begging her to stay . . . she blames herself."

He soothes Odette. She manages some more English. "My *sac*, I hold it so. He sees and fuh! I know he know."

And off she goes in French again. Agitatedly. Guillaume resumes his interpreter duties.

"Fournier is suspicious . . . even more when she will not release the purse . . . His fingers are in her arm like a . . . the crab—"

"A claw."

"Yes, claw. His eyes are like a savage animal's . . . Ah, then the elevator comes. She tries to get away. That is when she sees you. She cannot get free . . . Then the elevator doors close. Fournier is very agitated . . . He takes the bag and finds the camera . . . She can see his rage but also his fear . . . Three men come and they stop everything. Fournier tells her . . . 'You do not exist. Say what you want, no one will believe you.'"

Odette stops talking. She seems barely conscious. Guillaume asks her something in French. She can only manage one word in response: "Claude." Guillaume touches her shoulder gently and stands up.

"I ask how did she escape. You heard her answer, yes?"

"Claude, her brother."

"Yes, we will find out more later."

Lana feels a surge of admiration for the mental strength, the courage, the fire inside that took the young woman into that obscene lair. She envies it. Her little escapade, fired merely by curiosity born of elation, seems pretty pathetic now. If she had had any forewarning of the sleazy scenario that awaited her on the seventh floor, she would never have gone near that elevator. To go there willingly, toting a hidden camera, seems unthinkably brave. And then caught, tied up, interrogated, beaten.

They go downstairs. Guillaume speaks in a whisper.

"I think she will be okay tomorrow. She is wonnerful, yes? And still we have no evidence, no photos, only her words, which, against their words mean nothing." He looks meaningfully at Lana. "You are the only witness."

It would be so easy and feel so right to say yes to the question in his eyes. But Lana heeds a tiny warning voice.

"Guillaume, you know how people hate the way Americans interfere in stuff that's not really their business—especially the French, actually. And I totally buy that. You got an election coming up and it's for you people to decide. No matter what I saw it wouldn't be right for me to get involved in any way. Sorry. I mean, believe me I understand your frustration, but . . ."

Suddenly Guillaume claps his forehead and gives her the big smile.

"Oh, I am stupid. It is a problem with language. Lana, I am sorry if you misunderstand me. You think I want you to be a witness to change the election? No, no. This is impossible. We are nothing. Look."

He gestures around the messy space as if to confirm his epic unimportance.

"We are independent. Little. This project, I have been trying for a year. Maybe it will be another year. This is not a story
only about Fournier. He is a little part, yes, maybe a bigger
part, certainly, if he is already our president when we are complete. But no, this is a documentary . . . ah, a philosophical
investigation . . . to question the sexual politics of France. You
know we French like to say the public actions of a politician are
important only, not the private life. In fact for many they like
it when a politician is also seductive. D'Estaing was proud of
himself for this. You know what he said? He said, 'As president
I was in love with seventeen million French women. They felt
this love and they voted for me.' But there is a problem, yes?
This situation is good for men, especially for rich and powerful
men, but not for women. Chirac's wife, she must always ask
the chauffeur, 'Where is my husband tonight?' Well, perhaps
she was stupid to stay with such a man, but what about the case
of Mitterrand? What about his mistress and his secret daughter? Was it a private matter, his own business when Mitterrand
spent money from the state for his mistress and his daughter and
utilized the apparatus of the state to protect his secret? Interesting, yes? You understand, Lana. This is the story I am trying to
tell. It is a discussion most important.

"In France for men in powerful political situations, it is still
the time of Kennedy. Silence, secrecy. Sometimes this is good.
We are not puritans. But, ah yes, if the rules are not equal, if
the woman she cannot say no, if the man is not the charming seducteur, but something else? A predator, arrogant and
forceful. What then? This is a question. We ask your help for
this question, Lana. Decide the election in France? Dufour or
Fournier? No. Of course not. To make my little documentary

it is slow. Maybe another year, maybe more. We are idealists, we are dreamers. We hope, but we do not know. You were a witness to something very important tonight. It is better for our story that you are not French. You look with different eyes. Open eyes. Please, help us with this project?"

His arm is around Pauline's waist. When he finishes his speech he squeezes it and kisses her temple. They both gaze at Lana. Hungry puppies could not have been more entreating.

"So, this isn't some kind of election propaganda thing?"

"Lana. A French election is not like the U.S. We have no political commercials on television. It is forbidden."

"You're kidding."

"No, we cannot. It is the law."

"You promise me?"

"Of course."

Lana is sorely tempted. The contrast between the coiffed elegance of the TV politician and her memory of the naked old goat with a ferocious grip on a helpless young woman is stark and it angers her. If only people in France—women especially—had seen what she saw. Maybe it is the right thing for her to try to conjure up at least some sense of the violence of it: especially those blazing eyes. This Fournier guy is way past inappropriate. Maybe he is truly dangerous. What happened to Odette afterward was forcible abduction, surely?

"Okay. Tell you what. I leave Paris tomorrow evening. Let me sleep on it. If in the morning I still think it's a good idea, then yeah, sure, I'll do it."

"But you are here now. It will be only ten minutes."

"I know, but honestly, Guillaume, I'm exhausted. I have to think it through. Don't worry, I'm pretty well there with you on this and if I decide to do it, then you'll get one hundred percent. But I need some quiet time first."

"Sure, sure. I understand. Hey, why not sleep here? Then, when you wake—"

"No, I'll be more comfortable back at the hotel."

"But will you be safe?"

Guillaume says it like it's the most obvious thing. It hadn't occurred to Lana.

"Fournier's men tried to kidnap you. They tried to kill us on the street. They have your phone and the keycard for your hotel room. You don't think they will be waiting for you?"

But she has to go back to the hotel precisely because her passport and ticket are there. Maybe she should go to the police first, the real police? Explain the whole story. Hi, one of your presidential candidates is trying to have me killed. Could I have some round-the-clock surveillance, please? Not a good idea.

"But even if I stay here tonight I still have to go back in the morning to pay my bill and get my stuff. If they're waiting for me now, they'll still be waiting. Of course, you won't really care anymore once you get your interview, right?"

"No, Lana, please. This is not true."

"Okay, okay, here's a deal. Bring me to the hotel. If there's any problem, I'm straight back here with you. If not, I get a good night's sleep in my very luxurious bed and we'll talk in the morning."

Silence. Lana registers that odd something ripple across Guillaume's face again, a hint of the spoiled child thwarted. Not a man she'd automatically put her trust in, but right now what are the choices?

"Look, if you don't want to do this, I'll just go. Let me back on the street. I'll find my way to the hotel and take my chances, or go to the police—"

"No. All right. Of course we'll take you. I'm sorry, it's just I wish I can think of a better plan to help you."

Lana's not entirely sure why she doesn't quite buy that.

The yellow loaf—it was actually a classic Renault 4, Guillaume had proudly told her—is hardly the most inconspicuous vehicle to be arriving in should there be anyone on the lookout outside Le Chevalier. The last thing she wants is another crazy chase. So they pull in at the nearest corner, where another conversation begins between Guillaume and Pauline, so passionately intense they might have been arguing nature or nurture, but Lana's best guess is that they are only discussing which of them should check out the hotel lobby for anything suspicious.

Pauline jumps out. Guillaume, looking at her sashay brazenly under the arches toward the entrance, chuckles admiringly.

"Pauline, she is so clever. I say I will go. She says no, it must be her in this situation. She says if Vallette or one of his men is waiting they will know me for certain, but they may not know her. And if they do know her and approach, she says a woman can have the perfect solution for this problem. You know what she will do? Scream and scream, 'Leave me alone! Help, please!' There is nothing any French man can do in this moment. She says it will be fun making the scene."

Lana feels a little guilty that she's not more grateful for all the trouble this strange young couple is taking, apparently on her behalf, but somehow she can't rid herself of a vague resentment that this anarchic pair has trapped her in their own private made-up movie adventure. What she needs is a few hours' quiet to think through step by step everything that has happened and the best way to extricate herself from the mess. Right now the dull simplicity of meeting Brian off a plane at Dublin airport seems the most desirable thing in the world. The meds must really be kicking in.

Pauline comes skipping back and she and Guillaume exchange another unnecessarily long kiss before the excited babble begins. His translation is unusually, but mercifully, succinct.

"She thinks it is safe. To be certain we will wait for you. I will give you my number; you have the card?"

Lana hands him his business card. He scribbles a number on it.

"Call me from your room."

"I will. Thank you. Merci beaucoup, Pauline."

Pauline leans back and kisses her enthusiastically full on the lips.

The lobby and bar are more or less empty. No music at this late hour. Lana can't help glancing in the direction of the private elevator. She approaches reception and, given her presumption that anything that can go wrong tonight will, is surprised to be issued with a new keycard without fuss and with a smile. There's no sign of her hero bellhop, Odette's brother.

"There's a bellhop named Claude. Is he still on duty?"

The receptionist seems to hesitate before answering.

"Claude? No. He is gone home."

"Oh, that's a pity. I just wanted to thank him actually. He

was a big help to me earlier tonight. A real lifesaver. Maybe I'll see him in the morning?"

Again there's something uncomfortable in the receptionist's manner, her reply stilted.

"No. Claude will not be present in the morning."

Is it his day off? Had he been hurt tangling with Fichet—Vallette—and his crew? Had that lovely mouth got a fat lip on her account?

Lana feels nervous wings flutter inside her rib cage as the elevator doors open on the fifth floor, but the corridor is empty. She pauses at her room door. The old keycard had been in the purse that Vallette's guy had forced her to drop. Someone could be waiting in there. The flutter becomes panicked flapping. She scampers back to the elevator to confirm that it's still there waiting, then returns to 511, takes a deep breath, and slides the keycard in. The green light flashes and she eases the door open, peering into the darkness, anxious, alert. She reaches and finds the light switch. There's no one in the room. Of course there might be someone hiding in the bathroom, but at this point panic recedes, relief takes charge, and Lana tells herself not to be so ridiculously paranoid. She walks in with confidence, closing the door firmly behind her. Lying on the bed and closing her eyes feels exquisite. She begins to drift. Thanks to the meds, she should get something like a decent night's sleep. Is it possible that all the bad stuff is over? Perhaps Fournier and his friends have decided to leave well enough alone.

There is something she needs to do, but can't think what it is. Her brain is shutting down with the tingling pleasure of a masseur's thumbs rippling down her spine. Whatever the thing is, it can wait until morning. Everything can wait until morning. Guillaume will have to—Guillaume! Her eyes flash open. That's it. She'd promised to call and reassure him. Lana feels guilty, because, quite suddenly, the way she truly feels is clear to her: she doesn't want to see either him or Pauline ever again. All she wants is to get up early in the morning, spend a pleasant few hours wandering through pretty streets and pretty shops, and then fly home to safe old Brian.

As she reaches for the phone Lana notices the envelope on the bedside locker. Then she notices what is not on the bedside locker. Her meds. Isn't that where she left them? Yes, she is sure of it. Has anything else been touched? Now she looks around the room. Her bag, the jeans she had thrown on a chair, the catalog from the Hopper exhibition: everything is gone.

Room 511 has been cleared out.

It must be the cumulative effect of all the nerve-jangling experiences of the last few hours, but only now does Lana give in to hysteria. No matter the consequences, she so needs to scream. She opens her mouth and it seems inevitable that some awful primitive shriek will fill the room, but she can't make any sound other than short, urgent gasps. Her head swivels this way and that in a hopeless search. This can't be. She folds to the floor wishing she had someone to pray to. She wants to run and run, but can't even unclench her fists.

The awareness that Guillaume and Pauline are waiting for her call makes her finally reach forward and grab the envelope from the locker. "Madame Gibson" is neatly written on the front. She opens it cautiously as if it might explode in her face.

Madame Gibson, please telephone 0676589403
cordialement

She imagines whoever wrote it—Vallette?—enjoyed "cordialement." He might as well have scrawled "come out with your hands up." They have her passport, e-ticket, money, medication, cards. They hold all the cards. That's why they hadn't needed to waste manpower hanging around the hotel or lurking in the room waiting for her. She's out of options. What use are Guillaume and Pauline now? There's nothing they can do about this. What did these people intend to do with her, anyway? Lana always liked a good conspiracy theory—on the JFK assassination she was a grassy knoll woman through and through—but the idea that in this situation someone might think that killing her is the appropriate action seems utterly crazy, too excessive, unnecessary. How could she be that important or dangerous? Maybe they intend to kidnap her and keep her under wraps until after the election? Or bribe her?

Might it be possible to convince them that she's harmless, that it had all been a dumb accident as a result of her condition? They have the meds so they know that part isn't a lie. A woman on the edge goes a little crazy and ends up an accidental witness, but hey! She has absolutely no intention now of broadcasting what she saw, which was nothing anyway. In fact she's forgotten about it already. Put her on the plane and send her home. Best for everyone. Would they buy it? First things first, she'd better call Guillaume to reassure him, quickly before he arrives at the room to check on her. Lana knows she'll have to concentrate very hard to make herself sound truthful.

"Hi, Guillaume."

"I am in the foyer. I am coming to find you—"

"No, no, it's okay. Everything is fine."

"You were so long."

"Yes, I had to get a new keycard. It took a little while to sort it out."

Guillaume's voice suddenly becomes very quiet, very intense.

"Are you certain? Lana, if there is a problem and you cannot explain me, if there is perhaps someone with you now, just say, 'Good night, Guillaume,' and hang up."

Lana attempts a laugh, as if to suggest that he's being amusingly melodramatic.

"No, no, honestly, everything is fine. I'm just going to sleep now. But thank you."

"Okay. Good. You will call me in the morning?"

Lana feels more than a little guilty and is sure she sounds utterly unconvincing.

"Yes, of course. First thing."

"Perhaps I will meet you here early?"

"Sure, sure. Yes, why not?"

Finally he lets her hang up. She stares at the note for several minutes. There is nothing incriminating or sinister in it, but at least it's something on paper. If she brought this to the police wouldn't it show that she's not some crazed fantasist? But then what? Fournier is a powerful political figure and she's a foreign nobody. Grassy knoll time again.

She feels so utterly alone. Is there any point in calling Brian and crying down the phone, take some comfort from the sound of his voice at least? No.

Nathan.

Like a curl of smoke that takes shape the name drifts into her head. In this desperate moment, she allows herself to think about him. At least he is here in Paris.

Nathan. It's as if she had redacted all references to him in documents, consigned to the trash all files containing his name, yet somehow he has remained lurking in the hard drive.

Nathan. Nathan. Nathan. To entertain even the most fleeting notion of setting out to make contact with him at this hour seems utterly bizarre, reckless, hopeless, but, now that it's surfaced, she knows the idea is not going to go away. Given the hopeless situation in which she finds herself, wouldn't it be something to see Nathan again? But who's to say he's still living in the same place? After more than three years, the chances of finding him tonight, just like that, are minuscule. Especially without even a phone number.

But at this moment he seems like the only person she can trust.

2 AM

What Lana had promised herself would not happen on this trip, she is about to make happen. Yesterday evening her elated self had assured her that the Hopper exhibition was the perfect opportunity to go back and reclaim at least some part of Paris. To exorcise the ghost of her wicked behavior a few years ago. It would be uncomplicated, a short trip, a definite focus. There'd be no need even to think of Nathan and she certainly wouldn't indulge in foolish self-deluding actions like meandering over to the Left Bank pretending to be just another casual tourist, while secretly hoping to see his face loom miraculously out of the café crowds, or hear a voice from nowhere shout, "Lana Turner! Is that you?"

Circumstances had changed everything. Now she is about to go deliberately in search of him: trekking across the river to find his old apartment. So late. It's crazy and wrong. But it's all she has left.

Lana had sat on the floor in 511 for nearly an hour telling herself that this idea of taking off into the night without a cent in search of someone she hadn't seen in more than three years and who probably wouldn't want to see her, was the worst of the many bad impulses she'd acted on over the last few hours. What were the chances that Nathan was still living in the same apartment? How would she get into the building to find out? What could he do for her anyway, even if she did get to see him? All that considered, she still felt a desperate need for some kind of contact with someone who she felt . . . someone who wasn't a complete stranger. Surely he wouldn't slam the door in her face, no matter how she had treated him the last morning they'd seen each other? There was an even darker possibility. Was he the real reason she had worked up her unstoppable urge to return to Paris? No. No! How could that be? If the trip had gone according to plan she would not have made any attempt to make contact. But it was so much the opposite of going to plan and now she was alone and afraid.

None of this thinking and rethinking mattered. In the end, Lana could not bear to stay in her violated room any longer. No matter how tempting the bed was, no matter how exhausted she felt, sleep was out of the question. Even though she forced herself to take a shower she did so frantically, counting the seconds.

Now, crossing the lobby, Lana keeps her gaze well away from the private elevator. Is it her imagination that the night concierge seems concerned as he lets her out onto the street? Would Madame like him to call a taxi? Once outside Lana walks about twenty yards before stopping under the shadow of the arches to look around oh-so-cautiously. She waits to see if anyone emerges from the hotel. Are there shadows peeping out from anywhere? She scans parked cars for signs of surveillance. Jesus, she's thinking in words like *surveillance*. There are four people visible on the street and she observes their movement, but they seem like normal passersby. Fournier and his people are probably getting a good night's sleep confident that she has no options, nowhere to go.

But they don't know about Nathan. This is something.

Though he's very much on her mind now, it isn't until she turns right toward rue de l'Amiral-de-Coligny that she allows this walk to become a full-fledged journey of recollection, not so much a sentimental journey as a passionate white-knuckle ride. Straight ahead Lana sees the orange awning with LE FUMOIR printed in black letters along the fringe. She slows as she approaches. The bar is closing, a few patrons finishing their drinks. So different from the night she first met Nathan: It was just before the despised ban came into force in France and that night the dark-wood interior was bulging with smokers savoring the last of the good old days, a memory they would keep for their grandchildren. "Ah, what times they were. We used to crush into crowded rooms choked with noxious smoke. Our clothes stank and we coughed all the time. Wonderful." The sight of the impenetrable fug inside had made her smile for the first time since Brian and she had parted in tight-lipped silence earlier that day. Their long-planned, fabulously romantic Christmas and New Year's trip to Paris had crumbled to dust when Brian had gotten an urgent call from Seattle. He was needed immediately, which was how he was always needed. What pissed her off most of all was that it hadn't even occurred to him to discuss it with her before agreeing to return. Oh, he was disappointed, sure, hell, he was despondent. But, he said, that's the way the ball bounces and they'd get another shot at Paris. He'd been shocked to the point of disbelief when Lana told him, in a tone sharper than the windchill outside, not to change her flight because she was staying on. But . . . but . . . what would she do in Paris on her own? What about New Year's Eve? Lana had just shrugged. It was Paris. Five days would barely be long enough for what she wanted to see and

do. Brian's aggrieved accusation that she was being childish was
the wrong move. He'd adjusted, but then cast her as the cold,
unforgiving one while presenting himself as the true romantic,
whining that no matter where, they should be together on New
Year's Eve. It was also vital apparently that they should park the
Paris experience until they could return and enjoy it together.
Most ineffectual of all, he had tried wheedling. Come home
with him please, darling. He promised that they'd return at
the first chance they got, but she'd been implacable. The only
solution that would satisfy her was for Brian to tell his masters
that work could wait until January 2 as planned. So, after angry words that became chilly words that became silence and a
sleepless night, Lana had just wanted him to go as quickly as
possible.

She had spent the first few hours after he left smoldering
in the hotel suite. Then she wandered up to place Vendôme
and on to Madeleine, purchasing little beribboned gift boxes of
chocolate and macarons and perfumes in an effort to convince
herself that she'd been right to stay and was going to have a fabulous time on her own. She returned to the hotel, dozed miserably for a couple of hours, then decided what the hell, why not
get out, cross the river, see what the famous Latin Quarter had
to offer. She foresaw youthful street buzz, atmospheric bistros
with rude waiters, cool independent movie houses showing old
classics.

But she never got to the Left Bank that night. Smiling at
the puffing patrons of *Le Fumoir* Lana decided to do something she had often thought of, but never acted on before.
The bizarre French habit of panhandling cigarettes from complete strangers had always amazed her. Perfectly respectable-
looking, college-educated types would just walk up and ask

for—practically demand—a cigarette. She had never been able to refuse and had, ever since her first youthful visit to Paris, always wanted to do it in turn, but had never, ever had the nerve. Well, she was in just the kind of mood to do it now, and heaven help anyone who turned her down.

So she sauntered into *Le Fumoir* and looked around. After a couple of minutes of considering then rejecting a selection of potential victims, she recognized that she was just stalling, probably constructing an excuse to abandon the plan. Okay, she told herself, this is simple, just pick the best-looking guy in the bar and go for it. Almost immediately, she spotted him. Only his face was visible in the crush, but it was arresting enough. Either he had forgotten to shave this morning or he liked to look that way. The overhead light bounced off his luxuriant hair and the copper glow reminded her of a Lake Union sunset. Thick eyebrows hung over green eyes. The pale gold skin and mouth, wide and full, made the perfect French face.

Lana remembers staring a little too long, but more from surprise than procrastination. Then she wriggled through the bodies, tapped his shoulder, and made the smoking gesture.

"Une cigarette, s'il vous plait."

"I thought it was only Parisians who were allowed to do that. If Americans start begging ciggies there won't be enough givers for the takers."

His voice was such a shock. And a kind of letdown: a purring English accent, terribly classy.

"Oh, you're not French?"

"Are you disappointed? Of all the gin joints in all the towns? Actually, I am French. Well, a French citizen, with French parents, and although I was—but sorry, you don't want my life story, you want a cigarette."

He didn't stop talking as he offered one.

"Here's the thing. If you shamble off now with my cigarette, that's perfectly fine, but if you do want to hear my life
story while you smoke, I'd be perfectly happy to entertain you."

What could she do? Walking away was awkward anyway
in such a crush. Up close her flame-haired French fantasy was
even more attractive and the English accent had its own charm.
He might be Lana's age, but no more; possibly a little younger.
As she raised her left hand to accept the cigarette, she switched
instinctively and took it in the right hand instead and so kept
her wedding band out of sight as she lit up, sucked, and, holding
her cigarette hand high, blew a very cool thin line of smoke.
They introduced themselves and she reasserted some degree of
dignified independence by insisting on paying for the drinks he
ordered, while Nathan Maunier entertained her with his backstory. It took some time because of many asides, many good
jokes. He'd been born in England because his French parents
had moved there to work, and had been educated there all the
way to university in East Anglia, but had spent every summer
and Christmas in France. When his parents had retired back
home he'd followed a couple of years later to do a PhD in eco-
nomics and was now teaching at Sciences Po, specializing in
French and British colonial history, about which he was very
passionate. So much so he warned Lana to shout "boring" if
he strayed anywhere near this subject tonight. Boring was the
very last thing Nathan Maunier was and it occurred to Lana
what an alluring combination she had found: easy conversation
with a witty, louche Englishman, while feasting her eyes on a
ravishing Frenchman. When he walked her back to the Hotel
Regina she was drunk enough and buzzed enough to be so, so,
so, so very close to inviting him to her suite.

Lana can't remember now exactly why she hadn't, but had felt no guilt in agreeing to meet him again. Why not? She was alone in Paris, free, and, as far as he was concerned, single. Somehow, while not lying, she'd managed to omit marriage from her own résumé and keep the evidence out of sight. Why spoil a harmless, pleasantly flirtatious encounter?

On the Quai du Louvre Lana crosses to the riverside and peeks between the locked-up bookstalls along the quay wall. Halfway across, jutting out from Pont Neuf, a triangular park narrows to a point: the western tip of Île de la Cité, where Nathan had brought her the following evening. Despite the cold, all wrapped up, they'd picnicked on bread and saucisson and brie and grapes and wine and watched a winter sun, the color of his hair, tumble slowly into the Seine. Though she'd given it serious consideration, Lana, despite her anger at Brian, could not bring herself to remove her ring, so she had already decided to reveal the truth to Nathan and was shocked when he smiled and nodded.

"I knew there was a gap in your story. Some missing detail. It's a bit of a relief that it's relatively straightforward, I have to say. Also I rather like that you felt the urge to tell me. He's not lurking anywhere nearby, is he?"

She assured him he was not and nothing more was said about that. They'd shared a joint, the first she'd smoked in years, and he talked about the Chinese opium wars, which he said most people assumed had been all about the nefarious Chinese turning the West into junkies, when the real cause had been the British desire to flood China with opium from India. He told the story so passionately, elaborating on tiny details, gesticulating with precision and intensity, that it was quite a while before the polite Englishman in him remembered to inquire if he was being boring—even though the charming Frenchman in him knew quite well that he was not. He explained that early in his career he'd tried hard to be an objective historian but, for better or worse, could never really manage it. However, being anti-imperialist was inevitable now and to be a socialist in French academic circles was commonplace. By that stage of the evening he could have been the shoe bomber for all Lana cared. She fancied a little imperialist venture of her own and planted her lips on that wide warm mouth, laying claim to the territory and all its treasures. Later they wandered up to Odéon and after a few more drinks in *Le Danton*, it became inevitable that they would stroll together around the corner to his apartment overlooking place St.-André-des-Arts.

If he talked like an Englishman, Nathan made love as a Frenchman is supposed to, which, it occurred to her at one delirious moment, was definitely the right way around.

The memory is embarrassingly vivid in Lana's mind now, her straddling his thighs as he arches back, his hands on the bed taking the weight, his stomach and chest stretched, his head falling back and hair hanging almost to the pillow. Whatever light trailed from the window made the golden line of hair weaving from his navel to his chest glisten and spark. And she had screamed and finally laughed.

That was the first of the most reckless four nights and days of pleasure. It had so nearly been much longer than that. Halfway across Pont Neuf she remembers to stop at the narrow gap between the twin brick and sandstone buildings, to look beyond at the secret delight that was Place Dauphine and see if *Ma Salle* à *Manger* is still in business. Yes, there it is, just where the little passage fans out to an entrancing triangle. The chestnut trees are golden, unlike when she and Nathan had made the friendly little Basque restaurant their neighborhood hangout for three nights, including that languorous New Year's Eve.

Now Lana peeks inside. The staff are lounging, enjoying a little drink before going home. They haven't brought in the outdoor tables and chairs yet.

Despite the late December cold, she and Nathan had preferred eating outside because they enjoyed the serenity of the solid old seventeenth-century buildings that enclosed the triangle and protected it from the noise of the city quite effortlessly, and the storybook magic created by the lamps dotted about the park area that made curious skeletal silhouettes of the bare trees. After eating they always lingered, wrapped in shawls provided by the restaurant, sipping and smoking, savoring the manufactured delay before returning to his apartment, the anticipation more addictive in many ways than the sex that followed. Better even than what she had thought was the unstoppable, unsurpassable buzz of the Pumpkins live at the Oz back in October 1993, when the crush of the crowd had allowed her skinny teenage frame to float for most of the night and she'd wished her lousy virginity back just so she could offer it up to Billy Corgan. It was even better than those first weeks and months with Brian, discovering for the first time what it was to be properly, generously in love.

Lana had felt no guilt whatsoever during those few nights and the only uncertainty was about whether it should be left at that or become something more. She had seen little of her hotel room, returning only to shower and change and return Brian's calls. She mostly texted him back, which was safer, but yet when they did talk she was able to mute her mood of ecstatic excitement and find instead a cooler tone, one more suited to their ongoing standoff. She felt so far away from him, much further than Seattle, way beyond the nine-hour time difference. On a different emotional planet.

For the first time since leaving Hotel Le Chevalier, Lana feels a jolt of fear. Who is that man walking toward her along place Dauphine's cobbled road, his long moving shadow slinking up the wall of the buildings? She turns quickly toward the narrow Pont Neuf entrance and almost cries out when another man appears just as she emerges. But he pads by without a glance. When she looks back into place Dauphine the shadow man is no longer there, probably just a resident gone indoors. Still, she accelerates now to the far side of the bridge. Soon she'll hit the corner of rue de Buci and rue St.-André-des-Arts with its busy late-night bars. On that New Year's Eve three years ago, they had walked this same route and gone to see *The Apartment* somewhere along here, down a narrow street to the left. There it was. Halfway down rue Christine, she spots the battered old lit sign, made to look like a strip of film:

It had probably been there for fifty years, longer, since the golden age. She sees her ghost and Nathan's skipping out, arm in arm, babbling about Wilder's genius. The spectral couple come right at her and sweep by, rapt in their happy world. She pursues them to Buci and on to Odéon. She stares through the glass window of *Le Danton* at the exact banquette they had settled into, recalling, as though the thoughts are hers now at this moment, how much she'd hoped he'd ask her to stay on in Paris with him, knowing already that the answer would be yes. As it happened he hadn't said anything then, but later, in the sleepy dark, wrapped together, she heard a whispered, "Don't go."

"What are you asking me?"

"I know, I'm sorry, it's so bloody selfish, but I want you to stay, please."

"You mean for a few more days . . . or longer."

"I mean longer. Longest."

"All right. I'll stay."

Just like that. And made a liar of herself.

The apartment where Nathan had lived back then is only two minutes' walk away, but as Lana recalls how those few white-hot winter nights and days had ended, it's becoming harder to complete the journey. She turns away from *Le Danton*, but then just stops and stands there. Odéon bustles all around, but she is seeing nothing. Wretchedness overwhelms her. This idea of finding Nathan is both crazy and sad.

A young girl stumbles and friends react with teenage shrieks. Until this moment Lana had not noticed them. Suddenly the young girl is vomiting, convulsed and groaning. Some of her friends try to be of practical help, putting a comforting hand on her shoulder or tugging hair back from a drooling mouth. What's happening with Parisian girls? In Lana's experience, they never used to stagger around the streets in this condition. She starts to move closer. The girl is still on her knees coughing and moaning and now Lana notices that the teenagers are not wailing in

French. Just as she realizes that they are English, not Parisian, she spots a purse on the ground just beyond the vomit. It is scarlet and heart-shaped. Perhaps this style of purse is all the rage among English teenagers in Paris, but Lana prefers the less obvious conclusion that the girl on her knees really is the arrogant little bitch who had been so rude at the Hopper. She looks at her more closely, with more intense interest. Her clothes—what little she's wearing—are different, but of course she would have changed for her night on the town. The hair seems about the same length and color, but still, as she stops spewing and lifts an anguished face, Lana still can't be certain it is her. Then the girl speaks actual words. "It's okay, I'm fine, stop! Let me be, yeah." That petulant "yeah." It's her all right. Looking down at this shocking creature, her face green and gross, a thin line of drool stretching from her mouth, her skirt, already micromini, riding up so far her ass is exposed, Lana begins to believe that there might be a God and she is a kindly God who, to comfort Lana in her despair, sent her out onto the streets of Paris at this unlikely hour just so she can witness the humiliation and misery of this rancid little bitch. Lana taps one of the friends on the shoulder.

"Excuse me, can I help?"

"Actually we're fine, thank you."

"No, really, I'd like to help. You all have cell phones, I'm sure. If you let me use one I could get some great shots of you all. Wouldn't that be funny?"

The look on the friend's face certainly is, as far as Lana is concerned.

"No. Now just leave us alone, please?"

"But wouldn't all your Facebook friends get off on seeing this hilarious scene? Lots of Likes and LOLs? I could make a Vine of you, sweetheart, spewing. So sophisticated, real classy."

Horrified, the friends start to push Lana away. The princess tries to stand, staggers, and falls again. Lana is buzzing. All the crap she has had to put up with over the last few hours, the noxious mound of bile expanding inside her finally has an outlet and this spoiled, arrogant, mean girl is the useful target for all of it. Lana leans closer to her.

"You really are taking Paris by storm, aren't you? We met earlier at the Hopper exhibition. Remember me? No? You were snapping everything then, yeah? Now you're an exhibition all on your own. Yeah? Kind of living art."

Shrieks of revulsion and rage shock the Paris night. The girlfriends lunge at her. It's turning feral. Lana backs away.

"Oh come on, ladies, this should be recorded. Someone take some photos, please."

Parisians of the 6th strolling by shudder at the raw, ear-piercing Anglo-Saxon vulgarity. In the moment, Lana, buoyed by the effect of her taunts, doesn't care that she's probably coming off as as crazed and cheap as the young brats. The success of her vengeance propels her along boulevard St.-Germain, around the corner and in no time she reaches the corner of rue Danton and place St.-André-des-Arts. She looks up at the fourth-floor window. It is unlit, but that doesn't necessarily mean Nathan's not there. He might be asleep already. She approaches the heavy brown double doors. Naturally she can't remember the entry code, which surely has been changed in the last three years anyway. If she waits, will some resident leaving or returning let her in? Unlikely, especially at this hour, but she's here now, so she might as well stay and find out. It occurs to her she might not have to ask permission to enter. Lana remembers that the heavy doors are self-closing and swing very slowly. If anyone goes in or out she would have a few seconds to get to it and prevent it from locking. A Vélib' bike-share stand only yards away seems like the perfect place to hover without arousing attention. She can hang there looking at the map or reading the instructions as if trying to work out how to sign out a bike. No one passing would be remotely suspicious. She steps quickly toward the bikes, counting silently. It takes no more than six seconds. Time enough, surely.

The deflation comes soon. No one arrives at the doors or emerges from inside. Surely they're not all tucked up in their beds? Her hopes are raised and dashed, raised and dashed, raised and dashed . . . Each time someone approaches they just sail past the brown double doors. To lift her spirits she thinks about her encounter with the spewing princess, but this leads her to a very different memory: Lana Turner at the Regina Hotel packing her bags. The final moment before the shock.

She was all ready to check out and float back to Nathan's apartment, refusing to think about the painful phone call to Brian she would have to make later.

The nausea came out of nowhere. It rose quickly in waves and she sank, plummeted. On her knees in the bathroom just in time, head hanging in the toilet, breathing in gulps, she told herself it had to be some French thing she'd eaten, escargots, something. But she also knew she was almost a week late.

She found a drugstore around the corner on rue St.-Honoré and back in the hotel, curled in an armchair by the window, she waited for the verdict of + or −. The most surprising thing was that despite willing, demanding a negative, when the red plus sign appeared Lana felt an instinctive surge of what she knew was delight. That weird reaction evaporated almost instantly, but she could not dismiss its significance and how it changed everything. How many weeks gone? Not that it mattered, because it was Brian's, of course, there was no question of that. The hotel phone was a sudden, loud, alarming intrusion. A polite voice inquired if Madame Gibson was leaving today, as it was now after checkout time. She said sorry, yes, almost ready. Then she heard herself ask, would he mind booking her a cab to the airport? Her flight to Seattle would be taking off in less than three hours. Was she doing the right thing? Had the last few days been just a fantasy after all? Or worse, had she been playing a selfish trick on this poor guy, like one of those horrible women who enjoy stealing hearts? In the end she hadn't even had enough courage or grace to call Nathan, afraid that the sound of his voice might induce her to stay. That was what she told herself.

Bad faith creates bad karma. Lana had never shaken off the belief that there was a terrible link between her behavior in Paris and her miscarriage two months later.

The arrival of a cyclist interrupts these thoughts, which is fortunate, because by now she has the emotional equilibrium of an overpacked suitcase, ready to burst open at a touch. The guy makes her jump as he arrives behind her and brakes inches away. He grins, says *pardon*, and parks, rattling the bike to make sure it has locked properly. Then he heads toward the brown double doors. Lana steps after him immediately, but controls her excitement and holds back. The guy taps in the code. The door buzzes and Lana prays that he isn't a Cautious Christophe who'll stand waiting for it to shut. He disappears inside and instantly she runs . . . one, two, three, four, five . . . and stretches out a hand . . . six . . . and touches the brass handle. She holds it an inch from the lock and wedges her foot in. Hopefully the guy won't notice that there has been no door slam. She presses an ear to the tiny gap, listening for the elevator. When it seems safe she pushes the door open, steps inside, and lets it click shut. She checks the mailboxes. Yes! There's the name: N. Maunier. Slowly, quietly, with increasing heartbeats, she pads up to the fourth floor.

Lifting a little finger to the doorbell is nerve-shredding, as if it had NE TOUCHE PAS! emblazoned on it. Five forlorn rattles go unanswered, which feels pretty anticlimactic. Either Nathan's sleep is extraordinarily heavy, or he's out, or not in Paris at all. Of course there's a chance, and maybe a reasonable one, that he will be home shortly. Worth waiting to find out. Now that she's inside there seems little point in returning to the lonely streets just yet.

Lana sits on the steps leading to the next floor, not bothering to keep pressing the timer light switch. As she gazes through the gloom at the apartment door, their various comings and goings come back to her: the frenzied passion of their key-rattling arrivals, the languor and serene intimacy of their departures. On that last morning as she left to collect her belongings from the hotel he had presented her with a spare key. It was never used and was still in her purse when she got back to Seattle, where it stayed for several months, until one Saturday, finally, regretfully, Lake Union swallowed it up. At sunset.

She is pacing the landing when the rumble of the elevator and laughing voices send her back up the stairs out of sight. Two voices, male and female. The elevator arrives. She peeks but the dark forms are unidentifiable. A hand presses the timer switch and, as the landing light blazes, Lana hugs the wall. The voices mutter and giggle. Clearly it's been a fun night. A jingle of keys. She cautiously peeks again. It's Nathan all right. Even from behind, the hair, the frame are unmistakable. The woman's hair is satin-black, her thinness emphasized by a tight-fitting coat. Her high-gloss nails gleam crimson against his pale neck. How well do they know each other? How long?

The situation is impossible. Lana knows already there's no question of revealing herself to him with another woman there. The idea of lying in wait until morning, hoping that she'll leave early, is equally futile. There's nothing to do but let them go inside, then slink away. So near and yet so far.

But Nathan's gentlemanly manners offer Lana a last desperate whisper of a chance. When he pushes open the door he politely ushers the woman in first—a gesture that makes Lana think he might not know her so well after all—before stepping after her. She realizes that he will turn around as he closes the door. So, there being no time to think it through, she steps out onto the landing and whispers urgently.

"Nathan!"

The closing door stops dead. A startled pair of eyes flick and focus. His face framed in the gap registers shock for sure, but it is the shock of recognition. His mouth opens and seems about to say her name, but there is no sound. Then the timer light goes out.

Then the door slams shut.

f Lana has any inclination to rush at the apartment door and hammer on it screaming wildly, she doesn't act on it. Painful though it is, she accepts that she's got her answer and the answer is perfectly reasonable, given the shock of this strange sudden return after her even stranger departure and subsequent shameful years of silence. What was she to expect, ticker tape? "Darling, I waited and waited. I knew you'd come!" It's time to leave the building. Quickly.

Lana stares at the elevator. She wants to kick it, scream at it. At this moment it seems quite likely that she'll never use one again. In fact, taking a solemn vow not to do so seems a perfectly reasonable attitude right now. Though bereft of energy, psychological or physical, she can still trust her own tired legs to keep her safe and take her wherever. Walking down four flights will at least be a dignified snub to this hunk of malevolent engineering.

A few steps down, though, she hears his door lock click softly, followed by the muted squeak of a very cautious opening, followed by a voice whispering her name. When she turns back Nathan is already at the top of the stairs. It's too dark to see the look on his face, but he doesn't sound angry. On the other hand, he's not tumbling down, arms outstretched for a delirious embrace, either.

"So, it wasn't a ghost."

"No. Although I'm not feeling very human, either."

His voice now takes on a pace and urgency that, in the melodrama of darkness, makes it feel like lives are at stake.

"We haven't much time, so I won't even ask how you got in here. What brings you?"

"There's a lot to explain."

"Give me a headline."

"I'm in trouble. I'm alone in Paris and I'm in desperate trouble."

"Okay, you've got my attention. Any particular kind of trouble?"

"Maybe. I'm not sure, but someone might be trying to kill me."

"Christ, how Lana Turner that sounds."

It's a line right out of their past. The happy, jokey part. When she'd told him what her birth name was it had really made his day. He'd said it explained so much. From then on he used it to mark any moments of extravagance or melodrama. "What Lana Turner wants, Lana Turner gets." "I wouldn't do this for anyone else but you, Lana Turner." "Now don't go all Lana Turner on me." And she allowed, even enjoyed this, because his teasing sounded affectionate and, in a curiously pleasing way, he actually made her feel more Lana Turner.

"I know, but it's happening and you're the only person that . . . that I can trust."

"Trust?"

There was overt surprise in his voice. Was he reminding her how little right she had to use that word?

"Yes."

"You trust me?"

"Yes."

The female voice from the apartment is a sharp reminder. Lana has no idea what she's saying, but it has a question mark hanging on the end of it. Nathan barks a loud "Je viens" and then whispers quickly. "Wait up those stairs out of the way. This might not be pretty."

He goes back inside.

Lana's legs carry her very lightly up the stairs and she squats on a step out of sight, actually shaking now, relishing what she suspects Nathan is about to do and not caring much how the other woman will feel. Every second is agonizing. At first there are no sounds at all. Then, suddenly loud and clearly angry, a female voice. Far away first, then quickly closer and closer. Now Lana hears his voice, too, and knows immediately that, at such a moment, its calmness and evenness must be utterly enraging to the poor woman. The door opens. More accurately it's ripped open, slamming against the wall. And the decibel levels soar. Lana thinks how appropriate that the French have the best word for the geyser of verbal rage that is now erupting on the landing: a tirade. And props to the woman, she's giving it the full Sarah Bernhardt. Her delivery is so rapid-fire, her pitch so high, her tone so incandescent that Lana can't recognize any single word or phrase, not that she needs to. Could American anger ever sound so operatic?

Now from above another loud French voice joins in. Lana can't make out a word, though the rage is perfectly clear. A neighbor has been disturbed and he's not happy. What if he decides to come down for a confrontation? He will find her lurking on the stairs and expose her. Lana hears the unmistakable crack of hand on face. She leans out for a peek and catches a sweep of hair and a flash of swinging coat as the woman disappears into the elevator. She sees Nathan in profile, the mark of a hand pulsing on his cheek, gesturing for calm, trying to stem the flow but succeeding only in aggravating her more. Now the angry voice from above is getting closer and Lana hears footsteps pounding on the stairs. The elevator starts down, and the tirade continues, harmonizing with the clank and hum. At last Nathan hears the neighbor and, just as a large man in vest and boxer shorts appears around the turn of the stairs, grabs Lana's hand and pulls her onto the landing. She sees the black sheen of hair sink into the gloom of the elevator shaft. Nathan steps up to forestall him and Lana hears a duet of practiced moaning and apologetic replies. Over and back it goes until at last the neighbor's voice drifts upstairs in a fading cadenza of snorts and snarls. Nathan reappears and offers an odd combination of thin smile and shrug. On the floor above a door slams. Finally, improbably, silence.

"I hope this is worth it."

And he walks back into his apartment. It's not exactly "Alone at last, my darling" but he does leave the door open by way of invitation. She follows. Closing the door behind her feels like the most intensely relieving moment since her arrival in Paris. As if her car has swerved off the highway at speed, rattled down a ravine, and spun and tumbled and bounced before coming to rest and she finds herself miraculously still conscious, face buried in an air bag and relatively unhurt.

"I'm sorry, I didn't mean to—"

"I know you didn't. Don't worry about it. She was a bit too high-strung for my taste anyway—as you just heard."

Lana nods. Nathan kneels to clean up. Only now does she look around. The kitchen hasn't changed at all. It might have

been the same set of dishes piled in the little sink. This is comforting, though Lana's not really sure why. Nathan dumps the
shards of a coffee mug into the trash. His hair is ruffled, presumably the result of the woman's angry attentions, but it instantly
reminds her of how he always looked after sex.

"Actually, I was feeling very guilty until this flew past my
ear. Part of my favorite set too."

Now his smile turns into the one she remembers. The one
that flows from his eyes. It makes everything okay.

"Coffee?"

"Do you have enough mugs?"

"We'll manage. Actually you know, you do look a bit . . .
I don't know."

"War-torn?"

"Wild-eyed. Like you've been fighting off unwanted at-
tacks. Have you been mugged?"

"That's probably the only thing that has not happened to
me this evening."

"Do you want to—I despise the euphemism, but however—
freshen up? Or just sit and relax?"

"I'll curl up if you don't mind. Try to calm the wild eyes."

"Sure. This won't take long. Kick off your shoes. Flop on
the couch."

Lana goes into the living room, which is romantically lit with
the old tripod standing lamp in a corner. Next to her, exactly
where it had been three years ago, the little art deco banker's
lamp casts a green glow. The other woman had probably created this welcoming ambience while she and Nathan had been
whispering on the landing. These are the breaks. The room is as
pleasantly familiar as if she had sat in it the previous evening: the
wide back wall at one end tapering to the tall corner window

overlooking place St.-André at the other, the books overflow-
ing in piles on the floor, and, dominating the room as before,
the bulging brown leather behemoth of a couch, pre–World
War II, scratched and discolored, but inviting as chocolate cake.
Lana closes her eyes to see if she can remember what had hung
on the walls. Wasn't there a huge framed poster of Pontecorvo's
The Battle of Algiers at roughly ten o'clock? She looks. Yes! And
behind her, at five o'clock she's sure, a repro of one of Gauguin's
Tahitian women next to some framed photos of Nathan on
vacation with his parents and laughing group shots from his
college days. She turns. Once again it's all exactly as in her
mind's eye.

There is no doubt that it feels odd, a little embarrassing
somehow, to sink into the couch and remember, instantly and
vividly, the activity that item of furniture had been such an
accommodating part of those four wild days: the recollection
of one distinctly electric moment makes Lana grin. This is
definitely a very, very strange twist to the night. Nightmares
are usually only broken by waking up, but it's as if hers had
suddenly, impossibly vaulted clean into a whole other kind of
dream; turbulent, but not at all troubling. Quite sexy in fact.

Was it strange that there's been no whiff of any kind of
anger from Nathan? Maybe he's just holding it deep below the
waterline and it will emerge eventually? He looks even better
than what she'd presumed was an overromanticized memory
of him. Hadn't aged a day it seemed, still that year younger, of
course, as he always would be. She should be telling herself that
what appeared to be the miraculous evaporation of her troubles
was just self-delusion. Maybe so, but wasn't a little downtime
due after the hellish shift she'd put in? Maybe this isn't another
dream after all. Maybe she has actually woken from the night-

mare and is experiencing the relief of a warm bed—or in this case, couch—and the satisfaction that there are no actual terrors after all. Or, being here now might be the most foolish, dangerous dream. Oh shut it, Lana. Enjoy.

Nathan brings a tray with coffee and Breton cookies. She can't help thinking that he seems to stare briefly at her hand as she picks up a mug. A few seconds pass before it occurs to her that he may have noticed the absence of a wedding band. And why does he sit at the other end of the couch, leaving a pointed gap between them? He allows her a few warming sips before speaking.

"So, who's trying to kill you?"

Lana sips again, not playing for time, simply needing the coffee. And it's so good. As always.

"Do you really want the end of the story first? No context?"

"Fair point. Okay, start wherever you want to start?"

A difficult one. For some reason she wants him to know that this is her first time back in Paris since that other time, but that might take the conversation somewhere else entirely, somewhere she's not yet ready to go. And she doesn't want to tell him about her medical condition, which isn't needed to explain her behavior. To someone like Nathan, the Hopper exhibition is a perfectly good reason to come to Paris, so she can start the story from there.

"Well, lucky it's only three in the morning, we've plenty of time to kill. But are you going to tell me anything?"

Her silence had clearly been longer than she realized.

"Sorry, I just . . . it's very complicated."

"So, throw me a dramatic opening line. Or something cryptic."

"Did you know the Hotel Chevalier has this amazing penthouse called the Suite Imperial?"

"You're going for cryptic then. No, I'd have to delve deep into my trivia archive for that one. It rings the vaguest of bells."

"Then you probably weren't aware that the only access to it is by private elevator?"

"Correct. That priceless information had passed me by. Mind you, such an arrangement doesn't surprise me at Le Chevalier. Gotta keep the riffraff out."

Hearing him say it, Lana realizes that she had acquired the word from one of Nathan's casual monologues. She remembers it now: his riff on riffraff.

"It's actually Old French, fifteenth century: *riffler*; *rafle*, to spoil and plunder. And of course the mindset, the worldview lurking beneath the word is so very French. Nowadays no intelligent person would dare use it except in a funny voice and ironic quotation marks, but don't tell me that certain people don't still look at certain others and *think* the word, feel it, believe in the idea of riffraff. In France, probably even more than in England, the colonial mindset, the myth of innate superiority is far from extinct. Sorry, boring?"

When she used the word earlier, speaking to Claude, was Nathan already lurking in her head at that moment, despite herself? Is that how the subconscious works, making it more or less inevitable that she'd end up in his apartment regardless of the circumstances? Could it even be that she had deliberately behaved a certain way, created the circumstances, fueled this night's fire to a point that allowed her an excuse to reach out to him? No. This is crazy thinking. Focus, she tells herself, focus on telling him what she saw. Genuinely, she needs his help, right?

"Well, I arrived in Paris this evening and booked into the Chevalier—"

"Ah, the Suite Imperial?"

"No. A plain old junior suite; just for one night. I was going to the Hopper exhibition."

"Ah, very good. Still, I'm impressed. All the way from Seattle for Hopper."

"No . . . from Dublin."

The story is moving backward. Does she now have to explain the recent move to Dublin?

"Let's not worry about that; the point is, I'm staying in the Chevalier for a night and I find myself somewhere I've no right to be. I'm in this private elevator which goes direct to the Suite Imperial—don't ask yet, just let me get through this part—I'm in the private elevator, I mean I'm not planning to, you know, use it because it can only be operated by whoever is staying in the suite. Anyway, suddenly the doors close and it starts to go up."

"Someone in the suite has called it."

"Exactly! And, well, it arrives and the doors open and . . . there's really no other way to say this. There seems to be . . . there's an orgy going on."

Nathan starts to laugh.

"You mean a proper, actual sex orgy."

"Yes. Totally. I can see maybe a dozen people, I don't know, that's happening further off, inside the suite, but right in front of me, in the elevator lobby, more or less as close as you are to me now, there's this one naked guy—not young, I mean like, in his sixties—and he's holding this young woman, and I mean gripping her, and she's fully dressed and pretty obviously trying to escape, but there's no way this guy's letting her go. He's going to get his way, Nathan, and it's so shocking and . . . and disgusting that I'm just, you know, the original pillar of salt, I guess. I can't move. Then the doors started to close again and they both see me—oh yeah, and I have my phone in my hand so I try to grab some shots, but that doesn't work out and the elevator goes back down. Nothing I can do about it."

"Jesus. How long did this last?"

"The doors were open, maybe eight, ten seconds."

He's silent for quite a while. Then the serious questions begin. And of course he wants to know why she was in the private elevator in the first place.

"I don't really know. The bellhop had told me about it earlier, but he wouldn't say who was staying in the suite. Then later I see this guy going into it, but he has his back to me. And also . . . well, the young woman—the one I saw struggling with the naked old guy?—she'd been sitting next to me in the bar earlier and this little chinless guy came and escorted her to the elevator, which kinda made me really curious. Maybe I let it get a little crazy. Lately . . . my mind, I . . . Lately I've been . . ."

Lana pauses, not comfortable with where this is heading. Nathan waits, saying nothing.

"The truth is I don't know if Hopper was the real reason I came to Paris today. I thought that's what it was, I mean genuinely, but maybe there was something else going on . . . you know, subconsciously."

She shrugs and stops speaking. He doesn't fill the silence. It's up to her where the conversation goes.

"Nathan. You haven't said anything to me about what happened with us. You haven't even mentioned . . . why I never contacted you after . . . I mean how do you feel about that? Aren't you . . . I don't know, are you still angry with me? You've got every right to be."

Lana is surprised that he replies without any hesitation, as if he'd been waiting for the question: "It was a long time ago. I *was* angry, sure. I was in a blinding rage, totally livid, and inconsolable actually. For a few weeks, a couple of months maybe. But then . . . What was the point in staying angry? And after a while I was able to tell myself that you must have had your reasons."

"But didn't you—don't you want to know them?"

"Now?" He sounds genuinely shocked. Lana immediately guesses that what he would see as such a peculiarly American need to rake over the coals had never crossed his European mind. "No. But I do want to hear more about this evening. It sounds really extraordinary. What happened next?"

So Lana returns to her story, telling him about escaping back to her room, locking herself in, the knock on the door, the arrival of Inspector Fichet. Nathan does not interrupt until he hears the name.

"Wait, sorry. This guy called himself Inspector Fichet?"

"Yes."

Nathan grins.

"Did he show you any identification?"

"I never asked. Yes, doh! I know."

"Inspector Fichet. Very cheeky. Obviously the name didn't ring any bells for you?"

Nathan poses the question with such boyish pleasure, such an air of a magician setting up his big reveal, that Lana is quite pleased to get the jump on him.

"You mean *Les Diaboliques*?"

He looks duly surprised.

"Oh, you did make the connection?"

"Are you suggesting Lana Turner wouldn't know about *Les Diaboliques*?"

"Well, I suppose—"

"Silly Americans don't know their classic French movies, do they?"

"No, well, no. That wasn't at all what I was—"

She is enjoying his chagrin, but decides to let him off the hook.

"And you're right. It never occurred to me that the name was a little joke, a famous detective character from a classic thriller. It was explained to me later. But only after Fichet and his friend tried to kidnap me."

The punch line has the desired effect. It's she, Lana, who has produced the big reveal. As she explains what happened, Nathan's eyes fix on her with an intensity unusual even for him. As she describes Fichet and friend leading her outside, his hand instinctively inches along the back of the couch where hers is resting. Even as he continues to interrupt her with questions, he edges a little closer and, when she tells him about losing her bag in the struggle to clamber into the yellow Renault, he murmurs and touches her cheek. Lana doesn't dwell too much on Guillaume or Pauline, not even using their names, concentrating instead on the dangers, the near misses, her own internal panic at ruthless men hunting her down. She has no difficulty recalling the terror of it, so when suddenly she draws Nathan to her, the emotion is real. But it's he who takes the next step, with a kiss, full and heartfelt.

Lana doesn't stop him even though she could push him away and cry, "No! This is serious. I'm alone in a foreign city without a passport. My life may be in danger." But right now she doesn't care at all. Nathan is clutching her to him, Nathan is unbuttoning her blouse. Nathan is tumbling from the couch, pulling her with him. Nathan is ripping off his shirt and kicking his shoes away. His tongue carries the taste of some child-hood treat, his skin an almost-forgotten aroma of something delicious. She feels no pain when her flailing foot bangs the little table and the coffee mugs and biscuits spill across the carpet. They are both naked now, their eyes locked on each other, laughter in their short, frantic breaths, hands seemingly unable to concentrate, roaming, searching for that perfect spot. But everywhere is pleasure, intense and shocking.

And then all the frustration of this tumultuous day and night bursts inside her and floods every channel of her body. Her howl surely makes the whole building tremble, but Nathan doesn't try to stop her mouth. He's nodding and grinning at her, the green in his eyes sparking. Then he scrunches them and grimaces and Lana remembers how at such moments his mouth always opened wide, but his cries were never more than little wheezing coughs. Now he collapses, full weight on her. It's gorgeous, but, after a few seconds, uncomfortable. Mercifully he slides sideways.

When Lana drifts out of her doze she has no idea how long they have lain there. Nathan's breathing is soft, his eyes closed. Lana closes hers, too, and senses the sticky dried sweat of his skin on her palm. Her thumb touches the still-damp hair under his arm. His breath gently tickles her nose and she thinks, can't they just stay like this, never move again? Go away everyone. Everything.

At some point she feels herself being dragged, then lifted. Arms grip protectively, her body is now pressed against another, a neck and shoulder make a cushion for her head. It's all so easeful she feels no desire to open her eyes. Nathan can carry her to the window and drop her down onto place St.-André if he wishes. Whatever happens now, is what happens now.

The sheets are a cold shock but only for a moment. His body radiates heat. This time his lovemaking is slow and considerate; he seems to float above her, a shadow in the darkness, a friendly ghost. Afterward he remains hovering, his hands skating gently along her tummy to her breasts. Very soon she drifts into deep sleep.

SATURDAY

OCTOBER 27, 2012

The alarm had been beeping for two minutes before it dragged Ferdie from a black hole of painkiller-induced sleep. He needed about another six hours, but there could be no question of missing the appointment with Vallette. He resented that the lump of bandage around his foot made dressing a struggle—he lost his balance twice—and resented having to use crutches and having to take a taxi for the first time in as long as he could remember. More than anything, though, he deeply resented—and, if he was honest, dreaded—being summoned by a mad dog who would greatly enjoy doing him harm.

Vallette held court in Le Parthénon on rue de Courcelles between seven and eight every morning. There he outlined his plan for each day and snapped instructions to his underlings. Once or twice Ferdie had driven Monsieur Fournier there for an early-morning briefing. This was the first time Ferdie had ever been required to attend on his own behalf.

He still hadn't worked out how to play this and, as he extracted himself awkwardly from the cab, there was one more eye-catching cause for resentment. Parked across the road was his DS21, the car he would normally be using this morning to chauffeur Monsieur Fournier, the car that normally was his to take home each night, that for the last four years he had used pretty much as he pleased. In effect, *his* car, *his* Citroen DS21. Now that psycho fuck was swanning around in it. And Ferdie was very aware that his laptop was still under the driver's seat. The laptop with amusing photoshopped images of Vallette along with other files not intended for the eyes of others, especially those who might wish him harm. He would have to retrieve it this morning. But this was a lesser problem, the greater one being that he still didn't know what had happened last night and where he fit in. It couldn't be just megalomaniac rage that the chauffeur had dared bring a girl to the party without clearing it with His Eminence. Caramel Girl had caused trouble, that was for sure, and it was connected with the American and presumably the bellhop, whom Ferdie had sort of decided to protect if possible. Only if possible, naturally. There were limits.

He shouldered open the glass door. The place was empty apart from Vallette and the other two. Did he pay to have it all to himself at this hour? He was sitting alone at a banquette, eyes down, studying some file. Oscar and Marcel sat at another banquette, gobbling omelets and bread in silence, heads down, mouths in constant motion. The assault on Marcel last night hadn't dented his appetite. They looked around when they heard the crutches' click on the tiled floor. Ferdie was aware of smirks from the meatheads, but even more aware that Vallette didn't even glance up as he approached him, click, click, click. The journey felt a lot longer and louder than it was in reality and the slide into the banquette probably didn't need to be as awkward as he made it. When he laid the crutches aside one of them clattered on the ground and it required some wriggling and stretching to retrieve it. Finally he was settled, but Vallette's eyes stayed focused on his file. Ferdie knew that game and could wait, but it riled him enough to clarify his thoughts and decide right then that there was no way he was going to tell Vallette anything he didn't need to know. Bellhop would not be mentioned. He would say that he happened to meet Caramel Girl in a bar the night before and, after talking to her, had casually invited her to meet him in the Le Chev' bar. He wasn't sure she would come so he hadn't bothered to mention her, but guess what, she had turned up. Sure, Monsieur Vallette sir, was right, sir, it was all a bit too impromptu, but he would never have thought of bringing her up to the party if he hadn't felt very confident that Monsieur Fournier himself would decide if she was welcome or not and he had seemed *very* happy to meet her. Stick that in right at the end because Vallette would know it was true. Ferdie wouldn't need to describe the moment of introduction in detail: the way the boss's eyes had suddenly flicked to full beam and the tip of his tongue had pushed through closed lips like some sea worm wriggling between rocks.

If none of this worked with Vallette, Ferdie still had plan B. When the growl finally came it wasn't in greeting.

"Your whore was carrying a hidden camera."

Naturally he hadn't bothered to look up, but he adjusted his file deliberately, it seemed, to let Ferdie see that he was studying photographic material. Upside down and at an awkward angle it was hard to be sure what exactly the shots were, but there was no doubt that naked bodies in action were the main focus. Ferdie's insides lurched. A hidden camera. Such a thing had never occurred to him. Fuck. Fuck, fuck, fuck. This was really, really, properly serious. Oh Christ! And so much worse for him. He thought about Caramel Girl tied up and the blond American rushing from the elevator and Bellhop's pal in the porkpie hat whispering to him and Marcel unconscious near the overturned chair and understood how easy it would be for Vallette to insinuate him into this . . . cabal or whatever it was. Even if he didn't already hate Ferdie's guts it would be natural to suspect that he was involved. A hidden camera? Someone really was out to get Monsieur Fournier, out to destroy him. It wasn't just psycho guard dog Vallette manufacturing conspiracies. And Bellhop must have known about it. Had to.

Straight to plan B then.

Ferdie tried not to let turmoil show on his face, although it hardly mattered given that Vallette wasn't even looking at him. He would hear the fear, though, so Ferdie controlled his voice as best he could. He tried for innocent surprise.

"My God! Did you take it from her?"

Vallette's eyes shot up, probably despite himself.

"Don't ask me questions. I ask you questions." Now that he was finally looking at Ferdie he went for a long stare. It felt so weird looking at Vallette actually looking back at him.

"Just tell me everything about your part in this."

Plan B. The important thing now, the *only* thing, was to direct Vallette's attention away, far away from Ferdie.

"A camera? No. I knew nothing about that. Until last night she was, as far as I was concerned, just another party girl I'd . . . engaged."

"But you chose not to include her in the dossier with the others."

Ferdie did not want the conversation to move in that direction.

"I will explain that, of course, but first if I may, there is something you will want to know immediately. Last night, once I realized that this girl . . . was a problem, I decided to try to find out more. Too late perhaps, sure, but the guy who had introduced her to me, who had . . . arranged everything, works in the hotel. A young bellhop. You will remember him from last night, I think."

"That skinny child is her pimp?"

"Yes, actually I think they may be related in some way, brother and sister maybe, but I don't know for sure. Anyway, sir, I decided to follow him last night. I found out where he lives. May I give you his address?"

Ferdie was rather pleased with the way, at that moment, he pulled a pen from his inside pocket and held it expectantly, a little dramatic action that might help keep Vallette's attention where he wanted it. Vallette pushed a sheet of paper toward him. Ferdie wrote down the address and turned the page, holding it up.

"He's probably still asleep at this hour," Ferdie said, tempted to add, "as any fucking normal person would be at seven on a Saturday morning." But he held his tongue and watched Vallette for signs of which way he would swing.

It seemed a very long wait, but then without warning Vallette stood, snapped his file shut, and went to his boys. He muttered something and headed toward the exit with Marcel scurrying behind, while Oscar fumbled for money and threw some notes on the table before chasing after them. It was as if they had forgotten Ferdie's existence. This was fine as far as it went and maybe the smart thing was to say nothing and let them go, but he needed some reassurance.

"Monsieur! Am I coming with you?"

Vallette, almost out the door, turned and strode back toward the banquette. He leaned in close to Ferdie.

"When you are *fit* to work again, call me. If I need to talk to you before that, I will find you."

Left alone, Ferdie drew a long breath. Then he remembered his laptop. It was frustrating, but there was nothing to be done about that just now. Though his situation wasn't in any way secure, things had gone as well as he could have expected, which would probably not be the case for the poor bellhop. What was about to happen to him did not make Ferdie feel good, but like the laptop problem, there was nothing to be done about it. Actually, this was not absolutely true. The question was, would Ferdie be willing to do whatever he could?

8 AM

Negotiating the steps to street level at the Crimée metro station felt a bit awkward but was certainly a lot less painful than the night before. He had to be careful now. The crutches made him conspicuous and he couldn't be certain where Vallette and the boys might have parked. Maybe one of them had stayed in the car. He looked in every direction, then found an opportunity to cross the road, which was much busier now. At the corner of rue de Crimée he peered down, confident that the DS21 would stand out, but it didn't, nor were there any convenient cafés to use as a lookout spot. Ferdie wasn't stupid enough to go clipping along the street, making himself visible to whichever of the meatheads might be on guard in the car, bored at missing all the fun inside, and delighted at the opportunity to have some of their own at his expense. As he turned away, conscious that it was dangerous even to hover at the corner, he almost bumped into an old immigrant beggar woman bent at ninety degrees, shuffling. She jerked a plastic cup at him and just as he was about to pass her by an idea struck him. "Want to make twenty euro for one minute's work?" Though she remained bent over, her head lifted suddenly, eyes wary, mouth all scowling suspicion. Maybe this was a bad idea. But eyes, mouth, and wrinkles were all transformed at the sight of the twenty. On a scrap of paper he carefully printed the colors and number of the car and pointed down the street. "Find this car, and I'll give you this, yes?" She reached for the twenty and when it was withheld, the face sagged again and she wailed, presumably at the unfairness of life, which would never be any other way for those like her, but finally trundled down the street. As it happened, she earned her twenty so easily Ferdie felt foolish. No more than five cars down he saw her stop, check the piece of paper, and look closely at a car Ferdie could not see from his angle. She shuffled nearer and seemed to be staring in through the window. Clearly there was no one inside or by now the old bag would have been rewarded for her inquisitiveness with the slap of an opening door.

She returned, Ferdie noticed, at a much faster pace. Her face, wrinkled in ecstasy, hand already outstretched. She babbled in a kind of French. The car was the one described on the paper and there was no one inside. Once the twenty was closed in her fist she thanked him prayerfully, again and again, showing no sign of moving on. Perhaps now that she'd got a taste for such easy money she fancied another assignment. Ferdie had to wave her away very decisively.

He moved quickly along the street, aware that Vallette and the boys might step out of Bellhop's place at any moment. The sight of his car fed his resentment and spurred him on toward the entrance to Bellhop's building, which looked even grubbier in daylight. He needed a half-decent lookout spot. When Vallette and the boys emerged, it was reasonable to assume they would hurry toward the car with scarcely a glance in any other direction. Inspired by the old beggar woman, he squatted on the ground outside a closed Chinese restaurant and placed some

loose change in front of him. He dropped his head but kept his
eyes focused on the entrance to 187. He had earned himself two
fifty-cent coins by the time the men emerged. Oscar first, Vallette next, and Marcel last. As Ferdie had guessed, they moved
quickly to the DS21. Then he heard the familiar engine start
and roar away. Fucking car thieves!

The climb to the fifth floor was slow. He was embarrassed
at how puny his upper arm muscles were. Luckily the rest of
him was puny, too, so not too much weight to haul. His long
hesitation outside the door of what he assumed was Bellhop's
apartment had more to do with his disquiet than his tired arm
muscles. Finally he raised a crutch and poked. The door swung
open.

Bellhop didn't look like his sister anymore. He barely looked
human. He had been left sitting on the floor propped up against
a wall and didn't seem to have any plans to move from there.
It wasn't until Ferdie leaned in very close that he could be
sure the boy was even bothering to breathe. Just about. Blood-
matted hair, one eye closed, broken nose, the lower lip swollen,
and blood oozing and drooling from a hanging mouth. His
jeans were around his ankles and there was a wet patch on the
ground at his crotch. It seemed to be urine rather than blood.
Seeing him in this condition didn't make Ferdie feel any worse
about shopping him than he did already. Quite a few times in
his life he had had to choose his own safety over someone else's.
This was a particularly ugly example, but the principle was the
same.

It was hard to tell if Bellhop was even conscious of his presence as he took out his phone and snapped a few shots. He
didn't feel good about that either, and knew it wasn't evidence

of anything really, but something told him it was better to have them than not. Then he called an ambulance, which was, after all, why he had decided to come here; to return Bellhop's favor in kind. Sort of. The way it looked right now, he might even be saving his life.

When she opens her eyes Nathan's face is only inches away. It should be an enormous shock, but isn't. He had been in her dream, on the streetcar, the streetcar where, no matter where she sat, people insisted on talking to her. Not just talking, *gushing*. All thrilled to see her, all wanting to reminisce. *Remember* seemed to start every sentence. Remember when . . . ? Remember how . . . ? People from school, from Brian's office in Dublin, guys she didn't even know. Mostly it was very pleasant. Her stop, Pike, approached. She saw Brian waiting, but couldn't seem to get through the crowd to disembark, even though no one jostled or even laid a finger on her. When she turned away from one smiling face there was always someone else. Billy Corgan hugged her. Lana! Jesus! She could hardly believe how many people she saw on the streetcar. How did they all fit? It didn't look that crowded. Sometimes she was up top, sometimes down below. Pike came around again and again, Brian was still waiting. This time he saw her and waved, but the most stressful part was that even though it was an old kind of streetcar and the back was wide open so she could hop off at any time, she kept getting distracted.

Nathan had been smiling at her in the dream, too, but now,

eyes open, it's a relief not to feel that frustrating need to get away, jump off the streetcar. Nathan's breath has no odor.

"So, you were saying."

She laughs. "Did I fall asleep in midsentence? I can't remember. Or maybe I don't really care."

Because Nathan's hand is resting on her hip and the slightest move might start something, because his lips only have to ease in an inch or two, Lana is somewhat surprised that he chooses to do neither.

"Oh come on, I have to hear the rest. You were in a car with two complete strangers who drove like lunatics to help you escape two other strangers, who had pretended to be police and were now in hot pursuit. And the last thing you said was, 'The only thing I knew for sure . . .'"

Nathan lets his head slump, his eyes close, and he makes little sleeping sounds.

"Oh God, I have no idea what the end of that sentence was."

Nathan's eyes pop open. "Now I want you to relax. It's daylight, we've slept, and it's okay if you want to tell me now that you made it all up: that it was just a Lana Turner shaggy dog story."

"I'd love to. Yes, that's what it was. Just some crazy noir dream I'd had."

She's pleased that Nathan seems to take that at face value. His disappointment has a childlike quality. "Oh. Really?"

"No. I wish."

He brightens again. He accompanies the words with an encouraging tickle.

"So what happened? I'm particularly interested in the mystery of the two who saved you. What was going on there? I can't imagine it was just the kindness of passing strangers."

"Not exactly. The guy—Guillaume he said his name was—told me he was a filmmaker—"

"Uhff! This does not breed confidence."

"Don't jump to conclusions. He said he was making this documentary and the young woman I'd met in the bar, and who I saw being harassed by the old naked guy, she was working for him. Like his undercover reporter. According to him they'd planned a setup. She'd gone to this sex party with a hidden camera."

"Now you're just making stuff up."

"I promise. She was trying to get away when I appeared. I found out later the old guy took the camera from her, which meant they had no pictures, so I was an important witness to what had happened, according to Guillaume. He wanted me to go on camera and say what I'd seen."

"You didn't, I hope. You know nothing about this pair."

"No, I didn't, but I was tempted, especially when I found out who the old naked guy was."

"You know?"

"Yes. Guillaume showed me him on YouTube and right away—"

"YouTube?"

"Yes. And I recognized him—"

"So is he well known?"

"For sure, I'm told. Although the name meant nothing to me—"

"Not Gerard Depardieu, then?"

"No. But I guess you'll know him immediately."

"I'm touched by your faith in my knowledge of pop culture, but don't be so sure?"

"Not so much pop culture. I'm told he is a really well-known politician. You want to guess?"

For some reason Nathan pauses. He seems less amused.

"Oh. Ah . . . Tell me."

"Jean-Luc Fournier."

Lana had expected surprise, along with, perhaps, a cynical laugh. That would be Nathan. Instead he sighs and shakes his head.

"Oh Christ. No . . . no, no, no. . . . I don't believe it."

"Why not?"

"No, no. Unfortunately I do believe it. You know, as soon as you said 'politician' his name flashed in my brain. This is terrible. I mean . . . You know he's running for president?"

"So they told me."

"What is he doing, is he mad? Two months before the election? He has this reputation, you know."

"They told me that too."

"Who are these people? Did they say who they're working for? Everyone on the right would love to see Fournier destroyed."

Lana is a little puzzled at Nathan's attitude. Has he forgotten completely about what had happened to her?

"You mean like the way Fournier wants to see me destroyed?"

"Oh. I'm sorry. Yes, of course. I don't know what . . . It's incredible—sorry not incredible so much as extraordinary. These people, sure, they obviously helped you out of an awkward spot, but well, did you think, do you think they were trustworthy? I mean . . . do you believe everything they told you?"

Part of Lana wouldn't mind admitting that she does have some kind of vague, unformed doubt about Guillaume and Pauline, but the part of her that instinctively wants to slap Nathan down for not instantly pledging his sympathy and support wins out.

"What does it matter what I think of them? I saw the guys come after us in the car. I saw the looks on their faces. They would have been happy to see us crash and die."

"Right. Sure."

And now he pulls her to him and holds her close.

"What do you want me to do?"

"Nothing. I'm sorry I've thrown this at you."

"No, I'm glad. Really."

"I just felt so abandoned last night."

"Of course."

Lana would have been more than happy now to curl up in a cocoon of sex and for several long seconds it seems about to happen. Then Nathan eases away.

"I should explain something. You see . . . I actually know Fournier personally. Just a little. It's not like we go out dancing together or anything. He was teaching at Sciences Po when I started there. More than just teaching he was, well . . . he was a star. A brilliant mind. People who weren't doing his course would sit in on his lectures, just to be able to say they had heard him. So, naturally—"

"Does that excuse his behavior in other—"

"No, of course not. I'm not saying it excuses anything. I'm just I suppose . . . trying to be honest, declaring an interest. For example, I should admit that I—it would have been my intention to vote for him as president."

"And now?"

"Well, exactly . . . It's a strange feeling. I mean I've heard so many stories about him, of course. His reputation is no secret—"

"To the in-crowd."

"Well, yes, I suppose. But what I want to say is, your story makes me realize what a difference there is between hearing rumors at a remove, and finding out something like this from . . . well, from a primary source, I suppose."

"Is that what I am, a primary source?"

"No, I mean that in a good way. It means I believe your story completely, even though it's the kind of story that seems, I don't know, not unbelievable, but . . . hard to see why . . . I mean the sex party, that's one thing, and the girl, sure, but the part I find strange is that he'd allow you to be harmed in any way. Everything I know about him tells me he's not that kind of man."

"The violent kind?"

"Well, yes."

"But how well do you know him, really?"

"Of course, absolutely. It's just that I had never, ever formed such an impression of him. I mean in any way. You know how sometimes a person surprises you, but then it's not a surprise really—"

"If you'd seen him last night would that change your mind?"

Nathan nods, but says nothing more.

"And what about the fake cops? What do you think they were going to do with me?"

"I don't know, Lana. Is it at all possible it was a clumsy misguided way to bring you to meet him? They probably thought a straight-up invitation wouldn't work."

"Meet him? For what?"

Something about Nathan's shrug, his tone, makes her want to turn away, get out of bed.

"I don't know. To explain himself? One thing I can tell you for sure is that Jean-Luc has extraordinary confidence in the power of his own charm. Even more than most politicians do. That's why it's so hard to imagine him involved in any kind of violent response when he would probably assume that he could persuade you that what you saw was . . . harmless?"

"Harmless!"

"I'm speculating on what he thought. I'm not saying that—what I am saying is that from his point of view, the idea of causing you physical harm would just be madness. No logic to it whatsoever."

"Unlike the logic that tells him it's a good idea to have sex orgies in hotel suites when you're trying to get yourself elected president?"

"Sure . . . it's . . . it's kinda hard to understand, all right."

"I'm not sure I'm that interested in understanding it, Nathan."

She turns away and sits on the bed, legs dangling. Her posture makes her feel like one of Hopper's melancholy women. She stands and stretches.

"Mind if I shower?"

"Of course not, but listen—"

"And by the time I'm finished you might be able to explain the logic of this to me. When I came back to the hotel late last night, everything had been removed. My passport, my ticket. Luggage. These people, whoever they are, entered my room and took everything I own. If you want proof, *source material*, they left me a note."

She marches to the living room. Coming back, holding the envelope, her nakedness feels very strange. She misses the ecstasy of last night and the giddy wake-up of twenty minutes ago, but once it's gone, it's gone.

"How charming is this?"

Nathan reads the note quickly. The haste with which he jumps out of bed and comes to her, the urgency of his embrace, feels very satisfying.

"You must have felt so alone. Nothing gives them the right to try to scare you like that."

At last he seems to be getting it. And the smell of his skin is comforting.

"What do you want to do? Are you going to call this number?"

"No."

"Good. I don't think you should."

"What do you think?"

"Well, there's the American Embassy, but I'm not sure that they'll see you on a Saturday. I can check it out. If it's possible to get a temporary passport, then maybe you can sort out your ticket and still make your flight."

"So, I should leave as planned?"

"Oh. I thought that's what you'd want."

"I wish I knew."

"I suppose I'm assuming that if you leave Paris and they realize that you're not going to make any trouble for them, then it'll all blow over."

"That's also assuming I don't want to make trouble."

"Oh. Do you?"

"After what they've put me through? Maybe. I don't know. To be perfectly honest, Nathan, I'm not so hot on making that flight tonight."

It's a deliberate test. The speed and sincerity of his reply is gratifying.

"Okay. Well, personally speaking, I'm glad. Monday is probably a better day to sort this out with the embassy anyway."

"You think?"

"Definitely. I think."

Lana is liking his smile again.

"Of course, it's not just the passport. Remember, I have no money or phone or spare clothes."

"I don't see why that should be a problem at all."

"Monday seems like a plan then."

They kiss and somehow they're back on the bed again. As often happens the third time around, they don't quite get there. Well, they get there all right, but not *there*. Still, it feels entirely comfortable afterward lying together in a warm fuzz, as if the clock has stopped. Lost time. What she saw and all that followed, Odette, Guillaume, Pauline, Fournier and his cronies, it all seems irrelevant. And Brian? Poor Brian. Lana knows she should care more.

"You hungry?"

Nathan's question is a welcome interruption to her thoughts.

"Starving."

"Do you remember the market in Maubert?"

"Mhm."

"How about, rather than eating out, we go to the market and get some treats to bring back here? Maybe you could concoct something special?"

It's a perfect suggestion. Lana is a little surprised Nathan doesn't join her in the shower, but not too disappointed. When she floats back wrapped in his robe he's at his laptop.

"As I thought, nothing doing at the embassy. They don't make it easy: eight thirty weekdays only, with photo for biometric passport, use booth in embassy, DS-11 form, Social Security number, one hundred thirty-five dollars in cash or credit card. And a partridge in a pear tree, it seems."

"Can we think about that stuff later?"

"Sure. But I was thinking. There's some work I really have to finish today. So, would you mind if I do it now and we just ordered some takeout?"

"Oh. I don't mind waiting to go to the market."

"I'll be an hour or more. Sorry, but best to get this over with now and I know a really good Chinese."

Lana doesn't want to be a spoiled whiny little bitch, but going to the market and preparing lunch had seemed such a perfect idea.

"How about I go to the market by myself? By the time I get back you'll be finished with whatever you have to do and we can still make our own lunch."

"Oh. That'd be fantastic. You don't mind tootling off on your own?"

"Absolutely not. Well . . . there is just one little thing."

"What? Oh, sorry." He pulls out his wallet. "You've been cleaned out."

"And you'll have to remind me how to get there."

"That's two little things. And you'll need to remember the code to get back in. That's three little things."

He gives her a fifty and his directions to the market are simple: back onto boulevard St.-Germain, then left and four hundred yards straight to Maubert. He makes her repeat the code again and again, with a kiss each time. As she strolls to-ward St.-Germain, a sense of ease and security begins to flow through her.

NOON

The buzz is catching as she weaves around the stalls at Maubert: the colors, the aromas, and of course those luscious French voices talking food like there is nothing more important, not just on this Saturday morning, but always and forever. It's such a pity Nathan's not with her, but they'll have the rest of the day together; to lunch, to step out or maybe not; one of those take-it-as-it-comes carefree days.

Lana is tempted to buy something at every stall, but remembering she has only a fifty, tells herself to strategize, hang out a little, take it all in, check out the best on offer, plan an amazing brunch, and—okay, okay, okay, but look at those great hunks of creamy yellow cheese, have to have some of that. Can't just pass by. Way too much temptation. A pretty young girl with a beauty spot on her upper lip gives her a shaving of Comté Vieux and she buys a wedge of it, as well as a chunk of Beaufort and a thick triangle of Saint Agur and a few little cylinders of Chabichou. While the girl is wrapping, Lana's attention wanders to boxes of glistening salad greens at the vegetable stall. She wants some of those leaves. Does the girl really have to make such a ritual of wrapping a few pieces of cheese? Lana tells herself to relax, this is part of the pleasure of market shopping: the time and care taken. But she needs to get to those leaves before they're all snapped up. Come! On! Finally the cheeses are handed over. She gives her the fifty and immediately crosses to the vegetable stall and grabs a head of romaine lettuce.

"Madame!"

The girl is holding up her change. Lana goes back to her.

"Madame!"

The guy at the vegetable stall shouts, obviously concerned that grand larceny of a head of lettuce is about to take place, so she holds up her change by way of explanation. The smile he offers in response reveals remarkably gray teeth for a guy in his line of work. He's spindly and combs his hair forward in an unnecessary as well as unattractive way. Someone who cares about him should tell him it ain't working. She gives him the lettuce to bag and looks along the stall. Cheese and salad. The meal is already taking shape: a fat generous salad with wine and cheese to follow. What else? Vine tomatoes, obviously. She points. The spindly guy starts to bag them, looking to know when to stop. She keeps waving him on until her attention is distracted by the cucumbers. And fat radishes. And apples. And fresh herbs. She points at them all. Et là, et là, et là. This time, to avoid consternation, she hands over a ten before walking away as he finishes weighing and bagging everything. Lardons have popped into her head and she's on that trail now. And walnuts. Lardons and walnuts are what this salad needs. But a stall entirely devoted to saucisson makes her pause and quickly reassess: saucisson instead of lardons? Au Poivre, Au Pistache, Au Figues. Perfect. Sliced and tossed with the lettuce, tomatoes, tarragon, radish, cucumber, and the creamy Saint Agur in a giant bowl, if Nathan has one big enough.

The saucisson man is fat and wears glasses with oddly modish red frames. What little hair he has hovers above, a cumulus detached from his crown. He offers Lana a "gout" of chorizo and chuckles when she gasps at the heat of it.

And that's when, turning away to suck in cool air and glancing down, she notices the shoes: tan oxfords. Very elegant. Surprisingly so. Not Saturday morning at the market shoes at all. They make Lana look closer at the man, who's studying some farm chickens at the next stall. He's wearing a suit and carries no shopping bag. Nor does he appear to have bought anything.

While Lana tells herself this is pure paranoia, that she's just looking for trouble, she can't help remembering how she'd missed a similar signal the night before: the subtly expensive perfume of Fichet and his men. Okay, a guy being overdressed for the market is hardly a crime and maybe he's not here by choice. Maybe he's just hovering waiting for his wife, who'll appear in a moment laden with bags of fresh vegetables. Still, Lana feels it would be foolish to ignore those shoes. Okay. If her crazy brain is even halfway to being right, it won't be this guy alone. He'll have friends and maybe they'll stand out too. They would be . . . her eyes flick left and right and . . . yes, there's another one. A type like last night's fake cops, muscled with perfectly coiffed hair, also in a suit. And no shopping bags. He's gazing in total fascination at a selection of foie gras. Despite her accelerating heartbeat, Lana wishes she could get close enough to check out his shoes. Okay, she thinks quickly now, let's nail this. If there are two there might be a third. Maybe more. If there's another he would have to be . . . she stops at a dairy stall and fakes interest in a huge tub of crème fraîche, so thick it's pink-hued, while angling herself to check on her right. After a few furtive glances this way and that she nails him at the street end of the market, conspicuously sleek in a

double-breasted gray coat and a very expensive tie. And, of
course, no shopping bag. As far as Lana is concerned, there is
no doubt now. These guys are either some strangely elegant
gang of pickpockets or they're trailing her. She doesn't recognize any of them from last night, but of course she wouldn't.
What would be the point of having someone tailing her who
she'd seen before? But what do they intend to do? Watch and
follow, wait for the right moment to grab her? She feels panic
mounting, but so is the buzz and the buzz is winning.

Lana decides to test how they respond to whatever she does.
For the next minute she moves even more quickly, zigzagging
around the stalls, pausing to ask stallholders questions as cover.
Her trackers drift about and soon she works out that they're
keeping her locked at the center of a loose triangle. So she turns
suddenly and walks quickly, directly toward one of them. He
moves past casually, but immediately the others adjust to re-
configure the triangle. There can be no doubt. As she veers
close to the street side of the market, Lana realizes this might
be the kind of moment they're waiting for, if they do intend to
take her. Presumably they have a car waiting nearby. She turns
quickly, back to the safety of stalls and people.

Can she magic herself out of their sight long enough to con-
fuse them and get a head start? The Maubert-Mutualité metro
entrance is alongside one of the fruit and vegetable stalls. If she
can get down those steps before they react and cross the under-
pass to the other side of the boulevard, then she might have an
opportunity to lose them on the street. But how can she make
herself suddenly invisible? A short stallholder with big yellow
hair points at watermelons, asking if she wants some, they are
superb. Lana lifts one up, and its weight suggests the beginning
of an idea big and brash enough to tickle her. Forget invisibility,

go the other way: mayhem. She smiles and asks for two wa-termelons. As the woman selects and bags them, Lana turns in what she hopes seems a casual circle, as if savoring the pleasure of the market and the moment, as a tourist might, while actu-ally measuring with her eye the height of the railings behind her and figuring it won't be too much of a stretch to vault over them. But her watchers are positioned on both sides of the stall, making her plan to execute sudden chaos a little more compli-cated and uncertain.

The way the little stallholder with big hair smiles gives Lana a twinge of guilt about what she's about to do. By way of some compensation she hands over her remaining twenty to the poor woman. When she turns to her register, Lana pulls at a tower of boxes full of apples, scattering them on the ground in the direction of the guy in the oxfords. Now their eyes meet and he knows his cover is blown. He comes at her. Lana swings her plastic bags and lets loose. The watermelons fly at him like dodgeballs. One catches his shoulder but the other strikes full on his face and the muffled howl tells its own story. The poor little stallholder is now screaming and stretching to grab her. Lana goes for broke and sweeps everything—broccoli, carrots, potatoes, onions—onto the ground on either side. Then she clambers rather than vaults over the railings down to the metro steps, leaving the other two suits stumbling through fruit and vegetables, kicking aside boxes, leaping over their squealing-like-a-pig friend to get near the entrance.

At the bottom of the steps Lana shoots right to take her under the boulevard. Up ahead there's a left and right turn. Choose! Fast! Back up to street level or down to the metro platform? The open air and crowded boulevard seem safer, freer. She spins left and up. Back on St.-Germain she barges through a lot of people going the other way, but looking back they're not enough to shield her from the first of the three men appearing up the steps. Passing *Le Twickenham* café bar, Lana feels truly sorry for the old waiter who is outside, fastidiously laying lunch tables, placing wineglasses, knives and forks and napkins, but there's no time to apologize for upending everything as she passes, creating another obstacle for her pursuers. Too scared to check how close they are, she veers right, down a lane, trying to think ahead, trying to remember, to get some kind of picture of what streets led where in this area. She's pretty certain that somewhere between here and Nathan's apartment is the complex of cramped little pedestrian streets that is oldest Paris. In a straight runoff there is no hope of staying ahead of these guys for long, but that tourist-crammed zone might give her a shot at losing them. But this lane is eerily deserted apart from a Franprix store. The men still have not appeared round the corner behind her. She ducks inside and instantly regrets it. If the men stop and come in she'll be trapped. The little supermarket has no other exit. It helps that shelves go to the ceiling and the aisles between them are narrow, making it easier to keep out of sight. She scurries to the far end to catch her breath. Peering along the gap between walls of cans and bottles, she feels confident that there's no way they would have seen her even if they'd glanced in as they passed. The downside is that she can't see the entrance and can't be sure that they *have* passed. The space between shelves is so ludicrously narrow it's almost impossible for customers to move about without brushing one another. When the store is crowded it must be like some kind of human pinball game. Already the urge to escape this confinement is gnawing at her and she has to work hard to restrain her impatience. Edging

forward until the entrance/exit becomes visible, it's some relief to see that there's no one waiting, the aisle seems entirely
empty. Five minutes more should be long enough. Too long
for her liking, but still she counts it out, every irksome second.

Once she's decided it's safe to leave, Murphy's Law, which
she suspects is fast becoming Lana's Law, kicks in. As she arrives at the checkout, the guy in the double-breasted overcoat,
looking out of breath, passes the entrance, stops suddenly, and
steps in. Lana finds herself only a couple of arm's lengths from
him. His moment of surprise is replaced by a slow grin, like
an actor genuinely astonished to hear his name come after
"and the Oscar goes to . . ." Lana backs away, but he doesn't
follow; he's way too smart for that. He positions himself between the entrance and the checkout and slowly, deliberately,
his smile now wide and mean, takes out his cell. He knows
there's no other exit and is happy to play solo until the rest
of the band arrives. Lana has to do something fast. And, as it
often does, for better or worse, the buzz takes off and tells her
what to do. Which breaks more easily, more dangerously, a
wine bottle or an olive oil bottle? The olive oil shelf presents
itself first. When she grips a bottle by the neck, tight in her
hand, the buzz soars and breaks the scale. She's going to enjoy this—hell, she's enjoying it already. Mr. Double-Breasted
will so not expect this. Holding the bottle by her side, like
a firearm, Lana Turner sashays to the checkout and smiles at
Double-Breasted as she pays. Such a pity that the gorgeous
gray wool is about to be destroyed. The checkout girl starts to
bag it, but Lana stops her with a "Pas de sac, merci." She tries
to measure the distance between her and her pursuer. Only a
few feet. She holds a mental picture of his position as she turns
her back on him. Take one big step nearer as you swing, is

Lana's last instruction to herself. The moment has arrived and it feels scarily good.

Gripping the neck of the bottle, she taps the end against the metal checkout counter, and as it smashes she swings round and—with a step forward—rams the jagged bottle at the guy's face. The sound of shock all around her is gratifying, but the squeals of others are nothing compared to his animal howl. Blood and olive oil intermingle and smear down his face. Lana drops her weapon and runs without thinking about direction. Suddenly she's back on St.-Germain. Horns blare and voices rasp as she weaves and skips across the wide, busy road. One bellowing, gesticulating driver is silenced when she kicks his door and lunges in the open window to grab his neck, screaming faux-French gibberish in his face. Somehow she reaches the other side safely and keeps moving at the same pace until she stops dead and bends almost double, no breath left in her body. Looking up, there are two of everything moving along the great boulevard. She rubs her eyes. Only now does the full impact of what she's just done hit home. If her brain had been in equilibrium, would she have imagined herself capable of performing such a violent act? But undeniably it had been exhilarating, disturbingly so. She walks on at something more like a normal trot to the St.-Michel intersection and back to rue Danton, glancing carefully in every direction all along the way. Outside the apartment building she has a complete blank about the code, but by closing her eyes and summoning up Nathan's lips forming the numbers over and over, she remembers. And now comes a weird feeling of regret, disappointment, failure, that there would be no brunch, no glorious salad, or cheese or saucisson. She is limping home, empty-handed, with nothing more than loose change. Poor Nathan, does he really deserve all this hassle? Should she tell him everything immediately? Even about the olive oil bottle?

Thinking about it later, Lana will realize that when Nathan opened the door, she was so busy apologizing for the absence of treats from the market that she hadn't actually looked at him properly and so had no idea if his face betrayed any guilt or even nervousness. Had he performed brilliantly, like a poker pro? Perhaps, if she had been paying attention, there might have been something in those entrancing green eyes that would have warned her and allowed the tiniest opportunity to run. Not that she would have had any energy left to do it.

But instead, gabbling and still unsure how much to tell, she walks past Nathan and has almost reached the kitchen when she hears a repeated clicking sound. Lana freezes. No, no, it couldn't be what it sounds like. A moment later, Fichet—or Vallette, if Guillaume is to be believed—steps into view. Click, click. In a politely understated way his jacket hangs open just enough to reveal a gun in his waistband. Oddly enough it makes him look much less like a cop. Fichet—Vallette—stops picking his fingernails and gestures toward the living room.

"Step in, Madame Gibson."

Lana swivels. Nathan seems fascinated by his shoes. He doesn't intend to suffer an accusing gaze. She thinks, well, I need a rest anyhow. As she walks by Vallette, his now-familiar, discreetly expensive fragrance seems to mock her.

The first thing Lana sees when she opens the living room door is a leonine flourish of silver hair sprouting from the back of the couch. Vallette nudges her forward and a great spreading frame comes into view. Jean-Luc Fournier, squatting in the center, smiles at her and takes a deliberately languid drag from a long, slim cigar. He is fully dressed. Small mercies.

Madame Gibson . . . Jean-Luc Fournier."

Politely, he hauls himself up. Lana does not move toward the offered hand. Somehow through churning rage, bewilderment, and distress she manages to summon up a tone that resembles disdainful sarcasm.

"Oh . . . yeah . . . my apologies. As the old joke goes, I didn't recognize you with your clothes on."

Fournier behaves as if she has not spoken. He sinks down again, this time favoring one end of the couch, and gestures for Lana to join him. She ignores the invitation and takes her own sweet time before choosing a bentwood chair by the wall, forcing him to twist his neck around to look at her. Vallette leans against the wall near the door, while Nathan moves as far from Lana's direct eye line as he can manage. She doesn't bother to attempt any engagement with him just now. She feels too nauseated. Fournier's mouth is moving, the eyes and smile all for her. Lana makes an effort to tune in.

"I'm sure we will have much to talk about. I certainly hope we may. I love to engage with intelligent, beautiful women and you are clearly both. And, I suspect, much more. You are a vessel of rich possibilities, I think. It could be a very stimulating exchange. But . . ."

The pause doesn't suggest hesitation. It is entirely measured. He takes another long drag from the cigar, blows the smoke slowly, and waves a hand in what he intends to be an explanatory manner. When he speaks again, he's no longer looking at her. It's as if he's thinking aloud. Only now does Lana notice how clear his English is and how rapidly he speaks, as if to showcase his linguistic brilliance.

"I have one question of very great importance and I will ask it now, to take the issue off the table, as it were. There are those who in negotiation tend to favor moving slowly in decreasing circles toward problematic areas. I believe that is why so many bad decisions are made. By the time the most controversial matter is considered everyone is exhausted. It is always better to get to the heart of a matter without delay. So, I ask: who are you working for?"

The question is so out of left field that Lana's shock is genuine.

"I don't even know what you mean by that."

"It's a simple question."

"It's a dumb question. You might as well ask me my favorite color."

"I can only repeat: who are you working for?"

Lana shrugs.

"You say you like to 'engage,' as you put it, with intelligent women. Is this what you mean by engage: just keep asking the same meaningless question?"

"Jean-Luc, if I may—"

Lana can't believe that Nathan has stuck his head above the parapet and given her the opportunity to turn on him.

"Lana, if you can just explain to Jean-Luc how you came to be in the private elevator . . ."

She hopes her eyes are successfully projecting the iciest disdain. Look at me. Does this face suggest it has any interest in anything you might have to say? You're not even in the room. But Nathan surfs on, looking shaky, barely staying upright, yet weirdly proud of himself. It's as if he expects kudos for cunningly arranging this summit. Lana is annoyed with herself that it had not occurred to her, from the first moment Nathan mentioned his link with Fournier, that in institutions like Sciences Po, the boys' club would always hang together in a crisis. *Fraternité.*

Nathan sounds just a little strident now, insisting he had relayed her story and explained her actions, exactly as she had conveyed them to him. All Jean-Luc needs is a little more convincing. Eventually the ice in her eyes reduces him to spluttering incoherence and he tails off into a downcast and—what nerve, it seems to Lana—resentful silence.

She looks away. Had Nathan been suffering from a profound lack of self-awareness when he'd claimed last night that his anger toward her had lasted only a couple of months? Surely, because it's obvious he has no real appreciation of the complexity of his own feelings. The rage had merely lain dormant for a long time until her reappearance in his life, especially the manner of it—sudden, out of the shadows, late at night, prompting him to bad behavior toward the poor innocent woman he had brought home—awoke the poisonous worm in him. So is this little betrayal deliberate payback or does he even recognize the brutal vengeance in the act? His whiny, self-serving tone suggests he still needs to convince himself that he's looking after Lana's best interests, playing the honest broker between two warring, but essentially equally respectable parties. They should be begging him to sort out the Arab-Israeli conflict.

". . . All the elements point to a certain conclusion, you agree?"

Fournier has been talking all this time. Lana hasn't taken in a word, but she's fascinated by how his eyebrows are constantly on the move, resembling the silhouettes of two swallows in flight against the backdrop of a bloodshot sunset.

"Hm? Sorry, my mind wandered. I have no idea what you just said."

It's very satisfying that the calculated indifference in her tone at last draws a lick of flame from Fournier's eyes, a tiny flicker compared to the bushfire blaze Lana had witnessed the night before. For a moment she thinks the smartest guy in the room might just lose it, get up, rumble over, and punch her. She hopes he will. How quickly it would shift the ground rules, end this charade of the sophisticated, rational man, Descartes in a four-thousand-euro suit, trying oh with infinite patience to talk some sense into the crazily devious woman, who doesn't seem to recognize that she's been outmaneuvered. But the heat is quickly turned down and his eyes seem almost to change color as the cool, sympathetic—borderline patronizing—gaze resumes.

"I beg your pardon. Allow me to explain again. You are ready for me?"

"I'm totally there. Can't wait."

"Consider the matter from my point of view. A woman arrives in Paris alone from"—he leans forward and picks up a piece of paper—"Dublin."

He's holding her boarding pass, and—why had she not realized this earlier?—her purse, passport, and credit card are on the coffee table in front of him. The action of picking up the boarding pass was deliberate, to draw her attention to it and her other possessions.

"She books into the Chevalier. Soon she is showing great interest in the hotel's famous Suite Imperial, the means of access, and who is staying there. When she sees someone enter the exclusive elevator to the suite, she attempts to discover who it is. Later she speaks with a young lady who is brought to the suite, a lady who transpires to be not a lady at all, but a spy with a camera. Then this woman from Dublin, who is in fact American, somehow contrives to create a diversion. She gains access to the Suite Imperial for a few seconds and on returning to the hotel foyer assaults an associate. Then later, she joins two people, one of whom has a camera and who, according to her own story"—he gestures toward Nathan; Lana doesn't bother to look—"wishes to destroy my career and reputation. In the light of this, how can you think it unreasonable that we believe you are working for someone who, let us say, does not have my best interests at heart?"

Lana has to admit that from the perspective of an ambitious politician, on the brink of achieving or losing his life's goal, the events of the last twenty-four hours might indeed suggest a more conspiratorial narrative than the one she knows to be true. Nor can she help being curious as to who exactly Fournier might think she's working for. His political opponent? Or perhaps he's convinced himself that the CIA has targeted him. Tempting though it is to engage with him on this nonsense, she recalls instead that scene last night: the naked old goat and the white of his knuckles as he gripped the girl's arm. She thinks about Odette, curled up in the shadows, whispering about being tied to a chair and assaulted, which would have been Lana's fate if Vallette's attempt to carry her away last night or today's sinister surveillance had succeeded. It might happen yet.

"I have to admire your nerve, trying to make me the story.

But there's a little problem with this scenario of yours. It's not me who's into secret sex parties in exclusive hotel suites. I'm not the one assaulting a young woman because she refuses to strip and abase herself. I don't have muscle masquerading as police, which I'm guessing is a felony in France just like it is in the U.S., am I right?" She looks at Vallette, whose smirk suggests he's enjoying her outburst.

"Your cologne is way too high-end for a cop, by the way, and those guys this morning? Not dressed for the market. I'm surprised at such freshman errors, Inspector Fichet. Oh, sorry, no, Monsieur Vallette, isn't it?"

No one is trying to shut her up so Lana decides, what the hell, let it all out.

"So what is my crime? I accidentally got into an elevator at the wrong moment, and witnessed the nauseating reality of an old pervert who thinks he's the guy who should be running this country. Are you serious? You know what you should be doing, instead of warming your butt there like some puffed-up foie grass-fed COLONIAL OVERLORD?"—she hopes that description will kick Nathan where it hurts—"interrogating *me*, impugning *my* motives? You should be crawling, the way I hear you like to make women do, on all fours, imploring me to take pity on you and not breathe a word about your embarrassing, shameful freak show. Fuck you, Fournier!"

It feels so *good*. Like there should be applause from an appreciative audience. Lana is well aware that such a harangue will achieve nothing, but it can hardly do any more harm. Fournier, she figures, is one of those alpha males who pride themselves on what they think is their emotional intelligence, their mastery over petty responses. Words spoken in the heat of battle mean little or nothing. No matter how she lambasts him he'll keep his eye on the prize, which is presumably a clear, scandal-free run at the presidency. Lana can grandstand all she likes; that's all part of the game.

"An admirable tirade, Madame Gibson. I recognize the crude, cheap moralizing of the tabloid press, and I detect nostalgia for the Old Testament God of guilt and shame."

"Are you crazy?"

"Oh but yes, and I hear the debased sophistry of the American religious right. Perhaps this is the clue to your extraordinary behavior? Are you a devotee of Anglo-Saxon tabloid culture? Or perhaps an agent of some American right-wing organization, the kind that appropriates words like *freedom* and *liberty* in its title and is anxious to manipulate the democratic process? It is one thing to spend millions misleading voters in your own country, but to interfere in others? You moralize to me, but your use of language is meretricious. 'Assault,' you say? But your friend the spy was not hurt by me. And how would you behave, if you invited someone to your hotel room and discovered she was secretly filming your private world? No doubt you would say, 'Oh forgive me! In the future I promise to conduct my private behavior by your rules.' Ha! So I ask again, what is your agenda? Who do you work for?"

It feels a little like being on one of those political TV shows where the presenter keeps saying, "With respect, you haven't answered my question, so I'll ask it one more time." Lana wonders if this is Fournier's secret self-image: a fabulously coiffed, preternaturally bright, ruthlessly determined TV interrogator. Is he genuinely convinced that his suspicions are correct and confident that she'll break down and confess all in the face of his steely, dispassionate logic? Or is he just trying to panic her, make her beg, promise him anything in exchange for release?

If so, it's working. She's getting closer to that place than she would like to admit.

When Fournier speaks again, Lana notices that his voice has softened. He contrives to look caring.

"May I call you Lana? It is a delightful name and I cannot continue with this 'Madame.' Lana, why the obdurate silence? Why do you contrive not to vindicate yourself? You are like the old terrorist groups who always refused to recognize the courts. But you are not Action Directe and this is not a court. It is not even an interrogation. You must appreciate that I am only trying to protect my personal integrity—yes, integrity. I am not a hypocrite, I have never moralized about what others do. Nothing in my private affairs has ever interfered with the quality of my political work. The people of France vote for a president, not a saint. There are no saints, as you must know. You are too intelligent, too urbane not to accept this."

Silence. Fournier sighs, shrugs, gestures as if made helpless by her refusal to cooperate, and mutters something to Vallette, who leaves the room.

"Very well. I will be candid. It is my inclination to believe the story you told Nathan, despite its illogicality. After all, why would you lie? You were speaking to an intimate friend—"

Lana snorts. Nathan protests.

"Lana. Can't you give me even a little credit for—"

"And in my experience, this is life, yes? Random, uncertain, illogical. But if so, then why you say nothing to convince me is a mystery, when there are facts that might tally with your version of events. Evidence you could show—"

Vallette returns with Lana's bag.

"—ah, as we will see. You told Nathan you came to Paris

for the Hopper exhibition. And yes, you have a ticket and a catalog."

Vallette takes out the catalog and the ticket and places them on the table like they are court exhibits.

"So this is true. Would you waste this time if you were in Paris for some other, more notorious purpose? It is a little thing, yes, but there is more. Your medicine, Lana."

Vallette takes the bottles from the bag and gives them to Fournier, who holds them toward her.

"Interesting. Trileptal, Risperdal. Am I correct that this combination of drugs is normally prescribed to someone in the manic phase of bipolar disorder? In this situation it is normal for a person to be reckless, to spend too much, to act without considering the consequences, to believe that every foolish idea is inspiration. Do you not see, Lana? These pills are your best defense. If only you had told us what your situation was, it would have explained so much about your behavior."

The cruelty of the performance is breathtaking. Fournier's voice is utterly even, calmly sympathetic as a doctor's, his expression seems so understanding, flavored with a dash of tender sadness. And he's not finished yet.

"Embarrassment, perhaps? Of course, yes, it is normal. But we are sensitive people. It would have helped us understand you and your actions so much better. We might even be sitting here now, relaxing with a coffee, all matters resolved, conversing like old friends."

Fournier holds the bottle of pills toward her as if he's hoping she'll snatch at them like an embarrassed child. A phone rings. Vallette pulls his cell from his pocket and steps outside.

"So, yes, I can believe that you were merely in the wrong

place at the wrong time. But even so, how can I be certain you will just walk away? Don't you see? I would be happy to allow you depart quietly on this return flight tonight, but you have refused to help yourself, so that even if you promise now not to contact these people you were with last night—these people who are intending to destroy me—why should I believe you?"

Vallette returns, barking in French. Lana guesses from Nathan's reaction he is telling them about her bottle attack.

"Oh Jesus, Lana. What have you done?"

Fournier looks at the pills and shakes his head.

"A broken bottle, Lana? Reckless behavior, not caring about consequences: all, I believe, symptoms of your condition. The man you attacked is in the hospital. You really are not helping yourself. Fortunately his eyes are not damaged, but his face . . ."

"Lana, you have get out of France as soon as possible!"

She ignores Nathan.

"Then have me arrested, Monsieur Fournier."

"No. I don't want to cause you any—"

"You don't want me shooting my mouth off. And you know I will. You want me scared and silent. You want me to believe that without my passport and ticket and all the rest I am lost and the only way I can get these things is by promising to do whatever you want. But I can go to the embassy on Monday morning, report a stolen passport, and get myself a temporary one. I can arrange a new ticket and fly back to Dublin whether you like it or not. And as for your shock"—she turns to Nathan—"at how I defended myself, it's a good lesson in consequences, don't you think? You sent me out on the streets and then made a phone call. I find myself in danger and a guy gets himself hurt. You want to connect the dots?"

Nathan just shakes his head. Fournier sounds impressed.

"It's a very persuasive argument. I think we could all do with some coffee. Nathan, please."

The tone, the wave of the hand is that of a valued restaurant client instructing a waiter. Despite her disgust at Nathan right now, Lana hopes he'll show some backbone: "No, I am not your servant." But he nods and goes to the kitchen. The atmosphere has become as noxious as the smoke generated from Fournier's cigar. He seems to notice the smoke, at least, and goes to the window, opens it, and steps out. The noise of weekenders thronging the square and the St.-Michel fountain beyond reminds Lana how close by pleasant normality is. Fournier leans over the rail, seemingly captivated by the doings of the amusing little people below.

Alone with Vallette, she cannot not look at him. It seems that a pause in proceedings has been decreed. Is that to allow Fournier to reassess his strategy? Does she have him on the run?

How wrong. How pathetically, dangerously wrong.

"You are quite correct in all you have said, but to be correct does not always guarantee the victory."

Vallette's voice, oddly low and very calm, riles Lana. Why is he speaking now? Can he not allow her these few moments of merciful silence? Does he feel he has to fill the void?

"Paris is such a crowded city. So busy. It is surprising that there are not more accidents, no? But still, every day strange tragic events occur. Sometimes these events are no one's fault; they are just bad luck, fate. But sometimes . . . people make terrible choices, no? Sometimes these choices cause the death of others, but sometimes they end their own life. So sad, but impossible to prevent if the mind tells us, it is too much, this life. Americans, for example, love Paris so much. To come here and take your own life might seem to someone reading such a report like a very romantic tragedy."

Is Vallette insane or does he just have a peculiar sense of humor? Yet the choreography lends weight to his words: Nathan instructed to go make coffee, Fournier stepping out, leaning over, hearing only the noise of the street, leaving Vallette, the enforcer, to pass on the lethal message. But they cannot be serious. Surely Nathan, cringing collaborator though he is, would not be part of such a scheme? Of course not. Was that why he'd been sent from the room? Still, if any "accident" happened to Lana, wouldn't he piece it together and refuse to let it stand? Of course he would, before realizing that such a paranoid story would never fly. How would he back it up? The only forensic evidence in existence would be of her presence in his apartment and sexual activity between them. And how about the complicated backstory? Man has affair with married American. Years later the woman returns, spends the night with him, and then commits suicide. Man makes up crazy conspiracy to hide some other sordid truth. It would be not just foolish, but dangerous, for Nathan to speak out. And maybe the offer of a gig as some minor functionary in Fournier's future administration might help ensure his silence, having first allowed himself a little time to struggle with his conscience.

"Be sensible, Madame Gibson. I understand it is difficult. By the way, is it time for your medication yet?"

A face like Vallette's isn't constructed to look kind, but he manages a reasonable impression. It's still hard to digest that her life has just been quietly threatened. Nathan, such a handsome waiter, comes back with a large tray. Vallette shouts quite peremptorily to Fournier that the breeze is a little too chilly.

The potential future president of the republic smiles as he steps back inside, sniffing the aroma.

"Ah, superb."

Lana notices that as Vallette closes the windows behind him he discreetly wipes the handles with a handkerchief.

Ferdie woke in his own bed, naked, but with no memory of undressing. The trail of clothes led out of the bedroom and, in the hall beyond, he could see his crutches on the floor. He must have crawled on all fours to bed. Now he recalled squatting outside the Chinese restaurant to keep watch and confirm that the paramedics got to the bellhop in time. They arrived very quickly but were a long time in the building. When they eventually brought him out on a stretcher, Ferdie could tell by their demeanor and quick pace that the patient was alive, but the situation was undoubtedly critical. The taxi driver had woken him when they reached his apartment and he had only a muddled awareness of wallet-fumbling and stumbling on the pavement. Then, nothing at all.

For a few minutes after waking he enjoyed feeling rested. He stretched and his body tingled pleasantly. He curled up, a contented cat. But there was no question of drifting back into sleep; rather his brain began to spark and sizzle with thoughts that burned red-hot, all directed at Vallette. For a long time it had been Ferdie's casual mantra that something had to be done about this mad dog, but now it was critical: something really did need to be done and soon, now. The obvious option of bringing the matter to Monsieur Fournier's attention had dangers. Would what he told him just sound malevolent, if not deranged? More significantly, Ferdie could not be certain that Monsieur Fournier did not already know exactly how Vallette operated and considered it a useful, perhaps even necessary, part of the campaign, and would not particularly mind anything his guard dog did for the cause. Ferdie was honest enough to admit that outrage at the fate of the bellhop was less a motivation than was the certain knowledge that he would have no long-term future with Monsieur Fournier as long as Vallette was around.

Hanging around his apartment for the next few days brooding was not something Ferdie could bear. He briefly considered going to the hospital and trying to find out how the bellhop was, but he knew that any information worth having would only be given to next of kin. Anyway, what could he do at this stage; whatever would happen would happen. The deeper truth was that such a caring gesture was less interesting to Ferdie than the darker pleasure of striking back at Vallette. The thought of him cruising around right now in Ferdie's classic car felt particularly galling. And when he remembered the laptop under the driver's seat, the more unnerving thought of Vallette getting hold of that and being able to access so much private material was genuinely galvanizing. Ferdie had to get out of his apartment now, find Vallette, and do something to hurt him. It seemed clear that the bellhop had not given out any information to his attackers; otherwise he would not have been beaten quite so badly. So Vallette needed a better result, and soon, such as hunting down Caramel Girl or her associates; which made today an ideal day to keep track of him, if Ferdie could find him in the first place. But there was no way he could do it on his own.

Didi Bastereaud was the man for the job.

A grunt or two from Didi over the phone and some background noise indicated that he was doing nothing other than sprawling at home watching wrestling on TV. However, a few more grunts revealed that he was halfway through a six-month driving ban and technically wasn't available. So chauffeuring Ferdie around Paris for, say, the next twenty-four hours was out of the question? With his usual minimal word count, Didi indicated that nothing was out of the question if there was enough money on offer. Ferdie knew there was no point in doing this at all without being willing to pay a premium to get the most reliable and least talkative wheelman he knew. With Didi he was guaranteed discretion and protection, as well as driving skills.

The only complication was that, because of his ban, Didi could not risk using his own car, so one would have to be rented, but not in Didi's name; nor could he even be named as the second driver. And Ferdie could hardly arrive on crutches with a bound foot to collect a car rented in his own name.

The solution would involve some physical discomfort, but he had no choice. He told Didi where and when to meet him and then called a car rental company he had used before and booked a BMW Series 7. Then he ordered another taxi and, while waiting, removed the dressing on his swollen foot and slowly pulled on socks. Sneakers with the laces undone were the least uncomfortable footwear. Even so, the short walk from his apartment to the taxi was still very painful and got worse from the taxi to the car rental office. At least out on the street he could wince and whine, but once inside he had to keep his face composed and walk normally. When he reached the desk he suppressed a gasp, put his hands on the counter to take some of the weight, and eased the tortured foot from the ground.

Once he had produced his driver's license and two credit cards and signed all the necessary forms, the desk girl invited him to sit down while he waited for his car and clearly thought it odd when he smiled and said he preferred to stay as he was.

The journey from the office around the back of the building to the garage was almost unbearable, because the young guy who led him talked and moved at speed. Despite Ferdie's repeated expressions of satisfaction, he insisted on walking him around the car to check the bodywork, wheels, indicator lights, and headlights. Finally he was allowed to sink behind the wheel and he sat still, head down, breathing slowly, waiting for the stinging to ease. There was a tap on his window and he had to reassure the young guy that everything was absolutely, totally fine, but still the annoying little shit hovered as Ferdie started the car and took off, pressing gingerly on the accelerator. Back on the street he allowed himself a sustained moan, building in volume and intensity. Another hundred meters and he pulled in. Sure enough, the great hairy ape shape that was Didi appeared, offering a thumbs-up. Ferdie decided it would be easier to slide over to the passenger seat than get out and hop around. Didi heaved himself in. A nod and a grunt said how are you and where are we going? Already Ferdie had begun to feel better about the rest of his day.

Where were they going? He was relying on his knowledge of Monsieur Fournier's schedule to lead him to Vallette. He had an appointment at 4 p.m. at the Arab World Institute. Taking his cue from Didi, he wasted no words and just spat out the address. The odds were reasonable that Vallette would be traveling with Monsieur Fournier, and anyway, once he found one it would not be long before the other would appear. After that, who knew. But at least it felt a whole lot better than moping in his apartment, and he was determined to take any opportunity to make trouble for Vallette.

• • •

FOURNIER'S MONOLOGUE—IN FRENCH—ON THE QUALITIES OF NATHAN'S coffee goes on and on. The words are chosen so carefully, with such articulation and reinforced with lordly gestures, that his meaning is clear to Lana, though she doesn't affect even a scintilla of interest. She does notice, however, how pathetically pleased Nathan seems to be with the compliments. Vallette stands near the door, cup in hand. Lana avoids looking him in the eye. She believes he had meant what he'd said, but what isn't so clear is whether his threat is backed up by Fournier, or if she's dealing with someone who's playing by his own rules. Lana has a notion that it might be a little of both. The Fourniers of this world love having the loyalty of Vallette and his kind, the ones who know what needs to be done without explicit instruction. The bottom line from her point of view: if she gets killed, does it matter who gave the order?

So what now? Obviously she needs to stop being pain-in-the-ass girl and become can-I-help-you-with-that girl. Promise Fournier whatever he wants, her silence, whatever. Put it in writing if need be. All that matters is recovering her passport and ticket and everything else. Then she'd have just six hours in Paris to keep out of trouble. Maybe even enjoy herself a little. Yeah, right.

This is, without question, the sensible thing to do. Forget Guillaume and his documentary, forget Odette's pain, forget her disgust at Fournier. Just get herself home safe. She would hug Brian like she hadn't hugged him in a long time.

But . . . but . . . it feels like defeat. It pisses her off how much Fournier might enjoy her humiliation.

What are the alternatives? And would they result in her

taking a ride with Vallette to some wasteland in the banlieues? How about telling Nathan what Vallette had just said? Would he even believe her? And what could he do anyway? Still, it would be interesting to distract the two fine minds from their important discussion about where the finest coffee in Paris was to be had—or whatever debate they were now enjoying—and tell them, "While you were being a good little barista, Nathan, and you were out on the balcony, Monsieur Fournier, look- ing down on the little people, Monsieur Vallette quite casually threatened to kill me. He said it would be easy to make it look like suicide." She'd use the startled silence to add, "I presume you ordered him to threaten me this way?" If Fournier was responsible, then his denial would come wrapped in outraged tones and insinuations that perhaps Lana was desperate enough to accuse anyone of anything to sow confusion and uncertainty. If Fournier had no knowledge he might still react in a similar way—not wanting to seem disloyal to his lieutenant—but Lana is confident that there would be some little giveaway in his eyes or voice, something that would point to genuine shock at the discovery that he has a psychopath in his intimate circle.

Fournier is looking directly at her, holding the Hopper bro- chure and speaking. She tunes in and hears English again.

". . . so I envy you, Lana, this spirit of freedom. As you may guess, such things are impossible for me now. In normal circumstances there is nothing I would have liked better. There is a very special atmosphere around each of his paintings, so to be in the presence of so many all at once must have been utterly intoxicating. Ah! Maybe, Lana, perhaps, perhaps, per- haps Mr. Hopper affected you more than you realize. Such is the power of great art. Although for me, you know, restraint and modesty has always been the flavor of Hopper. So many people say that he created our idea of America and certainly it is true that he represented the particular urban architecture of the United States at his time. But his men and women are not who many Europeans think of as the typical, perhaps the stereotypical, American: brash, overconfident. I myself do not believe this stereotype and so, for many who see Americans in this way, Mr. Hopper should be a revelation. His characters are uncertain, modest, often with head bent low and eyes disappearing into the shadows. They wait patiently or go quietly about their work. They are little and alone in a big world. Yes, I would love to have the opportunity to see all these magnificent humane works. Perhaps they would make me fall even more in love with America. I spend a lot of time in your remarkable country, you know. I lecture there, I attend conferences, I have friends there."

Just as Lana is beginning to doubt he will ever stop talking he stands and changes tone abruptly.

"So. I have my commitments, Lana. Sadly, our time is finished. I realize that you are not . . . well . . . in the best situation now, so there is no point in continuing to engage in this way. I choose to believe that while you may be capricious, you are not malevolent. I am a man who likes to take a risk, to follow my instinct. But not without certain necessary precautions."

Can it be that Fournier is at last spooked by her aggressive silence? Is he going to cut his losses? Vallette begins to gather up all her documents.

"I have decided that you will stay here with Nathan. I'm sure you will enjoy each other's company for a few more hours. This evening at Charles de Gaulle, Arnaud or one of our colleagues will be waiting with all your necessary papers. If Nathan can confirm that you have behaved yourself, then you may take your flight just as you planned."

"Behaved yourself." Lana blazes inside. With just two words out of so many, Fournier has made a serious misjudgment.

"I won't even require particular promises. I will assume that once back in Dublin you will prefer to forget everything that has happened here. Arnaud, can you suggest a good meeting place in the airport?"

Vallette gestures and they step out on the balcony and lower their voices. Fournier nods energetically. They come back.

"Arnaud proposes the smoking terrace at Le Grand Comptoir, in Terminal One departures. At nine o'clock. But he also has one other useful suggestion. Purely as a gesture of goodwill, perhaps you would like to tell us one thing, Lana. These people you met last night, these interesting filmmakers. Where did you go with them? Have you an address?"

"No." How Lana manages to answer without revealing her rage she doesn't know. So Vallette and Nathan would decide if she had "behaved" or not. Surely Fournier understood exactly how stinging that had sounded, or was his contempt for women such that it hadn't even occurred to him? Right now Lana would not tell this coiffed ape the time, let alone give up Guillaume's address or any useful information.

"No?" Vallette's response to the refusal is chilly. Lana knows she has to hold herself in check. For now. "Behave" herself, if she can.

"It was dark, and it was a bit of a wild ride, remember." She smiles at Vallette as if recalling a fun evening together. "I had no idea where we were going. We stopped in a narrow street. I'm pretty sure we never crossed the river, so it was definitely on the right bank. Oh, and I remember, the front doors were purple."

Useless though this information patently is, Lana hopes Fournier will allow himself to be satisfied that she has made some attempt to be helpful. He gazes at her for what seems a long time, then shrugs.

"Not a problem. Nathan, I presume you are happy to be guardian to our guest until tonight?"

"Yes. Yes, I am."

From the way Nathan looks at her as he answers, she can see he wants an opportunity to be alone with her.

"Good." Fournier steps closer. "So this is goodbye, Lana. It is such a pity we did not meet in different circumstances. I think you would have formed a much better opinion of me."

How pathetic, unable to accept that he has failed to enchant her. This time she takes the offered hand. Limply. Fournier again stares, but finally seems to acknowledge that there is no point in pushing anymore.

In fact, right now Lana isn't even focused on him, distracted by what's happening behind his back. Vallette has picked up Fournier's coffee cup and is speaking quietly to Nathan in French. He seems to be insisting on cleaning up. As Fournier turns away from her, his minion is already walking toward the kitchen, cup in hand, to wash away any evidence of his master's presence in the apartment.

Now, not only is Lana insulted and enraged by the conditions of her "release," she doesn't for one moment believe it will happen.

And suddenly it's just Lana and Nathan staring at each other. Or rather Lana staring at Nathan, who looks away, then moves about the room and goes out to the hall to check that Fournier and Vallette closed the door properly as they left. Lana's gaze follows like a motion-sensitive surveillance camera, until he slithers out of sight into the little kitchen.

"More coffee? I'm going to make some."

The forced chirpiness in his voice seems to plead a truce, a cease-fire; that old story of soldiers coming out of the trenches on Christmas Eve for a few hours of peace and goodwill with the enemy. Without answering, Lana goes to the kitchen and watches him from the doorway. The clock on the wall says two forty. It might be a very long afternoon and evening. His eyes can't help flicking toward her, but he looks away quickly and focuses all his attention on espresso-making. Lana has no intention of letting him off the hook and there will be no preliminary chitchat. Subject: betrayal. You have as long as you like, Nathan, to explain yourself.

He holds out until after he hands her an espresso that is everything he is not—strong, gutsy, full of depth. Actually, the espresso reminds her of Nathan in one respect: it has a slight but distinctly bitter aftertaste. Lana sips, silent. He makes an apologetic gesture toward the living room. Does he seriously hope that a change of scene, the battered comfort of the old couch will relax the mood? What he hasn't picked up on is that, despite everything, Lana is feeling totally relaxed. In fact, up to a point, she's only toying with him. She's parked her rage, although she's not quite finished with it yet. But that has nothing to do with Nathan. It's all focused on Fournier now, and especially his "behave yourself" remark. Lana has already vowed that he'll pay dearly for that. At whatever cost to herself. So, truthfully, Nathan is just a sideshow, albeit a necessary one, because he stands between her and Fournier. Lana will have to bypass him, railroad him, or enlist him, and she's not entirely sure which one yet.

After another long espresso-sipping silence, he crumbles.

"Lana, I swear to you, whatever you may think, I was trying to look after your best interests."

"I get it. You thought I'd need some help carrying my bags at the market."

"Sorry?"

"Vallette's elegantly dressed gorillas."

"I honestly haven't an idea what you're talking about."

"Whose face did you think I smashed? Some innocent stranger?"

"Well . . . Lana, I don't know. Seems like there's lots I don't know."

And there it is, just the tiniest hint of petulance, of bitterness, of self-righteousness: what she hadn't told him, what she hadn't trusted him with. Nathan is going back over everything she said and did and reassessing it in the light of what Fournier revealed about her. So does he get to let himself off the hook and turn it all on her? She's manic, that's the solution, that's what this whole thing is about. Her story can't be trusted, nor her motivations, nor her actions, she's . . . she's . . . unstable. Lana can see how that version makes sense. But she tells him the crazy truth anyway.

"Three of Vallette's guys tried to kidnap me at the market. My question is, how did they know I was there?"

"What? Oh really! You think I—"

"I don't think anything. I'm asking how they knew I was there?"

"All I wanted to do was to see if this thing could be worked out."

"You know what? I don't like being here anymore. In this room. And I sure don't want to be a prisoner here for another six hours."

"You're not a prisoner—"

"Then take me out. Let's at least have something beautiful and real around us, while you explain exactly what you thought you were doing."

A little to her surprise, Nathan is desperate enough to seize on the idea. Is he scared of her, does he think it best to humor her in her condition? Lana, having so easily achieved step one, realizes she has to make the best of this opportunity. It will at least be more congenial to listen to whatever self-serving explanation he comes up with while enjoying the buzz of the streets. It would be sad if her last memory of Paris was the acrid disappointment hanging in the air of Nathan's apartment.

Outside, without really thinking about it, Lana steers them toward rue St.-André-les-Arts. The smell of street food, the cheerful faces of tourists, and the hum of French voices swirl around Nathan's low-pitched monologue. Their loud honesty only makes him seem more shamefaced and pathetic.

"I had this idea. I knew you wouldn't like it, so I thought, okay, I won't say anything, but I'll sort everything out and present it to her—you—tied up in a bow and then you'd be okay with it. My idea was to contact Jean-Luc directly, explain that you are a friend, tell him the story just as you told me, assure him that the whole sequence of events was just one of those peculiar accidents and you had no agenda. I was sure that he would understand and return all your—"

"*He'd* understand?"

"I didn't think there was any point in getting into a discussion about the right and wrong of the thing. This was pragmatism. My hope was that by the time you came back from the market I'd have your passport and ticket, everything, waiting for you—"

"You were anxious to get rid of me."

"No. I really hoped you'd stay on, forget about tonight's

flight, but I wanted you to be free to make a choice. Which would make it even better if you chose to stay on."

"And getting my own passport back was like some special privilege?"

"No, no, I know that's—no. Oh please, Lana. You have to admit it was a pretty terrible situation. I was just trying to find a way out that would satisfy everyone. I mean, you had thought that they were out to kill you. Have you forgotten that? Now I know better why you were having those cr—"

The hard *c* in *crazy* was as far as he got before hurriedly sucking the sound back in.

"—why you were . . . misreading the situation."

"So you didn't ask him to send three guys to hunt me down at the market."

"No, no! I promise you, I knew nothing about that."

"Right. He just somehow divined where I was."

"No! I . . . I mean . . . it was just . . . I think Jean-Luc asked at one point if you were with me, and I said not right now, and I probably mentioned the market, I don't know, maybe just casually, you know. I mean the context was—"

"So he or Vallette used this 'casual' information and sent those guys after me. You still think you can trust him?"

And the tiny hesitation is enough to tell her that Nathan might trust him more than he trusts her.

"I don't know, Lana."

"Or you don't want to know?"

"Maybe you're right. Can I be totally honest here? And I don't mean to be insensitive, but I have to admit . . . I've been thinking about Jean-Luc and the election. I live here. I know that the country can't take another seven years of neoliberal bullshit. It's been a disaster and Dufour will only make things worse: pro-privatization, anti-immigrant. Believe me, Fournier is the only man to stop all this, and I'm not saying that because he's an old colleague. He just is the right man for this job. His ideas are better. Sure, he has his flaws as a human being, and maybe these are more serious than I ever thought—"

"What if it's more than a flaw? What if it's a sickness? Have you heard of satyriasis?"

"Fine, give it some pop-psych name if you like—"

"Oh, right, the way we c-c-c-razy Americans like to."

"Please don't put words in my mouth, Lana! I just want you to believe that it wasn't ever my intention to do any harm. I really thought that I was helping. Can't we sit somewhere and talk? Things may feel better if we eat something."

They have arrived at rue de Buci, but Lana has no intention of planting herself in one of the cafés scattered on either side of the crowded street. Her object is to keep on the move, get farther from the apartment while she works out what to do next.

"You know something. I should go fix up my bill at the hotel."

"They have your credit card on file, don't they?"

"Sure, sure, but you know, I'd just feel better. And we can eat after that. How about Montorgueil?"

"Well . . . okay. We have time."

Lana realizes that if she can keep Nathan thinking about her as whimsical and manic, it won't occur to him to be suspicious of her intentions. They reach the Pont Neuf.

"All right, Lana, I admit my own ego made me act in what now seems like a . . . if you want to use the word . . . an underhand manner. And yes, I freely admit I wanted to be the good guy, the hero, sorting out this problem. If I'm at fault, then that was my sin."

Lana winces at the "if I" form of apology, but manages to keep her mouth shut.

"And yes, it hasn't worked out exactly as I'd planned, even though it does seem like things are going to be okay after all?"

"Maybe."

"Anyway, once I got talking to Jean-Luc I thought it was all going to be fine. He was very friendly, he listened very carefully and asked about you, and I was able to tell him really good things and he seemed to be relieved that it could be sorted out. I realize now that he . . . What happened was there were two calls. He thanked me and said he needed to think about what I'd told him and he'd get back to me very quickly. Which seemed, you know, perfectly reasonable in the circumstances."

"He got off the phone and called you back?"

"Yes. I mean I—"

"Which was when he sent his guys to find me."

"Well, thinking about it now, probably. Anyway, a few minutes later he called and said he was sure things could be sorted out and he would send your documents over. I gave him the address and not long after that he and Vallette turned up at the apartment. What could I do? Not let him in? I see now . . . Oh God . . . I'm . . . I'm so sorry, Lana."

At least this expression of regret has no "if" in it. Suddenly she feels, quite spontaneously, a spasm of pity toward Nathan. It's not an emotion that would ever have played even a walk-on role in their passionate past, but at this moment it's an improvement on disgust. His defeated expression seems genuine.

"I should have been more wary. But you know I'd contacted him out of the blue, so naturally when someone in those circumstances asks for more thinking time—"

"Sure. Why would it occur to you that he was organizing muscle to kidnap me?"

"Are you being—"

"Sarcastic? Actually, no. Not this time. I do understand. Why would you suspect such a thing about a man you look up to, someone you believe in?"

He is so sheepish he doesn't even notice that they are approaching *Le Fumoir*. Lana doesn't bother to point it out. What a twisting emotional journey it has been from here back to here.

"It wasn't about blind trust. I suppose my analysis was that here is an intelligent politician in a very awkward situation. A guy with Jean-Luc's smarts is not going to dig himself even deeper into the mire. I was offering him the quickest, easiest way out. I was his get-out-of-jail-free card, if you like. So when he wanted to meet you in person, that didn't seem, you know, all that surprising. Obviously I see now what was really going on. Fournier realized that you might evade his guys and come back to the apartment—"

"And he needed to get there before I did because once I found out you'd been talking to him, I wouldn't wait around."

"I should have been more suspicious when they arrived so quickly. I'd never met Vallette before. And I swear, it was only after you came back that I noticed he was armed."

They are under the arches now, only yards from the entrance to Le Chevalier. Almost twenty-four hours after her arrival, how much has changed. It's hard for Lana to enter without feeling she's being watched or that something bad is about to happen. The receptionist's English is just as smooth, but her smile seems to have even less of a welcome about it than yesterday. Obviously Lana's failure to check out by noon had not gone unnoticed.

"So sorry. My credit card, everything's been stolen and I was dealing with the police. But don't worry, I won't cancel the card until your bill goes through. You have my details?"

It's hard to pinpoint exactly what the receptionist does to express her disapproval. Is it in the particular incline of her head, or the force with which she taps the computer keypad, or the way she places an envelope in front of Lana as if it's an unsavory thing and she's glad to pass it on to its unsavory owner? "Lana Gibson" is scribbled large on it. Before opening the envelope, she checks that Nathan is sitting comfortably, paying little attention. It's from Guillaume; big, awkward writing, but easy to read.

LANA! WHERE ARE YOU? I MUST GO NOW. CLAUDE IS IN THE HOSPITAL! THEY BEAT HIM. IT IS SO TERRIBLE! CALL ME PLEASE! GUILLAUME

Hospital? A beating? Those anxious, amber eyes. *They are going to kill you, Madame.* Strolling ahead of her with the luggage cart, sinuous and beautiful. What have they done to him? Lana makes her mind up. Now she knows exactly what she must do. She folds away the note and composes herself to face Nathan.

"Right. That's done. Let's get out of here."

And once back on the street again she says, "Forget Montorgueil, let's go eat at the Danton. We'll take the metro."

She can tell he thinks it's another whim and he's happy to go along with it. They walk to the Pyramides station.

"When I saw the gun, I was flabbergasted, by the way. But then I told myself a presidential candidate would have a security person, of course, so that must be who Vallette was. But you know, it may well be that he's the problem here. He may have persuaded Jean-Luc that you had some kind of malevolent agenda."

It's the perfect time to tell him about Vallette's threat and also totally the wrong time. Lana just shrugs. "They wanted to scare me."

"Yes, but why, when I was offering him a simple way out?"

"You're assuming I would have agreed to it."

"Okay, yeah, sure." Nathan suddenly sounds uncertain. "But you would—wouldn't you?"

"Maybe Fournier knows me better than you do. Or maybe he knows himself better; just how sick and arrogant he is."

In the station Lana lets Nathan lead. The signs tell her they are going toward Gare St.-Lazare.

"Are you saying that if things had worked out as I'd hoped, if you'd come back from the market and found your passport and purse and ticket and clothes all safe, that you'd still have wanted to expose Jean-Luc?"

Lana speaks without thinking now, mere words to keep Nathan distracted.

"I'm only a foreign tourist. Surely the question is why you still don't want to expose him, after what you witnessed in the last hour. Don't you find it sinister?"

"Yes . . . yes . . . I admit my belief or my hope, whatever I had about this election, has been shaken. But you have to agree, you were not meeting Jean-Luc in normal circumstances."

"Sure, at least today he had clothes on, which was a big plus."

On the busy platform. *Prochain train, une minute.* Lana is so focused on her escape plan she scarcely notices that Nathan has fallen silent until his hesitant question completely throws her.

"When we had that time together . . . were you . . . had you already been diagnosed?"

What to say, why is he asking? She doesn't want him to think she'd hidden something so important back then, nor that he might have been the trigger.

"No, no. That happened a long time after."

"It's just I wish I'd known about it, to have had time to get used to . . . what it's like for you."

"Would you have wanted to?"

"Of course. Any opportunity to understand you better, Lana Turner."

Train s'approche. Focus. Think of Claude lying in the hospital. She mustn't let Nathan distract her now. Too late for that.

"Well, I wouldn't ever say this thing I have is easy to cope with, but there are times when I'm glad it's in me."

"Yes, I can imagine that."

The driverless train bursts from the tunnel. It's time to distract Nathan. Shock him.

"Especially when you have to deal with something like a murder threat."

"What?"

"Vallette. He said he's going to kill me and make it look like some sad crazy American woman had committed suicide."

"Are you making this up?"

The doors open. There is the usual crush to get on.

"When you went to make coffee, Fournier stepped out on the balcony and left Vallette alone with me. That's when he said it."

The warning horn blares. Lana pushes Nathan ahead of her. He twists his head around.

"But that makes no sense—if anything did happen to you, I'd know the real story."

"So why did Vallette insist on washing the coffee mugs?"

Nathan looks totally mystified at this, but he'll just have to work that one out on his own. She gives him a final nudge onto the train and follows, but hovers in the doorway. His back is to her. The moment the horn stops she lunges backward against the final anxious surge on board as the doors snap shut.

Nathan twists around, but the train is already moving. Lana looks at his fast-receding face with an expression intended to suggest that some terrible accident had separated them. Three teenagers come racing onto the platform, reaching for the train with theatrically despairing gestures and crying out French curses, even though they know there will be another in two minutes. Lana briefly notices the only other person standing on the platform, a guy in a newsboy cap, but her amusement at the teen dramatics and her own delight at escaping Nathan distract her from wondering how come that guy on the platform had also missed the train.

4 PM

It feels like the end of something. Even though her priority right now is to get to Guillaume and Pauline's apartment, Lana can't help thinking about Nathan's face as his train sped into the tunnel. He was actually openmouthed, still cute, but in the way a little kid shocked at being suddenly separated from his mother might: so different from that sophisticated mix of intelligent inquiry, inner wisdom, and physical beauty that she first encountered in *Le Fumoir* all that time ago. It probably *was* a pity they had ended this way, without an opportunity even to acknowledge that she had already begun the process of forgiving him for his stupidity. Would she also have told him that the passion that had defined their relationship and raged fiercely until just a few hours ago was now absolutely, totally vaporized? Phff! Maybe he realizes that for himself? Theirs had been a relationship that seemed to operate only in short bursts of high intensity. Now there's no time to dwell on this second separation. Lana has to figure out what train takes her close to rue d'Aboukir, but it's very hard to pinpoint the street itself on the metro map. She knows it can't be too far away from the Chevalier because it had only taken five minutes to drive there last night, but in what direction? Lana squints, moving her finger back and forth, regretting now that she had always left this sort of thing to Brian whenever they were in a strange city. Not only was he really good at reading maps, but even without them he had an innate ability to orienteer and loved showing off. She had enjoyed so many relaxing days just trailing about big beautiful cities, taking in the sights and letting Brian worry about where and how far and how long.

Rue d'Aboukir, rue d'Aboukir, rue d'Aboukir . . .

The next train comes and goes. Finally, by painstakingly tracing her finger along the map, half inch by half inch like a police search of a crime scene, she finally happens on the magic word, d'Aboukir. But she has no idea which end is the right one on what looks like a long street. Strasbourg–St.-Denis seems to be the closest metro stop and the least complicated journey from Pyramides. Change at Madeleine. Then five stops.

Once she's on the next train, the gnawing frustration recedes and the buzz begins to take over once more. She's going to make Fournier regret what has been done to Claude, regret the words "how you behaved yourself." She will allow Guillaume to record her testimony and, once safely out of Paris, she'll make sure Fournier finds out about it. His fear of this story becoming public would definitely mess with his head, undermine his campaign. And even if he still wins the election, this time bomb would keep ticking. It pleases her immensely to think of President Fournier living under the threat that some nobody, some clown-faced indie filmmaker, has a smoking gun and he will be in deep shit whenever Guillaume's finished movie hits the public. Sweet. So sweet. No more than his arrogance deserves. And his cruelty. She takes out the note again: *in the hospital*. Is Claude's life in danger? Guillaume will surely have more news of him. She cannot help feeling guilty. There is no escaping that the beating must be linked to the incident with her outside the hotel last night.

It's a long walk at Madeleine from line 14 to line 8. It briefly occurs to her that, had her trip to Paris gone as planned—what a bizarre notion that seems now—she would be spending the afternoon directly above, at street level, moseying around Fauchon and Hédiard, buying last-minute sweet treats before booking a cab to the airport. Instead she is creeping anonymously among these crowds through the series of identical white-tiled passageways, driven and focused. More than anything she's buzzed at having outmaneuvered Vallette: relieved too. The more she thinks about him the scarier he becomes. That calm-voiced murder threat may have been the nadir, but it reminds her of just how sinister everything about his behavior had been from the moment she had squinted at his distorted face through the fish-eye peephole of her hotel room. If only she had viewed him with suspicion back then. Was it he and the other guy who had beaten Claude? She could easily believe it.

At Opéra, a young Eastern European woman steps onto the train wheeling a karaoke machine. The backing track begins, too loud. Microphone in hand, the poor thing counts herself in and sings a ballad-type number that is so truly awful Lana guesses it has to be from the French hit parade. On the New York subway people would already be shouting abuse at her. On the London tube someone would have inquired rather stuffily if she was aware that this activity was not just illegal but socially unacceptable and so should desist. But on the Paris metro everyone just looks elsewhere and pretends it isn't happening.

At Richelieu-Drouot, the poor girl stops warbling and goes around the car looking for reward for her efforts. Of course everyone ignores her, which inevitably prompts Lana to dig into her pocket and offer whatever change is left from Nathan's fifty-euro bill. Almost immediately she regrets it. What if she needs to buy another metro ticket or use a public phone? But Karaoke Girl has already gone to the next car, not that Lana would have ever asked for a refund. Stupid, Lana. Stupid! As the train leaves Grands Boulevards she can't bear sitting anymore and gets up to hover near the doors even though there's one more stop before hers.

When she emerges from the station at Strasbourg–St.-Denis the day has shifted decisively from afternoon to evening and a gorgeous low sun is directly in her eyes. Lana tries to orient herself as Brian would: if she can see the setting sun then she's facing west, right? And she's on rue St.-Denis, right? So the question is, is rue d'Aboukir to the north or south? Oh, forget it.

When she finds it, what's most obvious—and disconcerting—are the bright lines of little fashion shops stretching out along both sides of the street. Many have eager names in brash colors and fonts: *Exaltation*, *M. Elégance*, *Miss Papillon*, *Mille et une Soirées*, and colorfully dressed mannequins pout from every spot-lit shop front. Disoriented and hungry though she'd been last night, Lana would certainly not have missed this 360-degree rag trade smorgasbord. She walks on quickly, desperate for the rainbow of teasingly feminine shop fronts to give way to something drabber and grubbier, which, memory assures her, is how the area around Guillaume and Pauline's apartment building looked.

Is rue d'Aboukir the longest street in Paris? Lana quickens her pace until she's more or less power-walking. At the rue du Louvre intersection, she sees that the block ahead has more of the shabby anonymity she recalls from last night. The purple doors have to be there somewhere, unless she's missed them already. Then, a flash of something recognizable: on her left is the beginning of a pedestrian street, and farther down, an awning

that looks familiar. She hurries closer to make sure. Yes, unmistakable: Bistro Le Tambour, where she'd wolfed down the
very welcome beef bourguignon. Now it's easy to retrace those
late-night steps and cross rue du Louvre. Within a minute she
is standing outside the famous purple doors, which look just as
battered and peeling as she'd recalled. Yes! Her mind had not
been playing tricks on her.

Of course, she doesn't know the code and cannot call Guillaume. How mind-bendingly dumb had she been to give away
her last coins to the hopeless karaoke singer?

Lana is set to combust. The frustration of another uncertain
wait like the one last night outside Nathan's is just too much to
bear. Of course someone would open those god-awful doors to
exit or enter; of course she would get inside and reconnect with
Guillaume and Pauline again. Eventually. But doesn't she deserve *something* to go her way? Shouldn't Guillaume or Pauline
or even Odette pop out for a baguette and suddenly appear on
the street? Instead it feels like the recurring anxiety nightmare
she's had for many years is being brought to dismal life: in this
nightmare there was always travel, and always just when the
end point, the breakthrough, seemed close enough to touch, in
whatever room or corridor or vehicle she was trapped in, she
would come up against that final locked door and there would
be no key, or a key that refused to turn, or a handle that rattled but would never open the door. And Lana would remain
a prisoner.

She finds herself pounding recklessly at the purple doors,
then hurrying across the street and staring up, praying for a
glimpse of someone, ideally someone on the fifth floor who
will see her flailing arms and recognize her desperate face. Not
that she gives a damn at this point, but it's probably fortunate

that the street is empty, so there's no one to witness this lunatic mime, except for one guy back at the intersection. But he's talking on his cell and paying no attention, not even looking her way.

His cell? Maybe, just maybe he'll let her use it. It's worth asking. She runs toward him. Close-up the guy is surprisingly ripped, broad-shouldered with a seriously chiseled face under his cap. When he sees her approach he immediately ends his call and starts to walk away quickly. Jesus! How wild-eyed does she look to make him so keen to avoid her? But she can't lose this opportunity.

"Please! Oh s'il vous plaît! Aidez-moi, Monsieur! Your cell, your phone!" What do they call a cell phone? "Monsieur, excusez-moi. Je veux téléphoner . . ." Then she remembers. *Portable.* Por-ta-bleu. "Portable, votre portable. S'il vous plaît. Pour une minute seulement."

Astonishingly, Muscle-boy halts. Lana slows, keeping a little distance in case she spooks him again. She points at the cell still in his hand.

"I . . . me. May I use, ah utiliser votre portable pour une minute. C'est un urgence."

The guy still seems very uncertain about handing over his precious phone. Lana pulls Guillaume's card from her pocket and shows it to him.

"This ah . . . Cet nombre. Peut-être vous—" The French verb to dial fails her. She mimes with her index finger. "Dial . . . pour moi." Then she remembers the verb to call. "Appeller . . . appeller. Je suis perdue. Je cherche un apartment ici, rue d'Aboukir."

She waves an arm to indicate the building behind down the street. Muscle-boy steps closer to check out the number and holds out his free hand to take the card. He dials. As soon as someone answers, silently he hands over his cell.

"Hello, is that Guillaume?"

"Lana. Lana, where are you? I am calling you at the hotel for you since very early."

"Sorry, I know."

"What is happening with you?"

"I can't delay, Guillaume. This isn't my phone."

"What? What is this phone, you are talking?"

"Just someone on the street. Listen, I'm here. I'm on rue d'Aboukir."

"You are here?"

"Yes, but I can't get inside the building."

"Ah. You want the code? I will come down."

"Yes, the code please."

"Hash 7918."

"Hash 7918. Great. Wonderful."

A miracle had happened. It was all going to work out.

"I am surprised that you are able to find us again."

"I'll tell you the whole story as soon as—I gotta go Guillaume, or I'll forget the code. Hash 7918, right?"

"I will come down for you."

Lana clicks off and hands Muscle-boy his cell.

"Merci beaucoup, Monsieur. Je suis désolée, mais je n'avais pas d'argent. Pas d'argent."

"De rien, Madame."

He walks away as if still anxious to put some distance between them; a strange nervous fish. Lana is keying in the code when the door opens and Guillaume sticks his head out. He checks up and down the street before wrapping her in a big hug and kisses.

"You find us again. You are extraordinary."

"Tell me about Claude. What's happened to him?"

Guillaume's face assumes cartoon sadness.

"It is so terrible. He is ah . . . en soins intensif."

"Intensive care?"

"Yes. His brain, it is a problem—"

"Oh Jesus no!"

"It may be okay, we do not know. Odette is waiting at the hospital."

"She's recovered then?"

It seemed to take a second or two for Guillaume to understand the question.

"Oh. Yes. Well . . . she cares about her brother, you know."

"Of course. And you know who did it?"

"You want evidence? We have no evidence—"

"What I mean is, how it happened, was he attacked in the street—?"

"No, in his little apartment. Someone came to him. Nothing was stolen. Of course I know who did this, but maybe you don't believe me."

"No. I think I do."

It really feels like she should hurry to the hospital, but Lana knows this would serve no purpose apart from making herself feel better. More useful now to do what she came to do. In the apartment, Pauline is waiting to indulge in some big-time kissing and shrieking and babbling. Guillaume translates.

"Pauline, she is saying she knew you will come. She understands you because you are like her. You must be alone in the first moment to consider a problem from every side, but when you make a decision, you are determined."

"Well, she's right. I've made a decision. And now I'm even more certain I'm doing the right thing."

"Lana, do you mean you want to tell your story?"

"Yes, I do. But I must ask you something first. I'm a little afraid. Can I stay with you until Monday, when I can go to the embassy to deal with my passport situation?"

Guillaume's reaction is reassuring.

"But of course, of course, Lana. We will take care of you until you leave Paris, leave France. There is no question."

Though he pretends to be in no hurry to do the interview and asks if Lana would prefer to relax a little first, have a coffee, eat perhaps, it's obvious that his anticipation is high to boiling over, so she tells him she just wants to take a shower and then get started.

She's never faced a camera before apart from those few weeks of renewal after she returned from Paris with news of her pregnancy, when—hauntingly—Brian had filmed her incessantly with his camera phone. Every other moment he recorded her doing the most ordinary things, filling the dishwasher, or reading a book. And always at some point he'd tilt the lens down and step closer to her growing belly. Had Brian destroyed all that footage? They'd never spoken about it, but she hoped so.

Pauline dries and fixes Lana's hair. When she looks at herself in the mirror, instead she sees a flash of Claude's beautiful face, bloodied. She says a firm no to the offer of startlingly scarlet lip gloss. She thinks of Fournier in makeup before that TV debate Guillaume had shown her. No doubt he had joked and flirted and gazed confidently at himself in the mirror, knowing he was going to be THE MAN tonight, that he would just kill it at this debate; maybe even lavish his attentions on the prettiest crew girl afterward. The twin images, a split screen in her mind, propel her rage: his face, tanned and pampered, and Claude's, pulped and bloodied. She will most definitely *not* behave herself.

The green on the wall behind her is so lurid that Lana can't help asking why Guillaume had chosen that color. He explains that the *fond vert* allows him to put background images on it later in editing.

"We are lucky there is no green in your clothes. If there was, the images would show there too."

"So, you can put, say, a giant image of Fournier stark naked behind me."

"Yes, perfect, if we had such an image."

He grins and opens a panel at the side of the camera and slips in a slim card.

"The memory card, right?"

"Very good. The most important item."

"Is that the same as the old roll of film?"

He slides it out and brings it to Lana.

"Exactly. There is no longer film for me, not even tape or disks, just this little card. Your interview will be on this, then I transfer to my computer. In minutes I can start to edit."

In the face of such nerdish enthusiasm, Lana does her best to look solemnly impressed. Guillaume slides the card into the side of the camera again. While he fiddles with the lighting, Lana becomes aware of Pauline in the dark corner of the room sitting on the bed. For once she is still and so seems a more powerful, watchful presence. Finally, Guillaume checks his shot and almost whispers.

"Okay, quiet everyone. You ready, Lana?"

She nods. It's disconcerting how suddenly it's happening. Everything she witnessed will no longer be just in her head; a visible, spoken record will exist.

"First, please say who you are and why you come in Paris."

When that is done he asks her to explain how it happened that she was in the private elevator for the Suite Imperial of the Chevalier Hotel.

"I know this will seem silly, because it was silly. Basically just foolish . . . well, nosiness I guess. Curiosity. You know how, in any hotel you assume that the elevators are for every guest to use. And that's how people meet people, going up and down. Sometimes you get to know them through, you know, seeing them in the elevator. So it was a thing, you know, that in the Chevalier there was this, like, special super-exclusive elevator tucked away in a little corner. Anyway, what happened was, I just happened to be passing near it when the doors opened and this guy, this man got out. So you know, I just couldn't, like, resist having a little look-see. I suppose I wanted to find out, you know, was it totally different from the other elevator, the one for us plain folk? But look, honestly? I really have no excuse, no good reason to be there except just plain old nosiness—very innocent and very dumb."

"So you did not know who was staying in the Suite Imperial?"

"Absolutely not. No idea. Obviously I knew it had to be someone very wealthy and I guessed it could be some celebrity. But that really wasn't on my mind when I stepped into the elevator. It really was just, you know, just, seeing what it was like. And then when the doors started to close, I couldn't figure out how to stop them aaand . . . it was going up."

Guillaume smiles and gives her a thumbs-up.

"Okay, now, when the elevator comes to the Suite Imperial, there was a shock when the doors opened, yes?"

There it is, the heart of the matter. It feels very different from telling Nathan the story on his couch last night. Guillaume's eyes are fixed on the monitor, the eye of the camera is fixed on her, the lights feel warm, Pauline's shape is at the corner of her eye. The words Lana speaks now will be her exact words recorded and replayed, heard exactly as she is saying them at this moment, in this mood. They will forever be her version of this scene.

For some reason the most insistent voice in her head right now is Fournier's, asking in measured tones how Lana would behave if she discovered a stranger filming her private life with a hidden camera. It would be so easy now, with barely any exaggeration, to describe a rampant man-goat, intent on havoc, and to paint, via Guillaume's helpful prods, a revolting portrait of sagging, crude, repulsive nakedness in contrast to the innocence of youth, clear-skinned and fully clothed. That had certainly been Lana's intention as well as being her genuine *feeling* about what she had witnessed, more or less. Knowing there are other factors, such as the hidden camera in the hands of the perceived victim, doesn't negate that perception: what Lana saw was what she saw. That it's not the whole story is a given. She was just witness to part of it and is reporting that part with reasonable accuracy.

But now, with the camera in front of her, she becomes more aware of how it will ingest every word and the viewing audience will gorge on every detail. Should she say he "held her" or he "gripped her"? Should his eyes be "determined" or did they "blaze"? Was Lana herself merely "shocked" or was she "unnerved" or "terrified"? Was Fournier no more than a man

enjoying high-spirited private pleasures along with other con-
senting adults, or was it a revolting spectacle of wrinkled lust
and patriarchal power? That Lana's eyewitness account might
be too carefully calibrated and hesitatingly expressed is clear
from Guillaume's increasingly regular intrusions.

"Had you ever witnessed such a scene before?"

"Was it clear to you that the young woman was desperate
to escape?"

"How violent were his efforts to stop her?"

"You said you were shocked. Were you frightened?"

Gradually Lana relaxes and, in her replies, gives Guillaume
more of what he wants, realizing it's what she wants, too;
Fournier as a baboonish granddad, still trying to reenact his
fossilized, male, 1960s notion of sexual equality, while at the
same time assuming his natural right to special privileges. Not
surprisingly it is the French who have the perfect phrase for
this, coined long before the sixties: *droit de seigneur*; socialist in-
tellectual by day, naked rutting aristocrat by night. No. There's
no way Fournier should be let off the hook.

"And you did not know who this person was?"

"Absolutely not. All I saw was some naked old man."

Guillaume's grin gleams at her from the darkness behind
the camera. He's clearly delighted with the interview so far.

"What did you think should happen? Did you feel, this is a
private matter, it is none of my business?"

"I certainly didn't think it was none of my business. But I
worried that, even though I didn't know who the man was, he
had to be someone wealthy and therefore with influence. So I
wasn't sure if any complaint I made would be listened to."

"Complaint. What do you mean?"

"Well, to be honest, at that moment I thought the police

should be called. It seemed to me—I don't know French law—but it seemed to me that this might be a case of violent assault."

"Would you say, rape?"

"No, I could not be certain about that. . . . No."

"The man you saw that night. Do you know now who he is?"

"Yes."

"Will you name him?"

She thinks, why not? Say it for the camera, honey.

"Yes. Jean-Luc Fournier."

. . .

BY 4 P.M. FERDIE HAD LEARNED THREE NEW THINGS. ONE: IT WAS POSSIBLE to have ham-hock hands and a stomach so protruding that it sank into the steering wheel and yet handle a BMW with the precision of a watchmaker. Two: Ferdie liked being chauffeured. For fifteen years he thought he had the better end of an arrangement where he had the pleasure of driving top-range cars while getting paid for it. It had never occurred to him that lounging in the back being driven everywhere could be anything other than unremittingly frustrating. Not that Ferdie sat in the back today. Instead he stretched his legs in the front passenger seat. Three: Detective work was more tedious than he'd imagined. The problem was not the inevitable hanging around, which he was used to doing, but in situations where he could read a magazine, listen to the radio, look at his phone, step out and have a smoke, and generally amuse himself; not stare fixedly at a building fifty meters away, conscious all the time of remaining unnoticed, afraid to glance away for fear of missing an important moment.

The first important moment happened a couple of minutes after four when his precious black and silver beauty approached.

He nudged Didi, who had dozed off. Oscar was driving and Ferdie couldn't quell the Catherine wheel of rage spinning and sparking in his brain at the sight of someone else sitting in his seat, but it burned itself out quickly and was replaced by a more satisfying tingle when, looking through the binoculars Didi had pulled out of his little tool bag, he saw two heads in the backseat. When, moments later, Monsieur Fournier got out with . . . yes, Vallette, Ferdie felt the special delight of having placed a long-shot winning bet, even though in reality he had only slipped past the bouncers to the casino's inner sanctum. He hadn't actually turned a card or rolled the dice yet.

Once Monsieur Fournier and Vallette went inside, Ferdie told Didi that these events usually lasted about an hour, but it could be longer if Monsieur Fournier basked a little too much in the inevitable adulation. Didi just nodded, then opened the door and heaved himself out. He walked in the opposite direction to the next corner and looked left and right. Ferdie had rolled down the window to watch him and Didi turned and made a gesture that could have meant anything, but which Ferdie interpreted as meaning he would only be a moment.

Only seconds after Didi disappeared around the corner, Oscar suddenly leapt from the DS21, one huge ear to his phone, and hurried inside. Something might be about to happen. Ferdie could not risk going in search of Didi, so he looked back and forth willing the huge frame to come waddling round the corner before anyone emerged from the AWI building. Where had Didi gone and what for? And why was he taking so long?

Oscar came back with Vallette right behind him, phone at his ear—all business, on the move. Ferdie, blood pumping now, saw Didi rounding the corner licking an ice cream cone and holding another. Ferdie did not dare make any move to

alert him in case it was seen. The DS21 pulled out and took
off at full speed along the embankment. Ferdie edged his head
out the open window and spat out "Didi! Didi!" as loud as he
dared.

He moved surprisingly fast and barreled into the driver's
seat, the two ice creams now clutched in one fat hand. He
shoved them at Ferdie, who took them, not quite believing
that in the circumstances Didi had actually held on to them. In
seconds he had the BMW moving.

"Over the bridge!" Ferdie shouted. As soon as they turned,
he was relieved to see a distinctive silver roof four cars ahead.
Didi's face relaxed and he extended a paw in search of his ice
cream. Ferdie gave him the untouched one and dropped the
other out the window, discreetly so as not to give offense. If
Didi could do the job Ferdie required of him and enjoy an ice
cream at the same time, he wasn't going to complain. Anyway, his thoughts were focused on a more important matter:
what had happened to cause this very obviously high-alert
response?

By the time Didi had licked his last while expertly reduc-
ing the gap to just one car, Oscar was swinging north onto
rue du Louvre. But when he turned left at Étienne Marcel, the
car between them continued straight ahead, so now they were
dangerously exposed. If Oscar threw even a casual glance in
the rearview mirror, he would surely spot Ferdie. "Not too
close, Didi."

They needed a car to pull out from somewhere and come
between them. Instead the DS21 turned right into place des
Victoires and then took another sudden right. Ferdie was confused when Didi didn't follow, but continued around the mon-
ument and came full circle. He pulled up as they arrived back

to the narrow one-way street again. Now Ferdie could read the name: rue d'Aboukir.

"I think they'll stop somewhere on this street."

Apart from this being the longest sentence Didi had spoken in all the time they'd known each other, Ferdie was astonished at the certainty in his voice. Didi traced an imaginary map in the air with his finger.

"Louvre, Étienne Marcel, here." Then he nods to rue d'Aboukir. "And there."

Ferdie got it instantly. Left from rue du Louvre, then right to place des Victoires and right again to rue d'Aboukir just led back to rue du Louvre. Why go that way if not to access rue d'Aboukir, which was one-way? Once again Didi heaved himself out and waddled to the corner and peered around it. Then he looked back, shook his head, and disappeared up the street. This was really frustrating for Ferdie. So much so he was seriously tempted to get his crutches and drag himself out, but common sense prevailed. If he was seen, then it would all have been a waste of time.

Didi was back in less than a minute.

"Yeah, parked."

"So, they've gone into some building?"

Didi nodded at the obvious and started the engine. He turned onto rue d'Aboukir.

"You think it's safe?"

Didi shrugged. "They're not on the street."

He nodded ahead to the DS21, although Ferdie had already spotted it. He'd also noticed three other new black C6s parked close together. As it wasn't a day for coincidences, this could only be Vallette's team. Three cars meant there could be as many as ten men. Something very big was happening here. Didi drove on to the next available parking space and pulled in. The DS21 and the other cars were no more than thirty meters behind.

"Those three C6s? Vallette's team. They've gone into some building back there."

"So, we wait."

Didi adjusted the rearview so Ferdie could use it, but he realized that if Vallette or any of his boys were leaving they would have to drive past and he would certainly be seen and recognized. It was safer in the back, where he could lie down. Didi stood on the path, his huge frame giving excellent cover as Ferdie hopped quickly out one door and in the other. Resting the damaged foot on the seat he stared out the rear window. After a few minutes' silent watching, Ferdie noticed that, unlike earlier, he was now waiting quite patiently: heartbeat normal, no tension around the neck and shoulders. Perhaps Didi's insouciant approach was having its effect on him. Obviously he would prefer to pursue Vallette into every corner, be privy to whatever was going on, moment to moment, but that was too dangerous so there was no point in getting wound up about it. Whatever was going on right now might have nothing to do with Caramel Girl or the events of last night, but surely it was much more likely that it had. He was getting more confident that whenever Vallette and his boys in suits emerged from whichever building, Ferdie would discover something useful. Useful, that is, in the sense of accelerating Vallette's downfall.

Lana is cruising in fifth gear now, chatting quite confidently.

"I'm embarrassed to say this . . . I hadn't really heard of Fournier. Or perhaps I had, but hadn't paid any attention. When I discovered that he was a candidate for the French presidency and saw him on TV in a political debate, I was taken aback, to say the least—"

She sees Guillaume lean forward and raise a finger very dramatically, clearly demanding silence. He frowns, as if he's listening to something, so Lana listens too. Sure enough, there are tiny sounds coming from below, impossible to name: a creak, a scratch of something. Movement? Maybe it's Odette returning from the hospital. Guillaume sprints to the spiral staircase. Pauline follows. As they disappear out of sight, shouting begins. By the time Lana reaches the top of the stairs, a scuffle has begun on the lower level of the apartment. Guillaume and Pauline are attempting a hopeless fight against several masked men, all carrying short, thick, sticklike weapons. Some of them are already beginning to smash equipment. Lana is about to back out of sight when one of them glances up and sees her. There is nowhere for her to go.

First instinct: grab herself some kind of weapon, do damage to whoever is about to ascend the spiral. The camera and

tripod seem the most effective option. She could crack some
heads with that, but by the time her hand is on it, a head has
already appeared at the top of the stairs. It's too late to stop the
guy getting to the attic room. She might be able to hurt him,
but there will be no escape. Even before he pulls off his mask,
she recognizes the eyes staring directly at her. When his face is
revealed Vallette has the look of someone dangerously pleased
with himself.

"Madame Gibson. There you are."

The memory card. Lana realizes that one important thing
he doesn't yet know is whether she has recorded her testimony.
Without the memory card, he'll have no evidence one way
or the other. There will at best be one shot at this. She spins
around, placing herself between Vallette and the camera, pleading silently that for once something will go her way, that the
memory card will be as easy to remove as it had been to insert.
Grabbing the camera with both hands, she uses the fingers of
her left to pull at the memory card—it slides out noiselessly—
while lifting the camera and tripod with her right and swinging it with all the strength she can manage before letting it fly
at Vallette, who pulls back and ducks. The improvised missile
does no damage, but creates the necessary distraction. Lana is
pretty certain he didn't notice her extract the memory card and
it's safe inside her firmly cupped hand for the moment.

Vallette is savoring his moment.

"Thank you for leading us here so efficiently. And passing
on the code to your pursuer was especially generous."

Lana feels ill: Muscle-boy, the cap. The man on the platform at Pyramides when she got away from Nathan. Of course.
Vallette and Fournier—well, Vallette at least—had understood
her mood and personality perfectly and guessed that she would

not sit tight in Nathan's apartment until the time came to catch her flight. Someone had been left at place St.-André, watching. They'd been tracked all the way, first together, then her alone. And she'd led them to Guillaume, just as Vallette had hoped. Lana is so ashamed at how easily he had played her. No wonder he hadn't been too bothered when Fournier had said she could go free. Or had even that been part of the plan? Is Fournier the one at the controls? The possibility that the "behave yourself" insult might have been deliberately calculated to goad her is particularly infuriating.

"I knew that without your medication, Madame Gibson, you would not be able to sit still for very long. Your anger, your mania would take over."

He moves closer and grabs her wrist. At first Lana thinks he's figured out what she's hiding and is going to force her hand open. But instead he turns and drags her down the spiral stairs, the precious evidence no more than an inch from his harsh grip.

"There is no need for you to stay here."

Downstairs Pauline is nowhere to be seen, but screams and hammering come from the locked bathroom. Guillaume is on the couch, clearly unconscious. Vallette's men—Lana recognizes the shape of Muscle-boy among them—are gathering files and disks and laptops and smashing everything else. Vallette barks something in French and two of his lackeys run up the spiral staircase. Then he gestures to another, who follows as he pulls Lana toward the apartment door, which now has a neat circular hole where the lock had once been.

He jerks her into the elevator. Her feeling of panic isn't helped by how crowded the little cage feels with three of them pressing against each other. The other guy pulls off his balaclava. It's Big Ears. Vallette lets go of her wrist, but she can't risk trying to do anything with the memory card yet, because any movement of her fingers will be noticed in this tiny space. But she knows she'll have to think of some kind of hiding place soon.

The elevator hits the ground floor at last and, when the doors open, Big Ears prods something into her side. Lana considers the possibility that it's not really a gun, but she has no intention of testing that theory. Vallette walks behind as Big Ears marches her across the weirdly calm street. Lana swings her arm as naturally as possible so as not to draw attention to the tightly closed fist. Big Ears pushes her into the backseat and Vallette moves in beside her, but fortunately her body is between him and her now aching hand.

"I do not know if your actions are entirely the result of your mania, or a natural element of your character. It is the American disease to know best, no? Anyway, you think I tried to make a fool of you? Perhaps. But these friends of yours have made a bigger fool of you."

A silence follows, which Lana has no intention of breaking. The time for verbal sparring is long over. It is hard enough to think about what to do with the memory card. She can't keep her hand in this position indefinitely. At any moment either man might notice some little thing, and once suspicions are raised it'll be too late. Just to give her hand muscles a break, she wedges the card out of sight, into the angle of the leather seat behind her. Okay for now, and easy to get hold of again. She puts her hands together on her lap in full view, feeling the tiniest bit more relaxed. The car moves at high speed and in the diminishing light, Lana finds it difficult to track where they are going. It seems like it's away from the center of the city. She can't bring herself to look at Vallette, who's not doing anything but whose presence is somehow becoming more sinister by the minute. As the landscape shifts from the solid familiarity of Haussmann Paris to the more uncertain architecture of the outer suburbs, Lana's nerves tighten. Where are they taking her? Not back to Nathan's apartment, that's sure, nor to any rendezvous with Fournier. Could this be the route to the airport?

Now Big Ears swings the car onto a wide road that seems more like a highway than a city boulevard and Lana sees a streetcar approach and pass by. Is this some weird dream of Seattle? It no longer feels anything like Paris. The road takes them over a river that must still be the Seine. If so, they are back on the Left Bank again, but a long way from the reassuring contours of the St.-Michel fountain or the Musée d'Orsay or the Eiffel Tower. Lana can see no recognizable landmark in any direction, but now they seem to have turned again toward the city—could that be? In this situation Brian would figure out exactly where they were headed. "Westerly. Southwest." Definitely she is aware of—on her right—the close, murky presence of the river.

A couple of minutes later, Big Ears swings right and coasts down a boat ramp until, almost at the riverside, a barrier marked PASSAGE INTERDIT prevents them driving any farther.

Vallette grabs her so suddenly, pulling her with him as he opens his door, that she has no time to decide whether to retrieve the memory card. His force is such that she either has to go with it or let her shoulder be yanked from its socket. Without a word Vallette pulls her past the little gap at the tip of the barrier and down toward the river. Now Lana is genuinely, seriously scared. Big Ears has stayed in the car and is turning it around, presumably ready for a quick getaway. Vallette's silence and determined movement make her feel certain that something already planned and very, very bad is about to happen.

• • •

"JESUS CHRIST!"

It was quite a shock to see the blond American being escorted from one of the buildings by Vallette and Oscar. So this was where she escaped to last night. Who did she know there and how had Vallette tracked her down? He looked back to the door they had emerged from, expecting others to appear, then realized that the DS21 was already on the move and approaching. He stretched out on the backseat just in time to avoid being seen. Then he heard Didi start the engine.

"Better stay down."

For the next while he lay there seeing only chunks of gray sky streaked with what seemed like blood. It was darkening very quickly. He also had the benefit of Didi's laconic commentary on their progress.

"St.-Martin . . . Voltaire . . . Nation . . . Picpus . . . Daumesnil . . ."

It was more than enough information for Ferdie's chauffeur's brain. He could follow the route precisely and when he felt a sharp right and heard the singular sound of a tram bell he knew where they were before Didi said "Boul' Poniatowski." So. They were about to cross over to the Left Bank. But why so far out of town?"

"Bruneseau . . . Quai d'Ivry . . ."

And then a sudden slowdown and stop. Silence. Ferdie waited for some word from Didi. Finally.

"Okay. It's safe."

He struggled up and looked around. He couldn't see the

DS21 anywhere. Didi nodded to his right toward the low wall separating the road from the riverbank and pointed over Ferdie's shoulder. Ferdie looked back and saw a gap in the wall.

"They turned down there. Will I take a look?"

"Be careful."

Now he felt frustration again at not being able to move freely, watching Didi peer over the wall, wishing he could at least see what he saw, instead of having to wait for information. Eventually Didi looked back and made a face, which Ferdie could not interpret, other than that whatever was happening was no big deal. More waiting. Then:

"Fuck me!" This was followed by urgent hand-waving, which Ferdie understood to mean he should come and look. Given the circumstance, it would be easiest on all fours. He tipped himself headfirst from the car, then scampered like a two-year-old across the path to the low wall.

The wharf is entirely deserted and scarlet shards cracking through dusk clouds offer the only light. A dozen or so trucks line up as pinky gray shapes. An industrial escalator rolls down to the riverside at a steep angle from the top of a tall tower. Vallette drags an increasingly resistant Lana past enormous heaps of what look like different grades of sand. She guesses the place must be some kind of cement plant.

It's clear that this is no scare tactic, not some last-minute warning before chauffeuring her to the airport. Vallette intends to kill her and make it look like the suicide of an unfortunate, mentally damaged tourist.

His strength is surprising. Even as she starts kicking and wriggling and flailing, he remains in easy control.

They are at the water's edge. Lana had often casually observed how at particular times the Seine thrashes about very violently. This is one of those times. The water is about three feet below the bank but still splashes over it. Lana is a decent swimmer, but there is nowhere near to clamber out. It is more likely that the turbulence will drive her hard against the river wall.

Vallette isn't about to waste any time with goodbyes so she grasps at the only ammunition she has left and gibbers, "I recorded an interview about what I saw."

"That is exactly why we are here now, Madame Gibson. You cannot be trusted."

"I took the memory card from the camera. I have it."

She feels his grip tighten involuntarily, then relax again.

"I understand you will say anything in this situation. If you have this memory card with you, then I will find it and then—"

"I don't have it on me. I hid it."

"Really? Well, it's nothing for you to worry about now. We will find it."

"You won't. Not without my—"

"That will not be your problem. Believe me, Madame Gibson, I do not dislike you. But . . . circumstances . . ."

He pushes with precise, unstoppable aggression.

The water is as cold and black as Lana had feared. Her arms and legs flail. She tries to hold her breath but why is the surface so far away? Why can she not reach it? Then her mouth feels air again and she sucks it in. Her shriek seems to come from somewhere else. Stop thrashing, she tells herself over and over, it's not helping. But she can't stop. There's no one to cry out to; even Vallette is no longer to be seen. In the distance, streetlights have come on. Why can't she get hold of herself, exercise some control? She dips below and pulls herself up and again dips below and pulls herself up, her mouth full of filthy water. She gulps and coughs and can't breathe. It's now almost as dark above as below. Lana is cold and shriveling, getting tinier, sinking down with only a forearm, a hand waving above water. Soon, sooner than she'd feared, Lana will no longer have it in her to haul her face back to the twilight air.

. . .

"YOUR GUY HAS DROWNED HER."

"What?"

Ferdie raised his eyes above the wall. Didi gave him the binoculars, but it was so murky dark that they weren't much help. He couldn't see Oscar or the American woman, but he recognized Vallette's shape and gait as he walked away from the river's edge.

"He just heaved her in."

"Does she have any chance of . . ."

Didi dismissed that with a snort just as through the binoculars Oscar came into Ferdie's view, moving quickly, waving his phone. Vallette snatched it. Then a few seconds later he waved a hand and snapped something at Oscar, who started running toward the river, kicking off his shoes and pulling at his clothes. Vallette followed him more casually, still talking on the phone. Oscar dived in. Ferdie shivered instinctively. It had to be very cold in there.

"Your laptop? Will I?"

At first Ferdie wasn't on Didi's wavelength. The drama down at the river had all his attention.

"There's no one near the car." The tone was demanding. Didi gestured for an immediate answer. "Now's the time."

Ferdie connected the dots and remembered his laptop hidden under the driver's seat.

"Yeah, sure, okay."

Didi stood up and, like a ball, bounced downhill gathering speed. Ferdie looked through the binoculars to check that Vallette's attention was still entirely focused on the river, then raised his head enough to peer down and watch Didi creep toward the car. He opened the back door and went in headfirst, and a few moments later his huge body began to wriggle out. When he emerged fully, he turned to show Ferdie the laptop clutched in his mighty paw. Ferdie wiggled the binoculars in acknowledgment, then raised them to see what was happening by the river. Vallette was kneeling by the female body splayed on the ground, but Oscar was no longer visible. Ferdie panned the binoculars quickly and found him, half-naked, holding his wet clothes in a bunch tight to his chest, *trotting back toward the car.*

Surely he would spot Didi now. Ferdie looked down and saw him on his knees crawling quickly inside, easing the back door shut behind him. Oscar came closer and closer. Ferdie imagined poor Didi, squeezed low between the front and back seats: a whale in a dinghy. Hopefully, in the poor light Oscar might not notice him as he passed. But what then? As it happened Oscar didn't pass at all. Instead he stopped at the trunk, threw it open, and pulled out some kind of rug or towel and started to dry himself off.

Ferdie remembered how exposed he was. In order to see the car below, his entire head had to be above the wall. If Oscar or Vallette glanced up in this direction . . . He dropped down quickly. What now? Again he cursed the injury that rendered him incapable of even providing a diversion. He listened intently and after some time heard what could only be the trunk slamming shut. Now Oscar would either get into the car—which would be bad luck for Didi—or return to Vallette. Ferdie waited, then just as he was about to cautiously ease himself up, a hand gripped his shoulder and pulled him around.

"Let's go," said Didi. He waddled round the BMW and got in. Ferdie scampered on hands and knees and hoisted himself into the passenger seat. Didi handed him the laptop, which he just tossed into the back, the last thing on his mind at the moment.

"When I saw Oscar coming back to the car and opening the trunk, I couldn't watch anymore. I was afraid he'd look up and see me. What happened?"

"Nothing, I couldn't see him."

"I think he was drying himself and putting his clothes on."

Didi shrugged. "Anyway—"

"He pulled the woman out of the water, but I don't know if she's still alive or not."

"—look what I found."

Didi held up a black plastic rectangle about the size of a credit card.

"It was hidden."

"Hidden?"

"Pushed into the angle of the backseat."

"The American woman?"

Didi shrugs. "I'd say."

Ferdic stared at the card and thought of the woman's delicate hand, sliding ever so slowly, secretly, to hide it, get rid of it. It must be a very dangerous piece of plastic.

• · •

HER EYES OPEN TO A BLACK SWIRL. HAD SHE LOST CONSCIOUSNESS? HER chest is exploding. For some reason she cannot move her arms and legs. A powerful arm is around her waist, but she does not know whose it is and she has no memory of when it took hold of her. The shock of cold air forces her mouth open and makes her chest heave. She coughs and spews foul-tasting fluid until her tongue and gums and the roof of her mouth feel like a recently emptied trash can. She still doesn't have the strength to turn and see whose body is pressing against her, but the cold, wet skin is hairy and there's power in the naked arm holding her, so that even though she resists spasmodically there's little chance of escaping her rough savior. Eventually, choking, she lets herself be a rag doll in a dog's mouth.

Then, suddenly, they are at the river wall, too far down to clamber back on land. A thin rope drops into view. A hairy hand presses her hand to it. A low voice says, "Hold on," and tries to close her hand around the rope, but when it's pulled, Lana feels it rip through her palm and she lets go and hears French gasps and mutters. Lana spews again. The French voice hisses urgently. "Hold with both hands. Hold for your life with two hands." This time she grips hard and feels the rope tug her upward. Below her, two hands on her ass whoosh her toward the riverbank. She's aware enough by now to press her feet against the wall to help lift herself. Knees and arms scratch against the concrete as she's dragged over the side onto safe ground. Lana lies facedown, coughing and heaving, but exultant too. By some providence she is still alive. Then she sees shoes, the most beautiful tan shoes. Shamefully scuffed. Who would wear Berluttis in a place like this? She feels a hand grab her hair and yank her face up.

"Where is the memory card?"

The waft of Vallette's sophisticated cologne is at odds with his venomous expression, dangerous growl, and brutal grip.

"Madame Gibson, can you hear me?"

Now she sees a figure, naked except for boxer shorts, shivering, running past them toward the car. The other guy. Big Ears. Had he saved her?

"It seems you have been clever, so we have brought you back from the dead. Do you want to stay safe or not?"

Vallette doesn't seem to get it that she can barely make a sound. Her teeth start to clack-clack-clack. A moan comes from somewhere deep inside her.

"What did you do with the memory card?"

Now Lana is afraid again. She wishes Big Ears would come back to protect her. Is Vallette going to throw her in again? For now he just jerks her head back.

"We will find it anyway. They are searching the attic room. It is only a matter of time. But if you save us even a little trouble, Madame Gibson, you can save yourself."

Even with her brain churning and bewildered, Lana knows the expiration date on that offer has long passed. She's too close to the water and too weak for Vallette to resist rolling her back in once she's given him the information. Especially when the truth would only take him seconds to confirm. Some tiny part of her can still find comedy in the fact that they're tearing an apartment apart up on rue d'Aboukir for a prize that's only a few yards away. When she coughs up more—only a dribble this time—Vallette lets go of her hair and steps back. She hears him mutter something and then feels that hairy grip again. Big Ears has returned and once more she's a rag doll in his hands. Away from the river, so that's good. Back to the car, please. Leather seats so soft and warm, they might even give her something to—Lana is dropped rather than thrown, but that doesn't make the grit and cold any less uncomfortable. It only takes a second or two for her hands and cheek to recognize the damp, soft, but rough texture: sand. He had dumped her into one of the sandpits. Now she's getting a forced facial scrub, accompanied by Vallette's voice, calm again, all outward anger gone. The real terror of it, returned.

"I cannot believe that you want to die, but you are about to."

Whatever the calm in Vallette's voice, there's rage in the

pressure on the back of her neck that holds her face helpless in the grit.

"Oscar, attrape-elle."

There is a switch of hands. Oscar's hold is a little more relaxed. Lana can hear Vallette speak quietly and rapidly. On the phone presumably, checking. Her only chance now is to keep this story alive and kicking. As long as they don't have the memory card, surely Vallette won't dare kill her. And they can't hang around here forever, right?

He finishes the call and barks something at Oscar, whose hand now roves up her body from feet to ass, between her legs and up her back. Then he flips her around and she watches Vallette do the same search on her front with unembarrassed efficiency. Only because she knows how lucky it was that she'd been unable to grab the memory card when Vallette had pulled her from the car does she manage to restrain herself from biting his hand as it passes from her breasts up to her hair.

"So, you do not have it, and every inch of the attic space is being searched. It won't be very long now."

"What about outside the apartment, or in the elevator? Or the courtyard? Maybe I dropped it there somewhere as we left."

The sand clings to her and she is chilled now, but the giddy pleasure of baiting Vallette almost makes up for the misery. He struts toward the car waving at them to follow. Little by little, she thinks, she's working her way back to some kind of safety.

It's a setback that Vallette sits in the back of the car on the side she had occupied, at exactly the spot where the memory card is: no chance of Lana recovering it right now. Oscar throws her a thick woolen blanket from the trunk and steers her to the front passenger seat, before settling in behind the wheel. But he doesn't start the engine. Instead they sit in silence for what seems like ten or fifteen minutes. She rubs her head dry with the blanket and tries to keep the rest of herself warm and considers how she might recover the memory card. There's certainly no chance with this seating arrangement and they won't leave her alone in the car. Without the card her strategy is little more than dangerous bluff on a tight deadline. Just now, damp and shivering and dirty, Lana actually finds it hard to care much. Behind her the clicking of fingernails begins, grating in the silence.

The way Vallette snaps at his cell when it rings suggests anxiety, which is good. As he talks, he pushes the door open and raises himself from his seat. Lana can guess what he's being told. The attic room has been taken apart, but no memory card has been found. He sits back, his hard ass right where the precious card is hidden, and spits into the phone. Then he ends the call, leans forward, and grabs Lana by the throat.

"Where is it?"

Lana's only reply is to match the flaming intensity in his eyes. Oscar puts a hand on his boss's elbow and the warning touch seems to bring him to his senses. But the bottle has been shaken, the cork popped, and real psychotic rage has spurted out.

Despite her fear that Vallette might yet be pushed too far, Lana's secret knowledge gives her the courage, or the foolhardiness to say, "And I'm supposed to be the one who's manic."

Now Vallette's demeanor shifts unexpectedly to weary admiration.

"All right, Madame Gibson. I give you the victory. Tell me where the memory card is and as soon as it is in our possession, you can go free."

"You really expect me to believe that?"

"You have no choice."

"Well, yes. Actually I have. We both know that. First things first. Take me away from here. I want to be somewhere I feel safer. Then we'll see."

She can feel his laser look at the back of her head for the longest time, as if in a silently deranged attempt to break her, impose his will. Then he seems to give up because Oscar reacts to a signal in the rearview mirror and drives back out onto the road. Despite her own exhaustion and fear, Lana can appreciate how wearying this must be for Vallette: right now, more than anything he'd love to swat this fly, but the more calculating part of him accepts that this is not a good option. Does his particular illness have a name? Maybe it's been diagnosed and he's taking something for it. She should handle things more delicately so as not to push him over the edge. But delicacy had never been Lana's thing and certainly isn't in her present mood. The meds would actually be very welcome now. It's going to be so challenging to keep her insolent tongue under control. If only she could channel some of Brian's caution. Right now it goes against her every instinct, but it's the sensible strategy.

To her intense relief it's clear that they're heading back toward the center of Paris. Traffic becomes heavier, and the cityscape ahead begins to assume a recognizable shape. The Île St.-Louis appears and, beyond it, the first sighting of Notre Dame. Even the bridges start to look familiar and soon they pass in quick succession, Petit Pont, Pont St.-Michel, and Pont Neuf, where, less than twenty hours ago, she had crossed to the Left Bank in search of Nathan and, instead of finding refuge and solace, had accelerated her free fall into peril. Yet her rage at his betrayal had calmed. Why? Because it wasn't real betrayal, more like the law of unintended consequences delivering a more than usually aggressive body blow. Of course, it's also because her conscience likes the idea of some punishment to atone for what she'd done to Nathan long ago. After today, they must be about even.

At Pont Alexandre, Oscar swings right and crosses the river once more. Lana guesses they are traveling north. Moving at speed now in dark dusk, she can't even read street names.

Finally, they pull up outside a row of rather beautifully maintained Haussmann buildings, and Oscar gets out, goes to a door, and speaks into an intercom. Then he pushes the door and holds it open. Vallette steps out, opens the front passenger door, clamps a hand on Lana's arm, and whips her very speedily into the building. Once they are inside, Oscar pulls the door shut. He remains outside with the car. And the memory card.

Vallette marches her silently up a curving stairway and guides her into a dark room. He flicks on the hard, sudden light to reveal an opulent bathroom.

"You will want to clean yourself."

He pulls the door after him. Lana hears a key being turned and doesn't even bother to confirm that she's been locked in. There is no tub, just a spacious enclosed shower. The only window has a frosted glass pane and is too small to climb through. She opens it all the same and sees a steep drop to a little garden with high walls. In the mirror Lana catches sight of her sand-spattered face and wild graveled hair. Perhaps it's the physical discomfort and general wretchedness of her situation, but she feels no vulnerability, no danger at all as she peels off her damp, stinking clothes. The shower is instantly hot and powerful, as is the pleasure. The grime of violation, a trickle of death stream down her body into the drain, down to the Parisian sewers.

She wishes Brian would come to her now, slipping in silently as he used to do, suddenly caressing her with soapy hands, fingers massaging her scalp. It's such a long time since he'd last molded his body against hers all the way from foot to calf, to thigh, his penis tickling, his heart thumping against her shoulder blades, his mouth breathing warm air on her neck, his tongue searching for her lobe; long before Dublin, way too long ago. Not his doing, he had merely picked up the signal that such passionate intrusions weren't welcome anymore. How Lana would welcome him now. She has so very little fight left, probably not enough at this point to attempt escape and get to the airport to board that plane. Her most comforting image comes from some old airline commercial: a slo-mo shot of a gorgeous but anxious boyfriend in the arrivals lounge, running to greet his fabulous girlfriend as soon as she appears. The delirious embrace, the ecstatic expressions on those perfect cheekbones. In Lana's mind the faces now become hers and Brian's. But another part of her cannot envisage such a scene ever happening. She no longer holds the ace card in her hand and sooner or later will be found out.

Stepping out of the shower, she discovers that, creepily, her clothes have been removed and a fluffy bathrobe has been placed on a stool. Who had entered while she showered? Vallette or some underling? She hadn't heard a thing. She wraps the robe tightly around herself. The door is still locked. She dries herself, then sits on the stool. After a few more minutes there's a tap on the door.

"Madame Gibson, are you ready?"

"I have no clothes."

"They are being cleaned. There is a robe."

"Yes, I'm wearing it."

"Then may I come in?"

"No. I want my clothes."

"It will be perhaps thirty minutes."

"I'll wait."

"I have a room for you. It will be much more comfortable to wait there."

"No, thank you."

Then she thinks, what's this game? He can open the door if he feels like it.

"But I can't stop you coming in, can I?"

"I would not do that."

Vallette actually sounds offended, which is a real hoot. He can drop her in the Seine without a twinge of guilt, but God forbid he'd enter a *salle des bains* without a lady's express permission. After a sufficient silence, Lana guesses that he has left soundlessly. She tries the door again. Locked. Now she regrets refusing him. She's stuck here until her laundry is done.

It feels like a very long half hour before there's another tap on the door and the click of a lock. Once again Vallette had approached without a sound.

"Your clothes are here."

Lana opens the door very cautiously. There is no one in the corridor. How does he do that, disappear without a rustle or creak? Her clothes, fresh as new, are neatly folded in a basket on the floor. Once dressed she leaves the bathroom and finds the stairway. Even though she tiptoes downstairs, as soon as she reaches the bottom step a door on her right opens.

"Come in."

Vallette is not alone. A young man wearing glasses with semi-rimless frames is sitting surrounded by at least five screens, a console, a keyboard, a sound desk, and several laptops. He smiles. A harmless, nerdy guy. Vallette's voice assumes its Inspector Fichet tone: polite, crisp, formal. Is this a performance for the young man?

"Sit down, Madame Gibson. You will remember that Monsieur Fournier and I explained to you that the people who you thought were your friends, were probably working for someone who is determined to prevent Monsieur Fournier's election. Since we finally identified Guillaume Pelletier and Pauline Garrel a couple of hours ago, we have been searching for information about them that might explain who they are and who's behind their company. He told you that he was a poor independent filmmaker trying to make an important documentary, yes?" Lana nods. "Alexandre, show Madame Gibson what you have found. YouTube, Madame Gibson. So full of dangerous nonsense, but occasionally an invaluable tool of democracy."

Young Alexandre brings up the YouTube home page on the screen. He speedily keys in some words, a little screen appears, and he clicks "play" before rolling back his chair as if to say "my work here is done."

The YouTube video is some kind of television report about Fournier's opponent, Dufour. There are shots of him looking impressive in a variety of situations; at official occasions, in the Chamber of Deputies, out with the public, campaigning. Lana has no idea what she's supposed to be looking for until a shot appears whose sickening significance she fully appreciates.

Dufour in a T-shirt, shorts, and running shoes, looking tanned and fit, is jogging in a park. Also in the shot, a cameraman, trotting backward, holds his camera at a low angle. The amusing porkpie hat at a cheeky angle, the body shape hunched over the camera leaves little room for doubt. It is Guillaume.

The voice-over is easy enough to understand. "Une image énergétique, vigoureuse. Mais quelquefois—"

Right on cue Guillaume loses his footing and tumbles backward. Dufour immediately stops running and holds out his hand to help him up. As he stands, Lana sees the familiar clown face quite clearly, but it's what Dufour does next that settles any residual doubt about their relationship. He claps him on the back and then waits for the cameraman to position himself to shoot again. Guillaume is clearly part of Team Dufour.

"You see? The interview you made with Monsieur Pelletier is not for some crusading filmmaker, but for Dufour's campaign to broadcast it on every possible social media outlet. Within hours millions will have seen it. You will be a sensation, Madame Gibson. Do you like that idea?"

Guillaume had lied to her. Pauline and Odette had unquestionably been part of the deception. Nathan had guessed correctly. More sickeningly, Fournier and Vallette had been right. In a life full of missteps and dumb moves, Lana has never felt such a fool.

Lana wonders whose home she's in. If it is Vallette's, did he hire an interior designer, or is he simply revealing his feminine side in the choice of warm pastels and natural fabrics for the room they now sit in? Is he married? She finds it hard to imagine him as part of a family. They face each other across a marble-topped sixties coffee table and listening to him talk it would never have occurred to a casual eavesdropper that he is the cold, killing one. Rather, he appears to be the sensible but sensitive type, on a mission to put this poor befuddled woman back on the right track.

"Of course it may be of no concern to you that you are helping our opponent so directly. But I also suspect you have no desire to see yourself on thousands of Internet sites, many of dubious reputation. So do you understand now how important it is that you help us find this memory card?"

Lana gives him a 9.9 for chutzpah. His manner implies she's either dumb or dangerous and under such circumstances his behavior is admirably patient and restrained. And the awful truth is, there's no use pretending she's not totally thrown by this recent evidence of Guillaume's affiliations. It's no bombshell that he's a rogue, but she had thought him a different kind of rogue, someone of her own spirit, if truth be told, an independent mind.

Instead he turns out to be just another follower, a mercenary, a paid deceiver. At least the crazy sitting in front of her has actual convictions.

"Is there still time for me to catch the flight to Dublin?"

He nods toward a freestanding clock. She hadn't heard it until now. Suddenly it's beating out time passing, time lost: tick, tick, tick: twenty after seven: tick, tick, tick.

"The flight is at ten minus ten? Yes. Let us say it is possible. But not likely. There is something you must know clearly, Madame Gibson, absolutely. I may be willing to come to an arrangement with you, but believe me also, if you continue to frustrate matters I will be very pleased to take you out again and finish our business."

Lana has no doubt he means it; relishes it, probably. The simplest thing would be to give up now, tell him where the memory card is hidden, trust that honesty would be rewarded and Vallette would take her to the airport and put her on the last flight. But the realization that even if such a solution was somehow guaranteed, it still would not satisfy her, arrives clear and fresh as her newly laundered clothes. Guillaume had lied, yes, but he hadn't tried to kill her, hadn't put Claude into intensive care, hadn't had Odette tied up and beaten. Then it dawns on her that she has only been told about these things. Guillaume had appeared in the apartment with Odette in his arms and her face was in shadow as she'd huddled on the bed. And she had absolutely no evidence beyond Guillaume's word that Claude really was badly hurt. If what she saw is even open to interpretation, then surely she must at least question what she had not?

No, no. She can't deal with Vallette under any circumstances, even if it makes her situation hopeless. But what can be done without him?

And in the uneasy silence, the way it does sometimes, an idea glimmers. Totally wild, of course, but better than sitting silently opposite a face she can't bear to look at anymore. It needs an accomplice for it to work and already she knows that there is no possible candidate except Nathan. Despite everything, he's still the only other person who might be on her side, although making him look foolish in the metro won't have helped. But surely he has no doubt now about the real danger she's facing? There is only one way to find out.

"I will not travel anywhere alone with you—"

Lana doesn't let his smirk deter her. She goes for it.

"At least, not willingly. And believe me, I will never give the location of the memory card to you. I will not deal with you anymore."

"But you *are* dealing with me, Madame Gibson, no?"

"I want Nathan Maunier to accompany us to the airport."

Vallette cannot keep the mockery from his eyes. Clearly he doesn't think highly of Nathan.

"Why?"

"For my protection. And I will give the information you need to one person only. Fournier."

"Really?"

"Yes. If you want the material, that is how it must be. Now I have no more to say to you."

His quiet words are preceded by the tiniest sigh.

"Where is the memory card, Madame?"

The effect of the blank eyes freezes her blood, yet somehow Lana's nerve holds during the long silence that follows, though her brain is a pinball machine. All or nothing. She has to believe Vallette is just amusing himself, daring her to push it. Nathan matters zilch to him and he can have no suspicion about what she has in mind or how significant Nathan's role might be. Now the clock ticks in an aggressive duet with Vallette's fingernails. He stands.

"Do you know how much I want to kill you?"

Lana manages a shrug.

"I will wait just a little longer, Madame, for you to decide to be sensible. But only a little."

He walks out. Once again she hears a key turn. What now? Surely, by walking away, leaving her alone like this, Vallette has only exposed the weakness of his situation. Of course! she thinks. Ha! He hasn't brought Fournier up to speed about the interview she'd recorded. He desperately needs to get hold of the memory card first. What was that maxim of Brian's? CEOs don't want to hear about problems, they want to hear about problems solved. Until Vallette solves this one, he won't dare touch her. So he's outside hoping she'll panic and give in. The only question is time, that clock ticking away. How long will it take for all this to play out? Is Vallette happy to let her go once he gets what he wants or will he think it safer to kill her anyway? Seven thirty. Lana really, really wants to catch that flight, but patience is her only hope.

At seven forty-eight the door opens. Vallette drags in her wheelie duffel, drops it next to her, and walks out. When Lana opens it she finds a credit card, purse, money, even the Hopper catalog, but no passport. Or ticket. Or phone. What now? Five minutes pass. The door opens again. Lana can't disguise her shocked relief when Nathan steps in.

"Oh my God . . . Thanks for coming."

"No problem. Bit taken aback. Just to clarify—no recriminations or anything—our unfortunate separation at the metro wasn't entirely an accident, was it?"

"No. Sorry."

"Smartly done. Where did you go?"

"Hasn't Vallette told you?"

"Yes, but can I believe him? I'm not sure I want to."

"If he told you that I went back to Guillaume's apartment, the filmmaker guy, and I recorded an interview about Fournier, then yes, you can believe him."

Nathan sighs and shakes his head. "Vallette says he has proof that this fellow and his friends work for Dufour?"

Lana nods. "I guess you told me so."

"Well, yes, but . . . wasn't it obvious? So anyway, why do you want me?"

Pause. She can tell he really wants to know. Words will matter now.

"Well . . . I think I'm going to need someone with me if I'm to have any chance of getting home safely. Someone on my side. You're the only one I can trust . . . I do trust you."

From the wide, wet surprise in his eyes, it seems this time she's managed to say just the right thing.

"All right. Okay, Lana Turner. So what's happening exactly?"

"I retrieved the only copy of the interview. So Guillaume doesn't have it. It's on a memory card. If I give it back Vallette says I can fly out tonight."

"Isn't that much the same deal as earlier?"

"I didn't believe that deal. And I was right. Vallette had someone watching your apartment. But now I have leverage."

"Fair enough."

"But I won't travel anywhere alone with Vallette."

"Why? Do you think he'll pop you?"

"Well, he threw me in the Seine."

"What!"

"Yes. An hour and a half ago."

"Are you—? Why?"

"To make his problem go away, I suppose."

"But . . . I mean . . . your clothes."

Lana realizes how fresh and clean they look. How crazy the explanation would sound. "Then he pulled me out of the water, drove me back to his place in that beautiful old Citroën, and did my laundry while I had a shower." It can't be about explanations anymore. She meets his gaze unblinking as she asks, "Do you believe me?"

It's obvious that Nathan hates being pushed into a corner like this. It's a struggle.

But he nods.

"Tell me what you need me to do."

• • •

OF COURSE DIDI HAD KNOWN SOMEONE WHO COULD DO WHAT WAS required and wasted few words sorting it out. Ten minutes after a twenty-second phone call a cheerful little 106 two-door pulled up.

Didi kept the formalities to a minimum "Guy, Ferdie." Ferdie shuffled himself and his crutches out of one car into another, babbling out instructions.

"Call if anything happens, okay? Anything. Any movement or—"

Didi smirked as he nodded and Ferdie felt so stupid for treating him as if he couldn't handle things. Without Didi today he'd be nowhere, lounging in bed, sorry for himself, future bleak to desolate.

Guy was as huge as Didi, but with added beard. Were they

part of some club? As they drove to his apartment, he showed him the black card and asked what it was. With no more than a glance Guy suggested it was a memory card for a digital camera, probably an Arriflex and, sure, he could access what was on it.

"What's the bitch saying?" Guy asked after they had watched the amazing interview enough times for Ferdie to understand most of it. Enough to appreciate why Vallette was on the rampage. Caramel Girl had not been a problem once her camera was retrieved, so there was no photographic proof of anything. But the blonde was a significant witness: a rich American whose evidence would be listened to. This recording could really fuck up Monsieur Fournier's election prospects. How had Vallette found out that she'd recorded this? It had to be what the rue d'Aboukir raid was all about. No wonder he was in a mood to drown her. It dawned on Ferdie that he was now in possession of the only reason Vallette hadn't let her die.

Who was this woman called Lana? After watching the interview so many times, Ferdie noticed himself feeling less snarky about the pain and suffering she had caused him with her vicious heel. He liked her face; her voice didn't grate on him as much as American voices often did. He admired her style, something audacious and playful in her eyes: exciting. Most significant, he believed her version of what happened. The way she told it made sense to him. Her involvement was random. She wasn't part of some mad conspiracy, even though there really was a mad conspiracy, one that had used him and maybe now was using her. It occurred to him that her situation was a bit like his: backed into a corner, she was ducking and diving, doing whatever it took to look out for herself. He was also aware that, thanks to this admirably reckless woman, he was now in possession of something very valuable. In the war with Vallette, advantage had suddenly tilted his way. Monsieur Fournier would have to be very grateful if Ferdie presented him with the memory card, while Vallette's failure to retrieve it would make him look very bad. How far could Ferdie go? He wanted Monsieur Fournier to free himself from Vallette. Was this material toxic enough to allow him to make it a condition? What a sweet victory that would be. Was he being naïve? Once he handed over the memory card he would have to trust Monsieur Fournier, the man who last night had thanked him for delivering him an adorable piece of ass and then said good night like he didn't expect to see poor Ferdie ever again.

He dialed Monsieur Fournier's private number. No answer. Voicemail. The familiar mellow tone, brief, but unhurried.

"Fournier. Leave your name, number, and your message."

Ferdie hung up just as his phone rang. Didi.

"The guy with the ears, he's just arrived with some other guy."

"Yeah, listen, not to worry. Change of plan. Come and pick me up."

A grunt indicated no further explanation was needed for the moment. He hung up and smiled at Guy.

"Thanks so much for this. Didi's coming to get me. Do you mind if I watch one more time while we wait for him?"

"I've got no problem looking at her again. Great lips. Is she on TV in America?"

"No, she's . . . she's an acquaintance. Oh, and while you're playing it back, maybe you can do me a last favor."

M onsieur Fournier has agreed to meet us at the airport."
Vallette's voice is deliberately emotionless. He leads
them to the front door. Lana's high had been climbing higher
for the last fifteen minutes. Now she almost feels sorry for Vallette. Nearly almost sorry. He has absolutely no idea what she
intends to do at the airport, how much trouble she's going to
make for him. And the nut job is facilitating it.

But parked outside is a brand-new black sedan, not the old
Citroën. And it's not Oscar holding the door open, but Muscle-
boy. They are going to Charles de Gaulle in a different car.
This scenario had simply never occurred to Lana. There is no
hope of retrieving the memory card. She freezes.

"Madame Gibson?"

What can she say without arousing suspicion? She hears
only desperation in what she wants to be a breezy tone.

"Hey, where's that gorgeous old car? If I'm leaving town I'd
like to go in style."

Vallette just stares. Nathan looks puzzled.

"Humor me. I used to see those cars in movies and dreamed
that someday I'd be driven around Paris in one."

She is conscious of babbling now: of danger. She can see
Nathan's expression change and knows he may be on the edge

of understanding. So she grins and sinks into the sedan. Vallette slides in after on one side, and Nathan goes to the other side. Lana manages to throw him a look that can in no way convey the turmoil inside her. She is so high and so low. The great plan is a bust. Whatever happens now, there will be no revenge on Vallette. They travel in dismal silence and somewhere along the way she notices, like it's taunting her, the little clicking sounds. Vallette, picking at his nails again, but with even more obvious agitation than before. What's going on? She catches the driver's eyes fixed on her in the rearview. He looks like he'd like to kill her too. Then the worst possible fear: had they found the memory card? Oh Jesus! Had Fournier even been contacted? Where are they really going? Surely Vallette isn't thinking of murdering both her *and* Nathan? At that moment she feels Nathan's questioning hand press against her thigh, but doesn't dare even glance his way. On the other side the clicking of Vallette's fingernails is getting unbearable and straight ahead the driver's eyes regard her with what looks to Lana like a kind of triumph. She has to stop herself from snapping, "Shouldn't you be looking at the road?"

Oh, to be safe on a plane. They're almost at the airport. If she's wrong and the memory card hasn't been found then she still has some collateral. Being able to reveal where it is might be just enough to get her on that flight out of Paris tonight. Right now she'd take that deal in a second. The car pulls up at Terminal One. The driver opens the back door. She steps out, looking straight into his eyes, and gets only the look of the blind in return. Vallette comes around and gestures rudely for them to follow.

The smoking terrace of Le Grand Comptoir is in the open-air central core of the circular building. High up, between them

and the night sky, is that famous seventies design flourish, the
intersecting tubular passenger walkways angled in the air, link-
ing opposite ends of the great circle, landside and airside. The
walkway home is hovering directly above, mocking her.

* * *

THE DS21 WAS PARKED OUTSIDE MONSIEUR FOURNIER'S BUILDING. FERDIE
felt yet another pang of resentment. *His* car. He should be the
one waiting at the wheel to ferry his boss wherever. Instead,
its presence probably meant that Vallette was inside. The
waiting driver was in shadow but the head had Oscar's shape.
As Ferdie pondered the next move, the front door opened and
Monsieur Fournier appeared, alone. The chauffeur leapt out
to open the rear door for him. Oscar, all right. Didi looked at
Ferdie. He nodded. Of course they had to follow. The old car
was really moving this time, but Didi made the pursuit seem
easy.

After fifteen minutes he said, "Charles de Gaulle?"

They were certainly going in that direction, but why? Very
soon after a swing right off the highway confirmed it. Ferdie
had to think fast. There was no way he could hop around the
airport in pursuit.

"When Monsieur Fournier gets out, will you follow him?
You can text me what's going on."

Three minutes later the DS21 pulled up and parked in
a corner outside Terminal One, illegally, Ferdie was pretty
sure. Didi quickly found a spot nearby and hauled himself out.
Monsieur Fournier and Oscar were already marching toward
door twelve, departures. Watching Didi catch up, Ferdie felt
frustrated, but if today had taught him anything, it was that
patience would be rewarded.

• • •

to have any meaningful communication with Nathan. She can
feel his eyes, searching, pleading for a sign. There's still no sign
of Fournier. At a nod from Vallette, Muscle-boy leaves without
a glance in her direction. Lana tries a wide smile with a confident tone in her voice. "Is our friend doing the coffee run?"

"No."

"How about you get us some?"

"No."

"I like that. Not even the pretense of politeness. Good for
you, Monsieur Vallette."

Her voice sounds so convincingly chipper that poor Nathan
probably thinks she has an awesome plan B. She tries to warn
him with a look. It occurs to her there is one piece of information worth gathering.

"I'm still disappointed about that beautiful old Citroën,
but I think I know why we didn't get to ride in it. Monsieur
Fournier wanted it, right? He says jump and you all say how
high? The king commanded, was that it?"

The way in which Vallette ignores her pleases Lana; it's a
kind of confirmation. At least if the old car is here at the airport
then the memory card is here too. Nathan's hand reaches into
his pocket and brings out two plastic containers. "Oh, I forgot.
You left these at the flat."

As he hands them over, his eyes are nervously questioning.

"Oh my God, thank you. Way overdue, actually. Monsieur
Vallette would agree, right? No chance of you getting me some
water, I suppose, Badoit for preference?"

Again Vallette ignores her. He's not going anywhere.

Then the glass sliding doors open. Fournier, with Oscar by his side. Lana sees only one pair of heads turn to acknowledge the star politician. Maybe it's mostly tourists in the smoking area or Parisians are just too cool to notice. As Vallette moves to greet him, Lana speaks quickly and quietly to Nathan.

"Sorry. It's not good. The memory card is in a different car."

She has no opportunity to watch the blood drain from his face. Fournier arrives and sits. Nods curtly. Probably displeased with my *behavior*, Lana thinks.

"So, Madame Gibson. You summoned me. Was that necessary to complete this business?" The hand wave suggests it's a trivial matter. He nods to Nathan. "Was he necessary?"

"Oh yes, he is vital to this conversation. But these gentlemen are not."

She nods pointedly toward Vallette and the others, relieved that she's able to project so much more confidence than she feels inside. Fournier seems puzzled.

"I beg your pardon?"

"Send them away, please. Oh, and would you ask Monsieur Vallette to get me some water. I have to take my medication."

"Take care, Madame Gibson. Do not exhaust my patience."

He speaks quietly to Vallette, who clearly wants to refuse but then growls an instruction to Oscar instead. Fournier turns back to Lana, his tone chillier than the wind now swirling around Terminal One's inner core.

"Do not think this situation allows you to start issuing commands."

Oh, Fournier, you just can't hide the old patronizing contempt, can you? Lana thinks, more determined now to prolong his suffering, just a little longer.

"But you are here on my command, if that's the word you want to use. Send your lackeys away, please."

"Madame Gibson—"

"Just out of earshot."

Fournier, trying to look like a patient man who simply doesn't want to waste any more time and so humors the capricious female, sighs and nods to Vallette. He opens his mouth to protest, but then, taking note of Fournier's stare, changes his mind and nods. He and Muscle-boy sit several tables away. Vallette stares into the night, the nail-picking quite savage now, but Muscle-boy's eyes are fixed on her as if he's participating in a staring competition.

"Well?"

Lana, allowing herself a moment to consider her choice of words, looks upward. Light spills from the Plexiglas top half of the passenger tubes hanging in the air. In one of them she's surprised to see a long line of disembodied traveler heads rolling along on what could be a macabre sushi conveyor belt and she imagines her own head rolling along up there with them. If only.

"First of all, let me assure you that I believe you know nothing about Vallette's attempt to murder me this evening."

Her hope that such shocking words would produce some involuntary reaction from Fournier is misplaced. Not a flicker. He waits with interest for her to continue.

"Nathan has pleaded your innocence in that regard. Anyway I cannot imagine how you'd be stupid enough to sanction or allow such a thing: it would be a dangerous mistake even to close your eyes to such a crime or attempt to place yourself at arm's length from it."

Though Fournier still tries not to give anything away, his

eyes have begun to shimmer all the same. Not so much fear as uncertainty, confusion, Lana guesses.

"In case you think I'm raving be assured, Monsieur Fournier, I was in the river Seine, only seconds away from what your loyal associate Vallette hoped would be reported as a tragic 'drowning accident.' It was Monsieur Oscar, I think his name is, who rescued me. Nathan?"

"I believe her, Jean-Luc."

His voice is steady. He had passed the first test. Appropriately, Oscar arrives with a bottle of Evian and places it in front of her.

"This man. You saved me from drowning earlier, didn't you?"

A thin smile and Oscar walks away without a word. Lana shakes a pill from each bottle, not quite knowing her next step. Undermining Vallette just might be a worthwhile exercise.

"Apart from considering if you have 'behaved' properly"— she can't help leaning on the word—"maybe you also need to check out the mental state of at least one of your closest confidants."

She pops one of the pills very deliberately and drinks some water.

"Believe me, I know what I'm talking about. I'd like to help you do that."

She pops another pill and takes another swig of water. Fournier leans forward and speaks very intimately. "I believe you have something that you think is valuable to me. I understand that you have promised to hand it over in exchange for your ticket and passport, et cetera."

"Yes . . . I'm willing to come to agreement with you. But you do see how important the bigger picture is, right? Getting the recording of my interview won't really help your cause if you're Nixon taking advice from Bob Haldeman. I'm sure you appreciate the historical analogy, don't you?"

"Can you show me proof for such an extraordinary accusation?"

"We're not in court here. Maybe Oscar will confirm my story, I don't know. I've warned you, now it's up to you. But I'd like to encourage you to do the right thing."

"I have heard you. Now, I am happy to make this exchange."

Lana knows she has run out of road. Nothing left but to reveal that the memory card is not in her possession, but actually has been in his for some time. It's clear that once they retrieve it from the backseat of the Citroën, she will be of no use to them. And may be a danger. What will the silky politician do then?

"Madame Gibson?"

Any moment now Fournier will realize that something is not right. His eyes shift slightly to look past her and while the surprise on his face is clear, it is harder to tell if it's pleasant or not. Lana turns and gets a shock too.

• • •

"VALLETTE IS IN THE SMOKING AREA WITH ONE OF HIS GUYS. AND THE American woman."

"What?"

"Your boss sat down with her."

Ferdie couldn't deal with any more unknowns. Events were drifting away from him. If Fournier was taking the trouble to meet her at the airport, that could only be because he thought he could get the memory card from her. Okay then. No more watching from afar, no more waiting.

"Get my crutches, would you?"

"Okay, but once you fuck with your boss, it's never the same after."

Didi was right. He and Monsieur Fournier were unlikely to go back to their former mutually advantageous relationship. Oh well, hadn't Monsieur Fournier already altered that last night when he abandoned Ferdie to Vallette?

He threw open the door and swung his legs out.

•   •   •

THE COUPLE WALKING TOWARD THEM IS CERTAINLY ODD ENOUGH TO draw the eye. The two men suggest to Lana a curious modern version of Asterix and Obelisk, the little one even thinner and more pathetic, clicking along on crutches. The contrast in the faces could not be greater, the confident hairy pumpkin head of one, presumably the boss, hovering above the weak-chinned moroseness of the other . . . Weak chin? Now she recognizes that and the cheap suit. Fournier's little helper from the hotel last night. Nervously she remembers her manic foot stamp. The swollen foot and crutches suddenly make sense.

Vallette motions to his people, but a gesture from Fournier stops him and then he surprises Lana with the warmth of his smile to Weak Chin. His "Bon soir, Ferdinand" and invitation to sit are perfectly charming, but the conversation then becomes more difficult to follow. Fournier is obviously puzzled at Weak Chin's—Ferdinand's—sudden arrival. Lana can't help thinking that Ferdinand is far too regal a name for this little woodland creature. He looks more like a Remi or an Émile; that cartoon skunk Pepé Le Pew springs to mind. And who is the other hairy monster? He certainly seems very relaxed. Ferdinand is doing all the talking, but his voice quivers a little and Fournier's expression is definitely intimidating him. Now he nods in her direction. She feels Nathan grip her elbow. He leans in and whispers, "Did you get that?" Lana shakes her head. "He says he has what both of you want."

Ferdinand nods to his big bear friend, who takes what looks very like the memory card from his inside pocket. Jesus Christ! He shows it to them briefly and, as he puts it back again, makes sure everyone at the table gets a glimpse of a gun in a shoulder holster. Despite orchestrating such a powerful moment of drama, Ferdinand still has the look of an animal nervous that the tasty treat he is drawn to is in fact a deadly trap. By contrast, Fournier's smile at Lana now radiates the confidence of victory.

Raising a hand again toward Vallette and company who had started to move in as soon as Weak Chin's friend had revealed the memory card, Fournier now chats in the most affectionate way to Ferdinand. To American ears it sounds like a seduction, as if at any moment he might lean forward and plant a kiss on the little woodland creature's twitching nose.

It's all over. She's at Fournier's mercy.

Ferdinand takes out his cell and, his hand still quaking, searches for something. He slides it along the table. From upside down Lana sees it's a face, pulped and bloodied. Then she hears the words "Hotel Chevalier" and she knows before Nathan's whisper that Guillaume had after all told her the truth about one thing.

"He's saying Vallette did this to a bellhop at the—

—at the Hotel Chevalier. Oh God, the poor kid."

Now Ferdinand is gesturing toward Lana. The longer he talks the more she is beginning to follow what is being said. It feels like the strangest lesson in conversational French.

"He's talking about Vallette trying to drown me, isn't he?"
How did he know about that?

"Yes. He's saying that both he and his large friend saw it
happen."

Fournier's smile remains, though all the warmth and sincerity have drained away. The friendliness in his voice is now
that of a politician ingratiating himself with a dissatisfied voter.
Something he has much practice at, Lana figures.

"Jesus, he says he'll give Fournier the memory card if he
agrees to get rid of Vallette and others from his team—"

Nathan's whisper shifts suddenly to loud interruption. His
words come fast and urgent. They are directed at Ferdinand
and she catches enough of it to know that Nathan is batting for
her, asking Ferdinand to make sure that she is allowed to leave
Paris. Lana is quite moved by the passion in his voice. Thanks
for trying, Nathan.

Right then he glances toward her and she remembers the
look on his face from a long time ago. She can't recall the exact
occasion or where they were, but it's such a look of . . . adora-
tion. Or something like that.

Ferdinand's stare suggests a different emotion. He rattles
his crutches and Lana is genuinely embarrassed about the foot
stamp. She says "sorry" and "désolée." He shrugs.

Ferdie wasn't angry with the American anymore. Nor did
he care much what happened to her. But he was beginning
to enjoy running the show. He liked having that guy plead
with him, he *loved* that Vallette was forced to stand back, helpless. And there was an undeniable buzz from telling Monsieur
Fournier what had to be done. But truthfully, although just
now it felt good, being the king didn't really suit him. After all

he had been through in the last twenty-four hours he figured he deserved this little moment of absolute power.

"And I guess, Monsieur Fournier, you intend to let this woman catch her flight. I mean why not, yes?"

"I think you know I'll do the right thing in that regard, Ferdinand."

"And Vallette?"

"What you have alleged is very, very serious."

"But you believe me—us."

"Yes . . . yes, I can see you are not lying to me. Of course."

"So . . . ?"

"Obviously, it wouldn't be appropriate to take action here, now. But I think I can assure you that your proposal is reasonable."

"By the time I return to work, he and the others will no longer be part of your campaign."

"You can rely on me."

And Ferdie knew he could not. Nothing in Monsieur Fournier's voice, of course, nor the eyes and smile, revealed it; perhaps it was something in a tiny shift of the body, a shiver rippling out from the fragment inside where his badly beaten soul still clung to life. And yet Ferdie knew like any dog does his master, instinctively understanding all his gestures and signals, that there was no way of guaranteeing victory over this man. Holding power over him actually felt embarrassing and he could not sustain the effort for much longer. So he was going to hand over the memory card and let the process of betrayal begin. It was sad. Monsieur Fournier was so nearly a great man.

He nodded to Didi. If Didi was surprised, he didn't show it. He gave Ferdie the card and he handed it calmly to Fournier, whose snatch at the little piece of plastic revealed the enormity of his relief.

And Ferdie was just a chauffeur again. Soon, it was odds-on he would not even be that, which would be disappointing. He had looked forward to being the president's driver. It would be interesting to see how his boss behaved now that he presumed the power was entirely his again. Fournier stood calmly. A big smile for Ferdie and nods all round. The redheaded friend of the American woman asked about her documents, saying there was just enough time to make her flight. Though Fournier replied in English, Ferdie recognized the tone of playful superiority with which he sometimes treated people of no importance to him.

"Oh, I'm sure it is no hardship for Madame Gibson to enjoy a few more days in Paris, especially in your company, Nathan. But remember, Lana, there is so much available to see in this city. Don't waste your time on what is not meant for your eyes."

What exactly had he said? Where were her documents?

"Monsieur, are you allowing the American lady to catch her flight?"

"Don't worry yourself about this, Ferdinand. Believe me, I know what I'm doing."

And he turned away. Ferdie now knew for certain that Vallette would not be dumped. Without pleasure, he spoke to his master's back.

"Monsieur Fournier. I have downloaded the material. I still have a copy of the interview."

Nathan leans in to whisper, but Lana nods to say she's got it. There are a few exchanges between the little fellow and Fournier, and even though his answers consist pretty well entirely of "Oui" and "Non," it is clear that his boss is getting nowhere. Fournier shrugs and looks at her.

"It seems that the man you assaulted has become your champion, Lana."

He goes to Vallette, who looks like he has clearly had enough and intends to deal with things his way. But Fournier grips his arm and Lana sees in that moment some secret message pass between them that has little to do with the present crisis: something under the skin of this relationship, the servant, the master, the who and the why of it. All she recognizes is that a complex subtext with a long, turbulent history exists between this pair.

Like a marriage, Lana Gibson thinks.

Vallette backs off. It's impossible to read what Fournier is feeling. Those restless brows quite still for once. It occurs to Lana that, even at such a critical moment, it could be that he's not thinking about this situation at all. He might be preoccupied with something much more fundamentally important to him, like the prospect of banishing the most loyal of old friends,

the potential hacking off of a limb. All at the behest of his unattractive little pimp of a chauffeur. The torment of that.

Vallette takes a bulky envelope from an inside pocket.
Fournier returns and places the envelope on the table in front
of Lana. Inside are her passport, ticket, and phone. She is whole
again. And almost at liberty.

Fournier stared at Ferdie as if a little disappointed in him.

"Are you satisfied, Ferdinand?"

"Thank you. Just to be clear, sir: I am anxious for everything to be as it was between us."

"Then we should work very hard to make sure that happens, Ferdinand. Good night."

Ferdie couldn't help but admire how, as Monsieur Fournier
returned to Vallette and the others, he was already smiling and
gesturing and his whole body radiated genial authority, as if he
had just spent a few useful minutes swinging skeptical voters
his way. He motioned the others to follow him and sauntered
off. Most satisfyingly for Ferdie, Vallette turned his stony gaze
directly at him. It was hard to resist taunting him with a little
finger wave. He had begun to convince himself—almost—that
he had won. The American woman stood and smiled at him.

"Well. We have to go. And . . . I really mean this. Thank
you. Merci très bien."

Without standing Ferdie took her offered hand. Well, why
not? They'd never see each other again. She even squeezed it a
little, which felt nice. They left and as Ferdie waited for Didi to
return, he thought about how hard it was to feel just one way
about something. There was elation, sure, no doubt about that.
He was ending the day a lot better than he started it, that was
certain. But he also guessed that his greatest wish would not,
could not be granted. After what had happened, things could

not go back to the simple perfect life he once had with Monsieur Fournier and his DS21. That had been shattered. And he had the feeling that whatever was to come would not be as satisfactory.

· · ·

LANA DECIDES NATHAN DESERVES A PROPER GOODBYE THIS TIME SO THEY walk together quickly to the shuttle that will take him to the RER station.

"You're incredible, Lana Turner, you know that?"

"Nice of you to say so, but no. I'm just out of control and I have to do something about it."

It being Paris, the little driverless shuttle is of course waiting, doors open in welcome. The warning beep starts. Nathan steps aboard.

"Well, when you have . . . when you're feeling calmer . . . why don't you come back to Paris and—"

"No. Nathan. This is a good ending, don't you think?"

"Well, not quite the atmosphere of *Brief Encounter* but—"

The automatic doors start to close.

"—it's a lot better than—"

They hiss shut and she barely hears, "—last time."

His grin and wave are tinged with something like regret or sorrow; found and lost and found and lost again. The shuttle rolls smoothly silent, into the darkness. Suddenly, heavily, Lana craves sleep. Can it be the meds kicking in already or is it just collapse, like at the end of an exhausting workout? "Ice bath time," Brian would always say after watching some particularly bruising football game.

By the time she arrives at the tube that will take her to the gate and is holding out her passport and online boarding pass

to a surprisingly friendly-looking official, Lana is already looking forward to returning to Paris. But this time with Brian.
They will have that holiday they'd missed out on. Even better
if they can make it a Gibson family holiday, she and Brian and
a baby. Yes, how about that?

A hand clamps on her wrist. Curiously, it's a female hand.

Pauline and Odette, standing side by side, offer the brightest
of bright smiles. Lana notes how amazingly well Odette seems
to have recovered from her interrogation ordeal.

"Lana. So you have your passport."

"You are free. Wonderful."

They each take a wrist. Surprisingly, Pauline's slim, frail,
blue-nailed hand coils more painfully. This is awkward. Lana
knows from those big, big smiles that they know everything
and figure, from her expression of petrified shock, that she
knows they know. In a millisecond Pauline's face dissolves from
welcoming delight into a pout.

"You know Claude is in the hospital. And Guillaume also
now. Is so terrible."

Panic shoots up Lana's spine, a thermometer line in a heat
wave.

"Poor Claude, he ask Odette, are you all right?"

"I'm sorry, but my flight, you see . . ."

"Stay one more day."

"Fournier's men . . . we lose everything."

"Please. Guillaume ask. He say you ah . . ."

Odette gets to the point.

"Make again the interview."

It's a request that plays like an instruction. Not so far away,
at the other end of the angled tube, through bored passport control, after the long, long, dipping, climbing, moving walkway,

past the posters of the girl with the Eiffel Tower hat on her head, beyond the tedious security circus, Lana knows there is a line of lovely ordinary people boarding a plane. Second by second that line is getting shorter. Any moment now she might hear that announcement in French, the one in which the name La-na Gib-son will scream at her and she'll know her time is up.

"Okay, sounds good."

The grips of the women do not relax. It's not going to be that simple. They begin to lead her away.

Lana looks directly at Pauline and speaks slowly. "Oh, one thing, Pauline. Remember last night? You. Dans l'Hotel Chevalier? Vous avez cherché . . . pour Vallette or any of his gang. Yeah?"

Pauline nods brightly, and Lana feels the hold on her hand relax a fraction.

"And you said. Vous ah . . . dîtes à Guillaume. You remember what you said? If anyone tried to interfere with you, you would scream. Scream your little butt off . . . yeah? Non? Vous ne comprenez pas? Scream?"

Pauline seems genuinely mystified, but Lana guesses Odette is merely pretending not to understand. Lana opens her mouth and mimes screaming. "Remember?"

Ah! Now Pauline nods and explains very enthusiastically to Odette, her hilarious idea that screaming her head off in a respectable public place like the Chevalier would scare away any nasty who might interfere with her. Odette smiles with forced amusement. Lana knows there is no more time.

"So, Pauline . . . Pauline. I guess, what I wanted to figure out was, does your idea work?"

And she opens her mouth and screams.

The initial shock makes both Pauline and Odette step back

as she drops to her knees shrieking. It's scary how easily this un-earthly howl of despair has erupted. Everyone on the concourse stops to look, but no one comes any closer. Pauline and Odette are frozen. Lana is about to make a run for it when men in uniform appear from several points, armed with what look like very high-powered weapons. She stops screaming and, in the sudden silence, one of the armed men barks at her. It sounds both commanding and threatening. She has to defuse the situation very quickly.

"Oh, oh. Here it is." Having dropped everything when she began screaming, Lana now picks up her passport and lifts it very slowly for the armed men to see. "I'm *so* sorry. I thought I lost it. My passport. Oh. My. God. What have I done? I pan-icked. Ah, je panique? Is that right, ah? . . . Hysteria . . . désolée, I am *so* désolée."

The armed men look completely bewildered. The one in charge lowers his weapon and, motioning the others to do the same, approaches. Slowly. Lana stands, gathering everything, keeping an eye on the two women. Pauline has lost her smile.

"Do I understand you, Madame? You are all right?"

"Me? Oh yes, I'm fine. I am so sorry. I totally, like . . . over-reacted. I thought I lost my passport, you see . . . my passport? Mon passeport?"

"I understand. Your passport. Is this all the problem?"

"Well, I'm running late for my flight and it's been a really stressful day and I . . ." Lana is beginning to enjoy playing the stressed-out middle-class American lady tourist. "You're not going to arrest me, are you? I mean I'm so désolée, Monsieur."

The man looks at the boarding pass Lana holds toward him. He motions with his weapon.

"Go now. Before it is too late."

"Really, can I? Thank you so much."

She moves quickly and hands over her boarding pass. There's a moment of tension as the nervous official scans it and everyone, soldiers, casual observers, Odette and Pauline, Lana herself wait for something to go very wrong. Then comes the relieving beep. She steps into the tube, onto the moving walkway that will carry her to the plane.

She turns back to Pauline and mouths, "Thank you. It works."

Because the last few passengers are still shuffling on board when she arrives at the departure gate, Lana turns on her cell and is surprised to find no messages from Brian, and even more surprised to realize that she doesn't feel relieved and pleased that, for once, he had followed her instructions and let her be. In fact, she's a little disappointed. More than a little. After all she'd been through since they spoke last night, it would have been comforting to know that he cared enough to ignore her instructions and send a steady stream of anxious texts. She'd have kind of liked to hear his voice again too.

But the most extraordinary and disconcerting thing of all is that when she dials, Brian doesn't answer. Instead his slappy-happy voicemail invites the caller to leave a message. A few seconds pass before she remembers to speak.

"Hi, Brian, sorry I'm late calling you. Just getting on the flight now. Ah . . . okay. See you at arrivals, I guess."

But now, despite assuring herself that it's the craziest idea, she's not so certain that he'll be there. This slightly unsettling possibility cannot prevent Lana's eyes from closing a few minutes after takeoff and even the landing bumps don't rouse her from a restoring, dreamless sleep. Someone is shaking her shoulder. When she opens her eyes, Jean-Luc Fournier is standing over her.

Before the scream comes, she hears him say, "Paris nightlife a bit too much for you, was it?"

Fluent English speaker though Fournier is, he doesn't have a strong Irish accent or such a kind smile. The genial blue-eyed, silver-haired man in the window seat just wants to get past her.

At passport control the man smiles and she returns it sleepily. It feels so relaxed and casual until, handing over her passport, her smiling Lana Gibson photograph reminds her that she isn't wearing her wedding band. She hurries through, pulls her bag into a corner, and, not caring how strange it looks, falls to her knees and searches frantically. She has pulled almost everything from the bag when she spots a little glint of gold as something falls from the back pocket of her jeans and it's such a relief; confirmation that finally, everything really is going to be all right.

Brian is waiting. Of course. As he'd said he would be. It's the best, deepest, most heartfelt kiss they have exchanged in a long time. She senses his shock in the first couple of seconds, then feels him go with the heat of it.

"Sorry I didn't answer when you called, baby, but would you believe I still hadn't left the office. I had to break the speed limit to get here on time. So . . . how are you? Would you believe just after we spoke last night I got a call to come back in? Code red. An all-nighter. So while you've been chilling at art exhibitions and fine dining in luxury hotels and shopping—speaking of which, where are all the bags? Where are Gaultier and Gucci and all those dudes?"

"Oh. I guess I didn't bother in the end."

Again Brian looks surprised, but pleased too. He squeezes her waist. They have arrived at the parking lot elevator. Lana stares, then turns away abruptly.

"Let's walk down. I wouldn't mind the exercise."

"Sure. So anyway, I've been taking meetings and calls for basically the last twenty-four hours straight. Have you eaten, by the way? I'm starving."

"So am I."

"Great. Oh Jesus, Lana, there was so much bullshit. Some of these guys, I tell you, you learn about people you know? Way out of line. I'm totally drained."

Lana squeezes closer to him. "Poor baby."

"Sorry, I know, I know. This work crap is boring. So, what about your trip?"

"Oh, nothing to tell. Your crap sounds exciting."

"You know, it was, actually. I've been kinda buzzing with it all, to be honest."

"Well then, I want to hear about it."

And all the way home she lets him talk, lets him enjoy recounting every detail of his crisis. She's too exhausted to think of making love tonight. But maybe in the morning? Definitely in the next day or so she'll start reaching out again. No pressure. Just do it, enjoy it.

Back at the house, after they grab a sandwich and milk, Brian says he's hitting the sack. She says she'll follow him in a few minutes, but needs some fresh air first. When he's in the bedroom she retrieves her cigarettes from her purse and goes outside. The rain spits and it's windy. No sign of the moon. Her thoughts dance about, but the weirdest thing is that, after all that has happened, what's mostly on her mind isn't anything to do with Vallette, or Fournier, or Nathan, or Claude or Guillaume and Pauline, or being trapped in the private elevator, or nearly drowning, but it's the young English brat on her hands and knees throwing up and those drunken friends lurching around in their ridiculous heels and microminis. Lana finds herself thinking, *poor thing*, and realizes what that means: she must be feeling better. What a relief it is not to be that young anymore. Thirty-five is fine, it's good; maybe it's the best time. A woman of thirty-five can handle a lot. She flicks away the unpuffed cigarette and goes to the trash. It feels quite easy to dump the pack.

Brian is sitting up in bed with the Hopper catalog. Lana is surprised to see his eyes are moist. She lies next to him. He's staring at *Second Story Sunlight*. The girl in the 1950s bikini sitting, brazen, on the edge of a sun-filled balcony of some Cape Cod summer home.

"Have you been crying?"

"What? No! . . . I don't know, looking at some of these I . . . I didn't cry. But I guess maybe I teared up a little. Very weird."

"Any idea why?"

"I don't know. Maybe I miss home."

A little to her surprise, Lana understands exactly what he means.

ABOUT THE AUTHOR

GERARD STEMBRIDGE is an Irish writer and director whose credits include *About Adam, Guiltrip,* and *Alarm.* His screenplays include *Ordinary Decent Criminal* and *Nora.* He lives in Dublin and Paris.

About the author

About the book

Read on

Insights,
Interviews
& More . . .

Meet Gerard Stembridge

Jim Guerard

There was a time when the only thing a reader knew about an author was his or her name, sometimes not even that. Crime and thriller writing in particular has a tradition of authors with (sometimes multiple) pseudonyms. It was not unknown to have a team of anonymous writers lurking behind the beloved name on the book cover. As a twelve-year-old I used to wonder what Franklin W. Dixon of Hardy Boys fame looked like. Nowadays readers are as curious about the person who wrote the book as they are about the book itself. Does this add significance to the name on the cover?

In Limerick when I was growing up, that full first name the reader of my books sees was rarely spoken: never Gerard, always Ger, pronounced "Jur." A second syllable was perhaps just too much effort. This was typical. Michael was always Mick; Thomas, Tom; Patrick, Pat. And as Mick, Ger, Pat, and Tom accounted for most of the Irish male population, this made social interaction very economical. An uncle who lived most of his life in Canada called me Gerald. I never knew why. Never asked. I liked the sound of it, though.

It was at university in Dublin that "Gerry" began. It just seemed to come easier to Dubliners. I had never thought of myself as Gerry, but I got used to it, at least in ordinary conversation. Somehow, though, I never really liked the look of it, written down. Many years later the Abbey Theatre was producing a play of mine and I found myself having a rather ludicrous argument with the marketing person, who decided it was better—and he really was insistent—that I credit myself on the poster and program as Gerry Stembridge. He was mystified that I should prefer Gerard. In the melodrama of the moment I harnessed my inner John Proctor and cried out, "Because it's my name!" On another occasion a newspaper columnist wrote "Gerry," then corrected himself, sardonically adding that apparently I was now calling myself Gerard, implying that he had caught me practicing some subtle deception on the public, trying to be someone I was not. Gerard indeed! The affectation of it!

This may account for the genuine relief I felt when, very recently, I discovered that my mother had kept an old poster (as mothers do) from my first college theater production. There was the credit, large (to be candid, rather too large) and proud: Gerard Stembridge. I really had always used my full first name.

By contrast the family name never posed any problem: the joy of difference. For as long as I can remember I loved how unusual it was. In my school there were many, many Gerards (or "Jur"s) but only one Stembridge. Our family was the only Stembridge in Limerick. There were no others in the phone book, I never encountered another in Ireland. With a name so particular it felt almost a duty to put it out there. Lack of skill rendered athletic fame out of the question. Neither science nor mathematics was ever my thing, so I was never likely to invent or discover anything. I might have tried politics, but luckily I preferred writing.

However, despite the pride in the family name, a pseudonym has always seemed an attractive, even romantic notion, even ▶

better if the real name can be buried in it. A full anagram of Gerard Stembridge is tough. I have thought of only one. How about Bridgete Remsgard? I like that it's female; the family name actually exists; the unusual spelling of the first name is acceptable (think of Karin, Annika, Jo, Leena); and, most excitingly for potential book sales, it has a Nordic noir ring to it.

Ice and Bone by Bridgete Remsgard. Great, except that Google informs me that "Ice and Bone" is already a title. Who'd have thought?

All right then: *Dead Elk in the Snow.*

Google concedes that one. Let's see how it looks in dramatic font and large typeface?

REMSGARD

Dead Elk in the Snow

I'm tempted. Seriously. Of course, there is the small matter of writing the book. ∾

The Origins of *What She Saw*

It began at the major Hopper exhibition in Paris in late 2012. Seeing so many of his greatest works for the first time all in one room was, as expected, extraordinarily atmospheric, but the greater and more surprising impact was discovering the profusion of narrative possibilities, in particular the stories of women: mysterious, mostly lonely stories, so many on journeys whether actual or emotional. And in every image a sense of place, so particular, yet somehow creating a profound yet elusive quality of displacement.

The effect was inevitable. Afterward on the real streets of Paris a woman appeared. First she was sitting outside a café—where else?—but not relaxed, her head twisting this way and that, smoking extravagantly. Then she was striding ahead of me, in a hurry somewhere. She hovered by one of those impressive Haussmann apartment entrances, waiting impatiently for someone to open it for her. She grabbed a bike from a Vélib' station and rode off without checking for oncoming traffic. Then I saw her gazing intently over a bridge into the turbulent Seine. Soon this woman had a name—and, very quickly, two names—and there was now a reason why she was alone in Paris.

That was when it became even more ▶

The Origins of *What She Saw* (continued)

exciting and purposeful to walk around this great walking city. Soon other characters emerged and with them incidents and encounters and a journey, a geography, began to be mapped out. The entrance beneath the green neon DULUC DETECTIVE sign on rue du Louvre was considered and discarded, but it led to Le Fumoir, only a hundred yards away, and a very different encounter. Always the question for me was, where is Lana going, and for what reason? There were trips on the metro, stepping out and stepping back and stepping out again until finally, the destination felt right. And soon it became clear that, whatever was happening, there had to be an urgency and immediacy to it; time was of the essence for Lana; the clock was ticking.

There is a moment when the needs of the character and the realities of the place coalesce and that vital element, the plot, takes shape. It is Paris, so of course language and food and art were always going to play their part, while the old standbys politics and sex mingle in a special way here, never more so than in 2012. Naturally there is satisfaction in finally reaching conclusions about what happens, because thrillers thrive on plot, but there is regret too in the realization that, for the author, much of the fun is over, the adventure of discovering who Lana is and what does she want and why—not just what she saw. Once the story is in place there are still many journeys around Paris, but these feel like a furtive return to the scene of the crime, confirming a detail or finalizing the choreography of an encounter.

But one pleasant mystery remains even now after the work is done: some characters live in places I have never entered, certain events occur behind doors never open to me. Unlike Lana, who could not resist stepping into the private elevator, I prefer not to cross these thresholds, so that it will always feel special to pass by a certain door or look up at windows on a certain floor and wonder, what *is* the story? ◠

Have You Read?
Gerard Stembridge's Favorite Kind of Thriller

Some thriller writers imagine the future, others like to re-create the past, and most prefer to stay in the here and now, the world they live in. There is another kind of thriller I love to read: the contemporary thriller from the past, particularly the mid-twentieth century. I recommend four, though there are many more just as brilliant. If you haven't read *Double Indemnity* (James M. Cain, 1936), *The Mask of Dimitrios* (Eric Ambler, 1939), *Strangers on a Train* (Patricia Highsmith, 1950), or *A Bullet for Cinderella* (John D. MacDonald, 1955), then considerable pleasures await you. They are great stories, written with deadly economy, but they have also left us a special legacy: the moods and colors of the world as it was then, the language and viewpoints of those living through that time. So in *The Mask of Dimitrios*, Eric Ambler, at the precise moment he wrote, was observing the mood of suspicion and dread in Europe on the brink of war. The Great Depression underpins the brooding tone of *Double Indemnity*, and *A Bullet for Cinderella* reeks of the angst of a generation that survived a world war only to end up dying in Korea. Highsmith's observation of and contempt for pampered, unpleasant young white men in the patriarchal America of 1950 is real and immediate in *Strangers on a Train*. None of these writers are looking back to an earlier time. They live in the world of their stories and have no idea what the future will look like. It was not remotely in their minds how readers seventy years later would respond.

This simple reality not only affects the prevailing tone, the broad sweep of politics and life in these classic contemporary thrillers, but also offers special delight in the throwaway descriptions of social behavior or daily routine that effortlessly put the seal of authenticity on these stories. Whereas the modern writer of period thrillers will carefully insert specific information as evidence of good research and the reader will admire the meticulously created "period atmosphere," contemporary writers from the past offer up quotidian detail without any sense that they are creating a kind of social history. When John D. MacDonald has the teacher, Leech, mention that "I once had eight Judys in one class. Now that name, thank God, is beginning to die out," he is not intending to offer the twenty-first-century reader a telling detail about the popularity of certain names in 1955, but simply having Leech say the thing he would be likely to say. When we learn that a character has no phone and must go to the corner store to make a call, MacDonald is not thinking how quaint this will seem to a reader decades later. ▶

Have You Read? *(continued)*

James M. Cain has his protagonist, Huff, tell us "I pitched my hat on the sofa," and later has him smoke on an observation platform at the end of a train, but he was not including these details because he divined that a time would come when few men would wear hats, there would be no observation cars, and smoking would be illegal anywhere on a train. Patricia Highsmith was not thinking of how readers now might yearn for the kind of train service where, like Bruno in *Strangers on a Train*, we could order "a delicious lunch of lamb chops, french fries and salad and peach pie washed down with two scotch and sodas." When Latimer in *The Mask of Dimitrios* buys a "pneumatique letter card . . . and drop[s] it down the chute," it is merely plot detail for Eric Ambler, not an opportunity to point out a curiosity of the Paris postal system.

It is in the accumulation of all these little gems—a fashion reference, the cost of a hotel room, the time of a train, an unusual piece of slang—that the world of these stories takes shape and comes alive. What I find intoxicating about these books is that instead of admiring a modern writer's brilliance in re-creating a particular period, I get to know it as if walked through it by a native guide. Beyond the considerable pleasure of the gripping yarn, these classic thrillers just feel *genuine*. The reader is connected directly to a voice out of the past, not remembering the past as a grandparent might, nor reconstructing it as the writer of period fiction does. These books are a primary source, alive and immediate. Imagine how our contemporary thrillers will read in 2080?

In *Strangers on a Train,* Highsmith has the killer, Bruno, ride a merry-go-round observing his prey, munching a hot dog as Sousa's "The Washington Post" march plays. It is a marvelous moment of tension (irresistible to Hitchcock when he made the film version) but is wrought from the most mundane elements of a 1950 amusement park. Highsmith probably strolled around one, enjoying her wicked imaginings.

Reading contemporary thrillers out of the past is a special experience. One to treasure.

Discover great authors, exclusive offers, and more at hc.com.